CRITICAL PRAISE FOR THE MYSTERIES OF WENDY HORNSBY

"*The Color of Light* is a fabulous book on many levels, well plotted and tightly written, with surprising twists in the plot. But the one thing that really makes this book special is the description of the multi-cultural neighborhood and how the various ethnicities contribute to the story."
—*Reviewing the Evidence*

"…complex relationships between the locals, multiple twists, and brisk pace…"
—*Publishers Weekly* [on *The Color of Light*]

"What a wonderful, completely captivating opening that is so visually rendered…. Maggie is a character who develops and whose life changes through the course of the series, including her relationships. *The Color of Light* is well plotted with a good twist."
—LJ Roberts, *I Love a Mystery*

"Well written and engrossing…"
—Roberta Alexander, *San Jose Mercury* [on *The Color of Light*]

"Edgar-winner Hornsby's enthralling seventh Maggie MacGowen mystery takes the documentary filmmaker to France…. Readers will almost be able to taste the food and drink the author so vividly describes."
—*Publishers Weekly* [on *The Paramour's Daughter*]

MYSTERIES BY WENDY HORNSBY

THE MAGGIE MACGOWEN MYSTERY SERIES

OTHER MYSTERIES

Disturbing the Dark

A MAGGIE MACGOWEN MYSTERY

Wendy Hornsby

2016
PALO ALTO — MCKINLEYVILLE
PERSEVERANCE PRESS • JOHN DANIEL & COMPANY

This is a work of fiction. Characters, places, and events are the product of the author's imagination or are used fictitiously. Any resemblance to real people, companies, institutions, organizations, or incidents is entirely coincidental.

The interior design and the cover design of this book are intended for and limited to the publisher's first print edition of the book and related marketing display purposes. All other use of those designs without the publisher's permission is prohibited.

Copyright © 2016 by Wendy Hornsby
All rights reserved
Printed in the United States of America

A Perseverance Press Book
Published by John Daniel & Company
A division of Daniel & Daniel, Publishers, Inc.
Post Office Box 2790
McKinleyville, California 95519
www.danielpublishing.com/perseverance

Distributed by SCB Distributors (800) 729-6423

Book design by Eric Larson, Studio E Books, Santa Barbara, www.studio-e-books.com

Cover image: Bernard Allum / iStock

10 9 8 7 6 5 4 3 2 1

LIBRARY OF CONGRESS CATALOGING-IN-PUBLICATION DATA
Hornsby, Wendy.
  Disturbing the dark : a Maggie MacGowen mystery / by Wendy Hornsby.
    pages ; cm
  ISBN 978-1-56474-576-7 (pbk. : alk. paper)
  1. MacGowen, Maggie (Fictitious character)—Fiction. I. Title.
  PS3558.O689D57 2016
  813'.54—dc23
                    2015029320

As always, this is for Paul,
without whom there would be no book.

—.—

I also want to acknowledge
the help and encouragement of
two dear friends we lost too soon.

Sharon Zukowski,
amazing writer, sounding board,
and the best travel companion ever;

Sgt. Richard Longshore,
Homicide Bureau, Los Angeles County Sheriff's Office,
story-teller extraordinaire,
loyal friend:

I miss you every day.

∽ MAGGIE MACGOWEN'S ∽
EXTENDED FAMILY

CASEY MACGOWEN, her daughter

ÉLODIE AND HENRI MARTIN, her grandparents

FREDDY DESMOULINS, her half brother

ISABELLE MARTIN, her biological mother

GÉRARD MARTIN, her uncle

ANTOINE MARTIN, Gérard's elder son

BÉBÉ MARTIN, Gérard's younger son

GRAND-MÈRE MARIE FOULLARD, née Dumond,
Maggie's godmother, Gérard's mother-in-law

MA MÈRE, the abbess, Maggie's godmother, Marie
Foullard's sister

JULIE FOULLARD BRETON, Marie Foullard's
granddaughter

JACQUES BRETON, Julie's husband

DAVID BRETON, Julie and Jacques's son

JACQUELINE CARTIER, Jacques's niece

DISTURBING THE DARK

— I —

Occupied Normandy, February 25, 1944.
Night. A waning gibbous moon.

FOR THE FOURTH NIGHT IN A ROW, Élodie watched Allied bombers stitch through the clouds, far out above the Channel as they headed home to their bases in England after blasting targets in Germany. She paused in the moon shadow alongside the cider house to watch them, sleek black silhouettes against the cold dark sky, as thick as flocks of geese flying north in spring. A sign, she hoped, that the long, soulless chill of life under the Occupation might end. That night, that moment, with fear hammering through her body, more than ever before Élodie wished she could open her arms across the breast of the wind and fly like a bird. Fly far, far away.

The din coming from the cider house surged and fell as the Germans inside grew drunk on the potent double-distilled apple brandy they were being served. On empty stomachs, they swilled the brandy like beer. Now and then, a raucous chorus of some German song was punctuated by bursts of laughter that sounded lurid to her ears, though after nearly four years under their thumb, even when they were sober everything the Germans said sounded lurid to Élodie. At that moment, as planned, the detested Boche were far from sober. Shouts for refills were quickly answered by the village women: As you wish, *monsieur le unteroffizier,* or *oberfeldwebel,* or, if he was really drunk, *mon chèr gros chien,* and then another generous pour from an earthenware pitcher. "The feast is coming, but first, how about another little sip?"

The women told the Occupation soldiers billeted at the Martin estate on the Cotentin Peninsula that tonight was a traditional winter festival. Come and celebrate the bottling of the year's brandy; the fall harvest was brilliant and what a wonderful brandy we've made. A delicious feast, the women promised, fat hens and good cheese, with plenty of strong drink. An evening of camaraderie. We are friends, are we not? Partners in this war. Not a single soldier turned down the invitation.

Élodie turned as the coal hatch at the side of the building opened on freshly greased hinges. Her school friend when they were still in school, Marie Dumond, peered around the edge, saw Élodie, and came outside.

"How many?" Élodie asked, handing Marie the basket of Camembert and bread she held over her arm, the first and only food that would be offered to the men inside.

"Only sixteen," Marie said, lifting the cloth under the cheese to make certain that the sharp, hooked pruning knives were hidden there. "Major von Streicher is still up at the house." And then, with a catch in her voice, she added, "And so is my sister."

"Go back inside, *chérie*, get underway," Élodie said, slipping one of the pruning knives into her apron pocket. "But leave the coal door ajar for me. I'll be back in five minutes."

"What are you going to do?"

"Take care of von Streicher."

Marie said a silent prayer and crossed herself before she gave Élodie a quick embrace. "Courage, my friend," she whispered before she slipped back inside.

The soldier who should have been standing watch over the stone-walled compound was missing from his post, lured inside for refreshments. Discipline among the Occupation troops had faltered as war news worsened for Germany. The Allies were in Italy and the Russians were in Poland, speeding toward Berlin. Dresden was a pile of rubble. As arrogant as ever, the soldiers had become rapacious, drunken, and even more brutal with every discouraging report. Élodie wondered if these men who before the war had been low-level clerks and government functionaries were having a last fling with power before the inevitable end of the war dumped them back into impotent anonymity.

Out of caution, in case one of the men came outside for a piss or dragged a woman out to satisfy a baser urge, Élodie kept to the shadows along the cold wall as she made her way toward the main house. Using her own key, she entered from the rear and slipped into the kitchen. Through the swinging door, she could hear two voices in the main salon: the officer-in-charge, Major von Streicher, loud and guttural; fifteen-year-old Anne Dumond, soft and frightened.

She pushed the door open enough to see into the salon. Von Streicher had his back to her, with Anne, struggling, clutched against him.

"Please, monsieur, I am still bleeding," Anne said, trying to pull out of his embrace.

"Can't you call me Horst by now, little Anna?" Von Streicher lowered his face to hers and spoke to her as if he thought she must somehow like him. "I don't mind a little blood. As long as you are bleeding we don't risk having that little complication to take care of again, do we?"

Élodie shoved through the door and walked boldly into the room.

"Take me instead," she said, putting her hand on von Streicher's arm. "After the procedure you forced on her, Anne would be too uncomfortable to satisfy you. Take me. I won't disappoint."

"What is this?" He grabbed onto her hand and she did not pull away. "Maybe I should have you both."

"You won't need us both, Major," she said, leaning into him.

He laughed and released Anne with a shove.

"Élodie, no." Anne, wracked by sobs, dropped to her knees. Élodie touched her hair. "Go now, *chérie*. Go."

"Yes, Anna, go." Von Streicher nudged Anne with his black boot. "So, what are you waiting for? Leave."

Élodie moved between them, pressing close to von Streicher. She reached up and undid the top buttons of his tunic to run her hand over his chest and up the side of his neck until her fingers found the rhythmic thrum of blood through his carotid. Roughly, he took her into his arms and pressed his face between her breasts as he began pulling up the back of her skirt. With his big hands busy cupping her ass, Élodie slipped the pruning knife from her apron pocket and drove the sharp, curved blade into his neck behind the carotid before she gave it one quick, practiced twist.

Von Streicher's hands flew to his neck as great jets of blood streamed from the severed artery. Before he realized what had happened, Élodie unholstered his sidearm, pressed the end of the barrel against his chest where there should have been a heart. And pulled the trigger.

Normandy. Late August. The present.

THE SKULL CAME UP out of the earth atop a scoop of rich Normandy farm soil. By the time I realized that this object I saw through the lens of my video camera was something other than a big round, dirt-encrusted stone, Olivia, the archeologist from *l'école du Louvre* in Paris, had raised her hand and started yelling for my half brother, Freddy, to stop his earthmover.

In the sudden lull, the farm's summer symphony of buzzing insects and rhythmic whacking of stout wooden poles against apple-laden branches in the orchard behind us was joined by a chorus of electronic taps and blips, as Olivia's five graduate students and my quartet of interns from the UCLA film school memorialized and sent out into the ether digital snaps and videos of the grisly discovery turned up on the edge of my grandmother's carrot field. The tapping and blipping was soon joined by the pings of incoming responses. As the harvesters in the orchard, a baker's dozen of international agricultural students working with my cousin Antoine, received messages from the dig-site youth, they dropped their poles and came running out through the trees like a pack of hungry pups called home for supper.

Freddy set the earthmover's hand brake and hopped out for a closer look. He was every bit as hopeful as Olivia was that during the excavation necessary to build his new housing development along the shoreline bordering the Martin family estate, he would disinter an artifact or two from a pre–Gallo-Roman village, or better yet, a Viking burial ship. A significant archeological find would certainly garner some free publicity for Freddy's development, and maybe draw some tourists who would be so charmed by rural Normandy that they would buy one of his cottages. All morning, as he dug a trench along the edge of the carrot field to lay a sewer line, he'd kept one eye on the ground and the other on Olivia, waiting for her *Eureka* signal.

Guido, my longtime film partner, who came running out of the orchard at the head of the harvester pack, raised his own video camera and zoomed in on the skull.

"Hey, Olivia," Guido said, then training his camera on her. "If you drop the skull into a bucket of bleach, by tomorrow it will be as white and shiny as a new pearl."

Olivia was aghast. After several tries, she managed to utter, "Never! Do you wish to destroy the integrity of this fragile specimen? It appears to me to be very old, very old indeed. Centuries, perhaps millennia."

I elbowed Guido as a warning. All morning, he had twitted Olivia at every opportunity as payback for the tongue-lashing she had given him the night before. If she caught him anywhere near Solange Betz, one of her graduate students, distracting the young woman— emphasis on *young*—from her work, Olivia promised she would rip Guido a new one. Or something to that effect. My rusty French had improved daily during the two weeks we'd been in Normandy, but even if I could have kept up with Olivia's verbal barrage I wouldn't have found some of her words in my pocket dictionary.

The approach of my ninety-two-year-old grandmother, Élodie Martin, in the little Kubota Rough Terrain Vehicle my uncle Gérard gave her so she could get around the estate more easily, added some bass notes to the general chattering and exclaiming. I saw the plume of dust trailing her as she sped along the farm's unpaved access road, coming from the general direction of the raspberry bramble. She was going so fast that I was afraid she would spin out when she reached the sharp turn at the end of the orchard, but she gunned the RTV's motor just as she hit the straightaway and held her course. Or stayed on target, i.e., us.

Grand-mère was out of the RTV and calling for Freddy before the dust stirred by her sudden stop had settled; she is amazingly spry for ninety-two.

"Freddy!" Grand-mère looked up into his face with an expression of reproach that could have chilled the fires of hell. "I told you, dig your sewer trench down the middle of the road."

"Yes, Grand-mère, but when we started digging up the road, Jacques said it was impossible. He has cheese to deliver and he's expecting a new whey separator for the *fromagerie*. He can't do without the road for ten days. But, as you see—" Freddy, nonplussed, waved his hand to show Grand-mère the course of his trench so far, a straight line running between the edge of the access road and the first cultivated row of the field. "We are not disturbing the carrots, Grand-mère."

Maybe Freddy, a banker by training and not a builder, hadn't set the little Volvo earthmover's hand brake properly, or maybe he failed to lock the scooper arm in place correctly, because just at that moment the apparatus suddenly jerked. That one sharp jolt was enough to start the skull rolling from its perch. There was a moment of absolute silence as it tumbled off the end of the scoop bucket and down into the trench, losing the lower mandible during its descent. When the skull finally rolled to a stop, it was upside down, grinning up at the clear blue sky. The chorus of digital taps and blips immediately resumed.

"So, Olivia." Guido looked up from the monitor of his video camera. "Who knew the pre–Gallo-Romans had fillings in their teeth? Is that bridgework on the molars?"

"Freddy." Grand-mère pinched his cheek to get his attention. "Don't you realize? This is where we buried the Germans."

⸺3⸺

AT THE BUTCHER, the baker, the *café tabac*, news that a body had turned up that morning *chez* Martin spread every bit as fast and wide as postings on the Internet had.

It was August, the month that French schools set their pupils free and urbanites abandon their cities and take off *en vacances* until September. Along the Normandy shore near Grand-mère's village, shutters had come off seasonal cottages and humanity poured in ready to relax and play. Except for local tradesmen who were happy to rake in the vacationer's euros, the residents of the area were generally too busy tending to summer crops and chores to pay much attention to the visitors unless some idiots, fueled perhaps on the region's potent Calvados, or more potent *eau de vie*, decided to off-road through the carrot fields, entangle their speed boats with commercial fishing nets, or wander among the livestock while looking for bucolic photo ops. If vacationers clogged the narrow village roads on market days, they also spent freely on the local produce, sausages, cheeses, and cider, so there wasn't much grumbling about their presence.

As nothing especially interesting had happened in the area since the carrot festival over in Créances a week earlier, villagers and summer visitors alike began to arrive for a look before the *gendarmes* from the local barracks had finished putting up blue police tape across the end of Grand-mère's access road and placed privacy screens around the area of Freddy's trench where the skull still lay. Cars, tractors, bicycles, and a pair of fine crossbred Arabian mares clogged the two-lane road leading from the village. There was such a large and festive crowd that if we were in California, where I live and where I work making investigative films for one of the big television networks, I might expect to see vendors working their way through the crowd selling churros, balloons, and frozen fruit out of bicycle carts. The French, who don't snack much, managed to have a good time without the ding of vendors' bells in the background.

Usually, the village's municipal policeman would handle crowd control. But something had happened to the poor man, so the district *gendarmerie* had taken over handing out traffic citations and maintaining civic order until another could be hired. The *gendarmes* did their best to keep the village road clear and the crowd from trampling the crop or falling into the open sewer trench, but with limited success. I watched a well-fed man wearing bright vacation togs venture beyond the blue tape, paying no heed to the crop he crushed under his flip-flops as he strained for a better look. Young Jacqueline

Cartier, looking crisp in her blue *gendarme* uniform, blew her whistle to get his attention.

"Monsieur, Madame Martin sells her carrots by the kilo," Jaqueline scolded. "Shall I have her send you an invoice?"

Properly chagrined, now stepping gingerly between rows, the transgressor moved back behind the tape where he belonged.

All four of my film interns were having a lovely time shooting background footage among the crowd. Antoine had herded his students back into the orchard for a discussion of the role of the bitter, inedible Binet Rouge apple in the blending of good hard cider. And Olivia, after the *capitaine* of the district *gendarmerie*, Pierre Dauvin, declined her offer to stay and advise his people about the proper method for excavating remains, decamped with her students to a far corner of the cow pasture where Grand-mère promised there were remnants of an ancient stone wall they might dig around.

After the masses had been pushed back, Freddy, Grand-mère and I, and Guido with a running video camera in front of his face, as usual, were with Dauvin, keeping vigil over the skull site until a decision came down from the local *Procureur de la Republique*, who functioned something like an American district attorney, about whose problem the skull was and what should be done not only with the skull but with a search for the rest of the carcass the skull had once been attached to.

Capitaine Dauvin was a local man, an old family friend, and probably a cousin of the Martin clan—and therefore me—somewhere along the way. His connections to the area and its people could be either an asset or a great hindrance in his work. While his platoon of officers snapped to attention when he was around, old friends did not. How his familiarity was going to play in the current situation had yet to unfold, though the problems he would face began to emerge immediately.

"I am sorry you are inconvenienced, Freddy," Dauvin told my brother. "But think, man, how lucky you were. It could have been a bomb. You know what happened at Jouet's when the dog dug up unexploded ordinance. *Kaboom!* Sheepdog parts blasted from here to La Manche, not to mention the tractor. No, my friend, think yourself fortunate that it's just more war dead you've dug up. If it is war dead, that is."

"Of course it is," Grand-mère said. "You know that perfectly well, Pierre Dauvin. And if you have any doubts I will call your grandmother and have her assure you of it, because she helped me put the *putain de cochon* into the ground."

"As you say, madame," Dauvin said with a courtly little bow. "But there are procedures that must be adhered to, *non?*"

"How long will it take before I can get back to work, Pierre?" Freddy was beside himself. "The plumbers are coming to install the sewer connections next week. If I delay the trench, I go back to the end of the queue and I won't see them until spring."

Dauvin shrugged. "What happens next depends on what Doctor Patel has to tell the *procureur* about cause of death. As I told you, she will decide how we proceed."

"Then I will speak with our Doctor Patel right away." Grand-mère aimed a finger toward the screened-off area of trench. "And now that *he* has been discovered, I want him gone from here right now. And the others as well."

Guido, who had been filming the entire conversation, froze in place. "*Others*, Madame Martin? How many others?"

"Sixteen more," she said with a dismissive little wave.

"You buried seventeen men here?" Guido gave Grand-mère a long look, as if seeing her for the first time. "*Merde.*"

"I told you the story," I said.

"Only in broad outline," Guido countered. "You didn't say there were seventeen of them."

"A broad outline is all I know," I said. "The locals took care of some rapacious German Occupation troops in 1944, and apparently here they are."

"And that is more than anyone needs to know," Grand-mère added.

"So, Pierre," Freddy persisted. "When German war remains were found under a collapsed wall near Pérrier a few years ago, some group of volunteers came from Germany and removed them. Can we call those people?"

"The German War Graves Commission—the *Volksbund*," Pierre said with a nod. "*Malheureusement*, as extravagant as the number of cadavers there might be here among the carrots, I understand that the *Volksbund* is so busy recovering German war dead in Ukraine now that they have finally been permitted to enter the Eastern sector, that unless we promise them at least fifty dead at this site, they simply haven't the resources to bother with removal."

I said, "Surely the German government has some apparatus for recovering their own combat dead."

Dauvin shrugged, meaning, I thought, Go figure. "It seems that the German government is still too embarrassed by Nazi war atrocities to risk having a presence in such an activity. No, retrieval and identification are left to volunteers. All they ask of us is that we save for them any dog tags we find."

"*Bon,*" Grand-mère said with an emphatic hand clap. "If the Germans don't want them, then we will call the priest and be done with all this before our little event becomes a scandal."

"*Becomes* a scandal?" I said, waving a hand toward the crowd. "A little late for that, Grand-mère. Everyone in the village knows what happened here."

"Yes, my Maggie, everyone in the village knows what happened. However, until this morning only four people ever knew where the bastards were buried. But now, look at this." She struggled to pull her mobile phone from her slacks pocket. "There I was, quite content this morning driving my little cart around, searching for late raspberries when this damn instrument your cousin Antoine insists I carry starts ringing. And there it is, a text from my friend Clara at the library in the village. You see?"

A video one of the young people had posted online showing the skull's emergence from the ground and its tumble back into the trench played on Grand-mère's mobile's screen. A scroll running across the top read, TRENDING, followed by a story update: "Archeological dig in Normandy unearths modern murder victim."

"Holy *merde*." I scrolled through various updates and versions in four languages before I turned off the phone. In one hour, one hundred thousand people had viewed the video.

"And it is not the truth," she said, returning the phone to her pocket. "It was not murder, what we did. It was an act of war. For the people of our village who know the circumstance, the way we dispatched those *bêtes lubriques* was both honorable and a little bit heroic. As to outsiders, and so many years later, what business is it of theirs where we disposed of them?"

I looked over at the mass of humanity being held back by *gendarmes*. Who was going to tell them this was none of their business, I wondered? I put my arm around Grand-mère. She leaned her head against my shoulder and took a couple of breaths. Calmer, she looked up at me, smiled gamely, and patted my cheek.

She said, "I saw what happened in Pérrier when those men were found. It was bad enough that ghouls came and dug up the ground looking for Nazi souvenirs to sell. But it was worse when possible survivors of those dead men arrived hoping that all these years later their missing papa or grandpapa would be identified among the remains. They hear about every discovery on Google alert, and they arrive with photos: 'Do you remember my papa? Did you ever see him?' To hell with them."

"You can understand that the family would want to know," I said. "It has to be awful to have a loved one go missing in action and to never learn how or where he died."

"Bien sûr, chérie," she said raising her palms to acknowledge a fact not in dispute. "But sometimes it is better to remain in the dark, yes? Will you be the one to tell a man or a woman the truth about what their sainted father did to the people of this village during the war? Shall I tell them how their father died? I say, put the earth back over them somewhere and leave them be. Let us say no more about them or that damn war."

Sounding alarmed, Guido said, "Mag?"

"Grand-mère," I said, feeling the same uncomfortable buzz somewhere in my middle parts that I heard in Guido's voice. "You know that the American television network that is financing the film we're making here expects us to include a conversation with you about what you did during that damn war. Have you changed your mind?"

"My dear Maggie," Grand-mère said with a wicked little smile, canting her head to watch me. "You know I only agreed to talk to you in front of the camera about what happened here during the war as a ruse to get you to fly over to visit your old Grand-mère this summer."

"I know," I said. "And I used your story as a ruse to get funding from my network so I could be here. Now, where are we?"

"Cat's out of the bag, Madame Martin," Guido ventured. "You can't put him back in."

"Perhaps. But I am certainly not required to let the beast back into my house," she said with a little shrug, linking her arm in mine. "Don't worry, children. We will talk. But lunch first, yes?"

"Of course," I said, not quite persuaded she would be very forthcoming when she did get around to talking for the camera about anything except farming. "Lunch first."

Carefully stepping around the police barriers, we headed toward her RTV. As I helped her in, she called out to Dauvin.

"Pierre, I'm afraid it might rain for your nephew's baptism party Sunday at the beach pavilion. When you pass through Lessay, will you please stop at the convent and ask Ma Mère to lend you the large marquee?"

"Of course, madame," he said with a little bow. And with a twinkle in his eye, he asked, "And shall I have some of my *gendarmes* erect the marquee as well?"

"No, no, just drop it off, please," she answered with a little wave as she started the cart's motor. "There are enough strong young bodies around here to put it up."

"Guido," I called, gesturing for him to hop into the back of the RTV. *"À table."*

—4—

AT THE STROKE OF NOON, everyone who lived or worked on the family estate washed their hands, combed their hair, and showed up at Grand-mère's old stone house for lunch, as was local custom. During the summer when there were extra bodies to feed and the weather was warm, long plank tables were set up under the rose-covered arbor that linked two of the three houses inside the stone-walled family compound. On any given day, counting students, family, and workers in the *fromagerie*, the fields and orchard, there could be as many as forty hungry people to feed.

Grand-mère always took the seat at the end of the table closest to the kitchen door so that she could oversee the two women from the village who arrived early every morning to prepare and serve the meal. The seat to her right was reserved for her old friend, Marie Foullard, called Grand-mère Marie by everyone. Other than that, there were no rules about who sat where. People tended to sort themselves out by age and occupation. I usually sat at the grown-ups' table with my grandmother, my half brother Freddy, Olivia Boulez the archeologist, Jacques Breton the cheesemaker and his wife Julie (née Foullard), my cousin Antoine, and various others generally over the age of thirty.

The seating arrangements were not entirely sorted by age, however. My daughter, Casey, a college junior, had become fascinated with cheese making that summer, and also, it appeared, with the cheesemaker's handsome son, David Breton, who had one more university term to finish before he went on to graduate school. On that day, Casey and David were seated at the far end of the table from me, deep in conversation, possibly about something other than cheese. My old pal, Guido, was at the next table, among the youngsters. Guido knew better than to put himself anywhere near Olivia's prize student, Solange, so instead he was holding a young local woman in thrall with, from what I gleaned by shameless eavesdropping, a rather enhanced version of his life working in American television. I heard him say, "Maybe you can help me with my French." In reaction, Olivia snickered. Solange pouted.

As everyone found their seats, my cousin Antoine came across the graveled compound from his house with Grand-mère Marie on his arm. I was told that Marie was present at my birth and stood as a sponsor at my baptism, but because I was spirited away to California when I was very young, I had no memory of her when I came to Normandy the previous fall to meet this part of my family for the first time since that happened. She was about the same age as my grandmother, though she seemed older. Her hips hurt and she wore a hearing aid when she thought to put it in. But, like my grandmother, she remained a force to be reckoned with.

Antoine looked tired, as might be expected because of the load he carried. He was the oldest of Grand-mère and Henri's grandchildren, the elder of my Uncle Gérard's two sons with his late wife, Louise, née Foullard, and thus Marie's daughter. After secondary school, he had gone to California to study agriculture, married an American, Kelly, fathered two children, and landed a professorship at the state university in San Luis Obispo, on the Central Coast of California. They were all very happy there.

After my grandfather Henri died, Grand-mère couldn't manage all of the estate's various enterprises on her own. Her adult children, Isabelle and Gérard, had careers elsewhere, as did their children. My Uncle Gérard, who had no interest in farming and had no intention of moving back to Normandy from his new home in London with wife number two, decided that the best solution would be to plow under the farm operations and replace them with a massive retirement community, complete with golf course. Gérard's plan had been far more ambitious and potentially destructive than Freddy's current development that made use of the non-arable land along the shoreline.

Grand-mère, appalled by Uncle Gérard's plan, appealed to Antoine to stop his father. Antoine and Kelly decided that the experience of living in France would benefit their children and be an adventure for them all. Once arrangements with his university were settled, allowing Antoine to maintain his tenure by teaching American students in Normandy through the university's campus abroad program and by mentoring graduate students in agriculture, he brought his family over. Two years, they thought. But now it had been five, and they wanted to go back. Kelly was currently in California with the children, spending the school holiday with her parents. Her husband missed them terribly.

After Antoine seated Grand-mère Marie next to my grandmother and took a seat next to me, grace was said, the back door opened and, to happy cheers, lunch appeared. Large platters of chilled rice and seafood salad, roast chicken with green beans and fried potatoes, and of course baskets of bread, were placed on the tables, along with carafes of water, cold apple cider, and red *vin ordinaire*. At the end of the meal, trays of cheeses were passed along with small glasses of Calvados, the local apple brandy, as a *digestif*. Altogether, it was a deliciously convivial break in the day.

Just as people were finishing, Pierre Dauvin drove into the courtyard in his blue-and-white Renault patrol car, with Jacqueline Cartier riding shotgun. I seemed to be the only one who tensed at their arrival, expecting that because they were still in full uniform this was an official visit. But they exchanged a round of *les bises*, the cheek kisses that are the standard greeting among French familiars, found places at the table, and filled plates with food. Jacques the cheesemaker poured a glass of cider for Jacqueline, his niece and namesake, and passed the wine carafe to Pierre.

Grand-mère gave Pierre and Jacqueline time to settle in before she asked, "You have something to tell us, Pierre?"

He nodded as he washed down a mouthful of chicken. "From the dental work, Doctor Patel concluded that the remains are early mid-century, quite probably German, almost certainly a war casualty. The *procureur*, as a formality, has arranged to have the skull sent to the *Institut Médico-Légal* in Nice for scientific examination. As soon as she hears back, and if Doctor Patel's assessment is supported and the remains are in fact German, she will send a formal request to the *Volksbund* to arrange for repatriation or instructions for re-interment of the remains. In the meantime, madame, though I do not wish to cause you further distress, she asks that you meet her at the discovery site this afternoon to show her where the others are buried. They must be removed and disposed of properly."

"How long before I can get back to work on my trench?" Freddy asked, looking distressed.

"All depends on what the *Institut Médico-Légal* has to say." Dauvin helped himself to more rice salad. "Remember that it is August and everyone is on vacation."

Freddy groaned.

"I will make some calls," Grand-mère said, catching Freddy's eye to reassure him. She knew that for Freddy working on the housing project was a very welcome distraction from the *Grand Guignol* mess his personal life had become. Putting work on hold until public offices re-opened in September would be a hardship for him on many levels. To me, she said, "*Chérie*, our conversation can wait until after I speak with *madame le procureur?*"

"*Bien sûr*, Grand-mère," I said, trying to sound like a local. "If you don't mind, though, I'll come along with you and Pierre to meet her. With a camera."

"I wouldn't dare say no." She patted my hand. "You are so like your mother, so persistent." From what I had learned about my birth mother, Isabelle, I was not at all certain that was a compliment.

As people finished their meals, they began to disperse. Some of the workers stretched out in patches of garden shade for naps. A group of young people, after figuring out transportation, headed off to the family's beach pavilion down the coast at Anneville-sur-Mer for a swim and probably a co-ed game of soccer. Guido invited some of the other young people, including his very pretty, very young luncheon seatmate, for a tour of the production studio we had set up in a little stone outbuilding that had once been an ice house.

Solange got up and walked over to a very handsome young man, tall and dark with a mop of black curls, and initiated a conversation. I wondered if she did this to twit Guido, but if she did, he didn't seem to notice. Her conversation with the young man grew animated and soon they moved together over to the back corner of Grand-mère's house where the curly-haired youth stooped to run his hand along one of the foundation stones, apparently as an illustration of something that she seemed to find intriguing. Or maybe it was her fellow student she found intriguing; the course of love between young academics, I thought, with a sigh, and wished that Jean-Paul, my current love, were there beside me.

Pierre and Jacqueline seemed to be in no hurry to get back out on duty. So, I poured myself a third glass of wine and sat back in my chair feeling thoroughly content and a little buzzed, enjoying the lovely breeze ruffling through the climbing roses overhead. During the short time I had been at Grand-mère's, I had come to love the place, its people, and all that it represented. I would be sad when the filming was finished and I had to go home.

Growing up in California, my notion of family was a nuclear model: me, Mom, Dad, my brother and sister, an uncle. As soon as my siblings and I finished school, we scattered to the winds and began lives largely independent of each other and of our parents. The Martins, in contrast, were a collection of intertwined family lines and enterprises, all having the estate in Normandy at their center. Though most of them had homes and careers elsewhere, everyone remained closely connected to the land and to each other in ways I had never experienced before. Their notion of family was a revelation to me.

Labelling the family home an estate makes it sound grander than it was. And to say that it belonged to Grand-mère was not quite correct, either. Ten years ago, when my grandfather, Henri Martin, died my grandmother, Élodie, his widow, became the lifetime guardian of the large farm property that had been in the Martin family since some time in the fourteenth century, before the Hundred Years' War. Grand-mère could legally profit from the estate, make improvements to it, had the privilege of paying taxes on it. But, according to the arcane French inheritance laws, because Grand-mère was not of Henri's direct bloodline she could not sell the property or any part of it unless all of the potential heirs for the next two generations approved.

One day, after Grand-mère slips off this earthly coil, primary ownership or guardianship of the place will pass to me and my half brother Freddy, as the heirs of Isabelle, and to our Uncle Gérard. The strange part of that is, I did not know my biological mother, Isabelle. I did not know that she, or Grand-mère, or Freddy, or this place existed until after Isabelle died. Indeed, it was because she died that I learned about this part of my family at all. Sometimes I felt like an interloper. A well-fed and currently quite content interloper, but an interloper nonetheless. Everyone there was generous and kind to me, but I did not know what resentments they might hide in their hearts.

The *procureur* interrupted this quiet moment when she phoned to say she was on her way from St-Lô and would meet us at the site in an hour. My interns were at the beach, so I headed off alone toward our little temporary studio to gather up Guido and the equipment we would need for filming that afternoon.

The building was in a corner of the compound, behind the house that Isabelle built for her and Freddy when she was working on a project nearby. As I was coming around the side, headed toward the single door, I nearly collided with the young *fromagerie* worker Guido had been so attentive to at lunch. Her cheeks were already flushed, but when she saw me, her face flamed red. She ducked her head and ran past.

I felt my own face flush; with chagrin, yes, but also with dismay and anger when I recognized what the rosy cheeks and glassy eyes meant.

Guido was on a stool in front of a digital editor when I walked inside. I couldn't see the image on the monitor until I shut the door, blocking the glare. I expected to see something lewd, but it was only a close-up of the skull. When Guido turned to greet me he didn't try to hide the self-satisfied little grin on his handsome, chiseled, aging face.

"We had a talk before we left L.A.," I said as I pulled camera battery packs off their chargers. "You promised."

"What?" All innocence.

"I saw young Delphine from the *fromagerie* on my way in."

"Nice kid, huh?" He swiveled on the stool, following my movements as I gathered necessary equipment. "So, what are we doing now, Mag?"

"I don't know, Guido." I dumped the battery packs into a duffel and added four remote recorder hook-ups. "What the hell are you doing?"

"You mean Delphine? For crap's sake, Maggie, she's an adult. I'm an adult. The rest is nobody's business."

"It is my business, Guido." I hoisted a video camera onto my shoulder. "I don't want your inability to manage your zipper to get us into trouble again. Not here, and not with these people. When we finish this project, you can ride off into the sunset and disappear, but I can't. My situation here is already strange enough without you complicating things for me with the locals."

"What the hell? Nothing happened."

"Nothing happened, yet," I said. "The look I saw on that kid's face I've seen often enough that I know what comes next, Guido."

He shrugged: so what?

"When we first worked together," I said, "watching you chase eighteen- and nineteen-year-old girls was just annoying. But that was twenty years ago. Now that you're old enough to be their father, your pursuit of the same eighteen- and nineteen-year-old girls has become, frankly, icky."

"You should talk," he said. "You're going with an older man."

"Yep, same thing," I said. "Jean-Paul is fifty, and I'm forty-three, the same age as you."

He tried again. "If you hadn't noticed, Miz MacGowen, we're in France. People here aren't as provincial about sex as Americans are."

"If you hadn't noticed, sir, we're in provincial France."

"To hell with you, Maggie." He hopped off the stool and stormed out the door. I was at least as steamed as he was, but I finished packing up and went outside, locking the door behind me.

I came around to the front of the building in time to see a burly, middle-aged man I recognized as part of the *fromagerie's* milking crew raise a giant ham of a fist and deck Guido with a practiced right cross. Though I didn't understand some of the man's vocabulary, his meaning was clear enough: Stay away from my daughter, you lecherous old bastard.

After the man, clearly young Delphine's father, stomped off, Guido just stayed on the ground where he'd landed. I let my partner rub his jaw and collect himself for a moment before I went over to him.

"You going to lie around all day?" I asked. "Or are you coming to work?"

He moaned, but he got to his feet and followed me across the compound. Grand-mère and Freddy were waiting for us beside her RTV. They had seen the entire bout and though wicked little smiles passed between them, they said nothing as Guido, still rubbing his jaw, loaded our gear into the backseat of the cart and climbed in beside it.

With the film gear taking up space, there wasn't room for four people in the four-seater cart. Freddy volunteered to walk, and I offered to walk with him. Guido needed a little space to cool off, and I was happy for the opportunity to be alone with Freddy. Since my arrival, there were times I thought my half brother was avoiding me. Indeed, it seemed that he was avoiding being alone with any of us. Embarrassment over the implosion of his personal life, resentment about my presence or about having to share our mother's inheritance with a veritable stranger—me—or just the stresses of divorce and sudden single fatherhood along with the management of a large construction project? Maybe all or none of the above. Whatever was on his mind, he was keeping it to himself.

Freddy and I walked out through a side gate in the compound wall, across the bottom of the summer kitchen garden, past the berry bramble, and came out on the farm road between the apple orchard and the cow pasture behind the *fromagerie*. I waited for Freddy to speak first.

"I hear you've been summoned," he said, looping his hand around my elbow.

"I have," I said, leaning in to him. "Jean-Paul's mother has invited me to come for tea tomorrow."

He chuckled. "Does she want to know what your intentions are for her son?"

"Apparently. Are there local customs I should be aware of? Do I need to bake her a cake or something?"

"Leave that to Grand-mère. I overheard her and Grand-mère Marie discussing what they should put into the gift basket they'll send with you. They also discussed which car you should drive, Grand-mère's Range Rover, or my Jaguar."

I laughed, visualizing the two grandmothers at their matchmaking. Grand-mère hoped I would marry Jean-Paul and live happily ever after with him in France so that I would be near her. That might be lovely. And though love might conquer all, so far I—we—had not figured out how love might conquer geography.

When we met, Jean-Paul was the French consul general to Los Angeles, where I live. But recently, he was recalled home to France, marking the end of his appointment. I hated that there would be six thousand miles between us, but following him seemed impossible. My work was in California, where my daughter would be in college for at least two more years and where my eighty-year-old mom, meaning the woman who raised me, not Isabelle, was increasingly dependent on my help. Then there was that other little problem: Jean-Paul and I had not discussed the possibility of happily ever after.

I said, "Antoine said I could borrow his Mini for the drive. It gets good gas mileage."

"Where are you meeting Madame Bernard?" Freddy asked, taking out his telephone and opening a map app. I gave him the address of the Bernard family's summer cottage in Villerville, which I was told was on the coast near Honfleur.

Freddy let out a low whistle as he showed me a highlighted route across the Cotentin Peninsula then over toward the estuary where the Seine meets the English Channel.

"She's making you work for it," he said. "Villerville is over a hundred and sixty kilometers from here. You'll make good time on A84, but with summer traffic along *Route du Littoral*, the beach road where you turn off, the trip will take about two hours. Be happy that she invited you for tea instead of breakfast."

"Maybe I'll come down with a cold tonight and postpone the visit until the weekend when Jean-Paul can join me."

"Don't be a coward," he said putting away his phone. "Do take my Jag. It's more fun to drive, and Antoine's Mini doesn't have GPS aboard."

When we made the turn past the hedgerow that separated the apple orchard from the access road, we could see the village road on the far side of the carrot field. I was relieved that the morning crowd had decamped, though I had expected that they would. Early on, I learned that in rural France lunch was served between noon and two o'clock. If you missed that time window to eat, you were just out of luck until dinner at seven. And forget hitting the drive-through, because there wasn't one. Lunch, then, I surmised, had been more compelling to the curious than old bones were, and everyone had gone home to eat.

There was, however, a little cluster of people and cars on the access road next to Freddy's trench where the discovery *du jour* had been made. Parked in a line, there were Grand-mère's little RTV and Pierre Dauvin's official blue-and-white Renault Mégane, two bicycles, and a dark Honda Fit. I cringed to see that Olivia was there with her student Solange, but when I saw that Guido was staying clear of them, busy with camera setup, I relaxed a bit. Pierre and three of his *gendarmes* sort of milled about, keeping their eye on things.

I bent my head toward Freddy and gave a nod toward the one person I did not recognize. He whispered, "*Madame le procureur*, Renée Ferraro."

The *procureur* was a willowy woman maybe in her fifties, elegant in an immaculate blue cotton sun dress and black rubber muck boots as she stood in the middle of the sewer trench, studying the place where the skull had emerged that morning. Olivia, dressed in the style of Indiana Jones, knelt on the gravel road beside the trench and with broad arm gestures explained to Ferraro about the primitive state of World War II archeology and, therefore, the necessity for an academic like herself to be present for further excavation at the site so that nothing was destroyed for future study. Young Solange, fair hair pulled back into a ponytail, cheeks sunburned, nose already peeling, stood beside her professor and offered up her sketches of the skull to show how useful they could be.

As she listened, *Mme le Procureur* nodded or shrugged from time to time, but remained noncommittal. On the other hand, when Grand-mère introduced Guido and me to her, and explained that we were making a film, Ferraro shook our hands firmly, offered pleasantries and asked questions about our work. As she shook Guido's hand, she touched her jaw at the place where Guido now had a shiny red-and-blue lump emerging on his. She said, "*Ça va?*"

"He met the father," I answered for him. Smiling, she clucked her tongue and turned back to the business at hand. And so did Guido. He clipped a cigarette-pack-sized remote recorder unit to Grand-mère's belt and attached the tiny microphone to her collar.

The *procureur* agreed to hold a recorder because there was no place on her dress to attach it. She seemed amused as Guido clipped the microphone to the top of her dress. Pierre, with a little shrug, allowed a third recorder to be attached to his utility belt, with the mic on his shirt placket. Guido handed me the fourth recorder to hook up to myself. When everyone was wired to record, Guido connected the external recorder to the camera, checked that sound and video speed were in sync, raised the camera to his shoulder and began filming.

A sleek black Mercedes of a certain age turned off the village road onto the farm access road, a great pillar of dust swirling behind.

"Ah, *bon*," Grand-mère said as she watched the big car approach. "Gaston is here."

I had met Gaston Carnôt, the village's elected mayor, during my previous visit. His job involved managing public facilities, overseeing festivals, advising the appointed village police chief, and generally making certain that his constituents were orderly and happy, as they generally seemed to be. He was an old family friend, my grandfather Henri Martin's first cousin twice removed, an aging roué with a great appreciation for the finer things in life. Grand-mère adored him, and though he was twenty years younger than she, I wondered if once there had been something between the two of them. Maybe there still was. No argument, he was charming. But the first time I met Gaston, I learned not to turn my back to him.

"Madame Martin," the *procureur* said gently when the technical preliminaries were finished, "will you please show us where the German soldiers were interred in 1944?"

Grand-mère looked around for a moment, apparently getting her bearings. She turned and studied the hedgerow. Then she walked about three yards down the road, looked again at the hedgerow, went to the edge of the carrot field and dug a divot with the heel of her shoe into the soft soil in the first planted row.

"From here," Grand-mère said. She stayed where she was until one of the *gendarmes* had driven in a post to mark the spot. After giving him a nod of approval, she paced back toward us, past the marker where the skull had been, and then made another divot in the soil about ten feet farther along. "To about here."

Pierre looked from one end of the area she defined to the other, and asked, "How wide?"

"One meter," she said pointing into the field. "More or less."

He seemed skeptical. "And how deep, madame?"

"So high." Grand-mère stood up straight and drew a line across her chest with the side of her hand. "Of course, the soil has built up over the years with composting and so on."

"But you say there are seventeen men buried here. How is that possible in such a small space?"

"Well," she said, raising her palms. "How much space would you expect a pile of charred bones to take up?"

Renée Ferraro let out an involuntary little *"Merde."*

"I saw no evidence of charring on the skull found here this morning," Dauvin said, watching Grand-mère through narrowed eyes.

She paled. "Yes, one man was not in the cider house when Henri set it on fire. We put that one into the hole last."

The *procureur* surveyed the area, looking for something. "Where is the cider house from here?"

"At the time, it was inside the compound wall," Grand-mère said. "My son Gérard later built a house on the site. You know my grandson, Antoine. He lives there now with his family."

Seeming dubious, the *procureur* asked, "You transported the remains of those men all the way from the compound to here? Quite a distance, yes?"

"It was winter," Grand-mère said, sounding as if she thought the answer should be obvious. "The ground was very hard. Except here. The field had been plowed for turnips, and so here we could dig."

"If the men died in the fire," the *procureur* said, "why not simply leave the remains in place for the Nazis to deal with?"

"Because the men didn't die in the fire." Grand-mère ran a finger across her neck. "We slit their throats first. There would have been reprisals."

"Ah," was all that the *procureur* managed to say, nodding as she considered what she was hearing. After a glance at Dauvin, perhaps to record his reaction, she stepped up out of the trench. "*Monsieur le capitaine*, I believe that it is safe to expect that after a fire and some seventy years in the ground, it will be unlikely that any of the remains can be identified. Except, of course, for the one that escaped the fire, and even then—" A little Gallic shrug finished the sentence. "It is clear to me that no crime was committed here, so there is no reason to delay popping these remains out of the carrots, *d'accord?*"

"*D'accord,*" Pierre said, agreeing with her. I thought he seemed relieved, perhaps because his own grandmother had been an active participant in putting them into the ground. "When you have a signed order, please send me a copy. Will you notify the *Volksbund?*"

"Gaston?" she said, turning to the mayor. "I believe that is within your purview, yes?"

He nodded. "Yes, I will call the Boche. And I can tell you what the *Volksbund* will say. They will request that in the process of disinterment we set aside any items we find that might lead to an identification. Dog tags, wallets, photos, and so on. I doubt anything useful has survived, still—"

"You've done this before?" I asked.

The mayor nodded. "Not as often anymore, but yes, from time to time war remains are still found."

"What will happen to the remains?" I asked.

Gaston glanced at Pierre Dauvin, received a little shrug in response to an implied question before he answered. "Probably into a new hole in the German cemetery over in Orglandes or at La Cambe, a few miles east of here. There is still room for a few more stragglers, I hope."

"Well then," Grand-mère said. "We are finished here, yes?"

Pierre nodded. "For now."

Gaston, ever gallant, bowed to her. "May I drive you home, *ma chère* Élodie? It is so warm out here, and you forgot your hat."

"Thank you, yes. But first I need a little word with Pierre." She unclipped her mic and recorder, handed them to me and with Gaston holding her arm, went over to speak with Pierre.

I was collecting recorders and putting them into the duffel when Solange came up close beside me.

"All of this is very interesting, is it not?" she said, tucking her notebook under her arm.

"In a gruesome sort of way, I suppose it is," I said.

"You have it all on film," she said. "Will you make a documentary about the discovery?"

"We'll see," I said. I was expecting her to offer her expertise if we did. But she had something else in mind.

"I think that I may be in some of your footage," she said.

"Possibly."

"I wonder, if you did film me, might I have a copy?"

I shook my head. "I'm sorry, but our footage is proprietary. We don't, actually we can't, give it away without a release from the network. But if you want to share what happened out here with friends and family, I'm sure you can capture images off the Internet. At least half a dozen people posted videos and still shots. Anything on the Web is fair game."

She nodded, but clearly my answer did not satisfy her. "The quality of the footage on the Web is substandard."

"I'm sorry," I said, and started to move away. She tagged along.

"I suppose that finding war remains might seem so commonplace to the layman that it wouldn't be of general interest," she said. "Maybe it interests me because my family once lived not far from here."

"Oh?" I said, winding my grandmother's mic cord before stowing it.

"Yes." She pointed over her shoulder in the general direction of the village. "They left a long time ago, but they speak of it. I know that what Olivia is hoping to discover on your family estate this summer is some evidence that the Viducasse people had a settlement here. You are familiar with them? They were Celts, or Gauls as Julius Caesar labeled them. The blond people of the woods, the Romans called them. Olivia would be quite excited to find Viducasse relics here. And such a discovery would make the university happy, as well as the acquisitions department of the Louvre."

"Would it?"

She shrugged, as if dusting off the lot of them. "But I think we would be breaking new ground if we focused instead on evidence from the great modern wars with Germany. Think of it, over three different generations the Germans pushed into France. First the Prussians under Bismarck, then the Great War of 1914, and last Hitler. It is an epoch too long ignored by archeologists. We could break new ground here, Miss MacGowen. Certainly such a study would make a magnificent topic for a documentary."

"Something to consider, I suppose." I found her intensity to be a bit off-putting. I looked around for an escape and saw Olivia scowling at us. I said, "Does your professor want a word with you?"

She glanced over, shrugged. "In case you aren't familiar with her work, Olivia is the premier expert on the Viducasses. I have one of her articles I will be happy to share with you, though I'm afraid you would find it quite dull."

I told her I would look forward to reading it, and excused myself. I was taking a still shot of the hole in the trench when my grandmother walked up close beside me. In a low voice, with a nod toward Solange, she asked, "Do I know that child?"

I gave her the only answer I could: "Her name is Solange Betz."

"Betz?" Grand-mère shook her head. "No. Not from around here. But there is something about her—"

Gaston, offering Grand-mère his arm again, asked if she was ready to leave. With a smile, she slipped her hand through his elbow and the two of them started down the road towards Gaston's vintage Mercedes, heads bent close in quiet conversation. After a moment, he turned back toward the cluster of people at the trench.

"Tonight I am uncorking an exceptional Calvados, *hors d'age*, very old," Gaston said. "But first, a meal. Please say you will join me. At seven?"

Freddy was the first to answer. "I would never turn down an invitation to dine with you, *Monsieur le maire*. Jacques has made a very special cheese in the style of a *Pont l'Evêque*, aged for three years; very strong. Perfect with brandy for the last course."

"Wonderful," Gaston said with a dramatic bow. "And make sure you bring your lovely sister and her..." He seemed at a loss as he focused on Guido. "And her helper. Renée, Pierre, you will join us?"

"Delighted," Renée Ferraro said, offering him a broad smile as she returned his bow.

Pierre demurred. "I am so sorry, Gaston, but tonight my Gus has a swim meet in Pérrier, the summer finals. Another time, I hope."

"*Dommage,*" Gaston said, Too bad, and seemed very sincere when he said it.

With another wave, he and Grand-mère continued to the car. He said nothing to Olivia or Solange. Were they included?

"Helper?" Guido said as he put the camera's battery packs into the duffel with the mics. "Maybe if you'd introduced me to the guy when he got here he'd know to call me general dogsbody, not helper."

I patted his cheek, the uninjured one. "Poor Guido has had a rough day. But tonight should be fun. Put on a clean shirt and a happy face, my friend, and join the grown-ups."

"Yes, do, Guido," Renée Ferraro said, seeming very sincere when she said it.

─5─

THE LONG TIDE of the local seacoast had been fully in for about an hour before we arrived at the mayor's for dinner. His house sat atop a small rise on the village outskirts. As we drove up in Freddy's Jag, we could look across the expanse of green fields crisscrossed by hedgerows, the gray roofs and spires of the village, and see the shimmering ocean beyond. Fishing boats were still making their way toward land with the day's catch. There was no boat basin. The fishermen rowed or sailed into the shallows until their boats ran aground, and then they waded to shore, hauling their catch on sledges pulled behind them. When the tide receded in a few hours, their craft would be mired in the mud until the morning tide refloated them, and another fishing day began.

A battered old Isuzu pickup followed us up Gaston's long gravel drive and pulled in next to us on the grassy car park beside the massive gray stone house.

"It's Luka," Grand-mère said. When we were all out of the car, there were noisy greetings and introductions. Luka, who was maybe fifty, had a very strong Norman accent, but I was able to follow the conversation well enough to understand that he was a fisherman just in from the sea and he was delivering our dinner straight off his boat. He opened the truck's back gate and lifted seaweed off the tops of several buckets so we could see the mussels and whelks, spider crabs and Carteret lobsters, and flat Dieppe sole he'd brought for us. All of it, he said proudly, was still alive and moving.

Guido and Freddy each took a bucket and followed Luka, who carried two, around to the broad veranda behind the house. Gaston came out to meet us. After a round of *les bises*, he shone his attention on Luka.

"Ah, my friend, what have you brought us?" he said, taking one of the buckets from Luka and hoisting it up onto the countertop of his outdoor sink for a look. There was much exclaiming over the catch and some back-and-forth about the best way to prepare each creature, though I thought Gaston probably had all that figured out long before we arrived. Our host was just as enthusiastic when Freddy presented him with a round of the stinky *Pont l'Evêque*-style cheese and Grand-mère showed him the apple tart she had taken from the oven on our way out the door. Gifts were rewarded with a round of drinks.

Luka was given a good dose of strong Calvados to refresh him after a long day's work. And a second for good measure. After a chorus of good-byes, Gaston tucked two bottles of Calvados under Luka's arms as payment for the catch, and waved him on his way.

For his dinner guests, Gaston had chilled several bottles of a summer rosé to the temperature of a castle dungeon, he told us. It was a perfect summer wine, dry and crisp, with hints of tart fruit and sweet clover as it slid down my throat. Gaston waited for my reaction.

"Delicious," I said. He kissed my cheek, patted my bum, and gave me a wicked little wink. To make up for Guido's hurt feelings that afternoon over being called my helper, as Gaston poured wine for him I made a bit of a show about formally introducing Guido, explaining that he was my longtime film partner. They were deep in conversation about our various film adventures when Renée Ferraro arrived bearing a stoneware jar of homemade *foie gras* she'd brought home from a visit to her mother in Épernay the week before. She exchanged greetings all around, accepted a drink, and very pointedly trained her considerable charms on Guido. She neatly separated him from the rest of us for a stroll through Gaston's extensive gardens. Something she wanted to show him, she said. Guido seemed a bit nonplussed, but he went with her. She was a few years older than he and I, certainly older and more sophisticated than his usual female interests. I wondered how that might play out.

Watching them go, Freddy seemed a bit wistful. I said, "You like her?"

"She's interesting." He gave them a last glance before turning away. "She can talk about more than cheese and cider."

"She's also prosecuting your wife, isn't she?

He shook his head. "No, her case was handed over to a *juge d'instruction*, so Renée isn't involved anymore."

"You aren't quite available yet, Freddy," I said. "How's the divorce progressing?"

In the extensive vocabulary of French shrugs and head bobs, I read his to mean something like, so-so. More or less? Yes and no? I didn't press the topic further.

Antoine arrived with my daughter, Casey, and handsome David Breton. I took Freddy's elbow and we walked across the veranda to greet them.

Casey looked radiant, tan and buff. Working in the *fromagerie* all summer seemed to have agreed with her. It helped that David, who was Jacques the cheesemaker's son, was working with her, or at least near her. I had to admit that they made a lovely pair, both of them six feet tall and athletic. Lately, I had noticed, when they stood together I couldn't see daylight between them.

"Helping Jacques turn the new cheese?" I asked, exchanging *les bises* with all three of them.

"No. Talking him out of this." Antoine held up a bottle of thick, yellow cream from the morning milking at the *fromagerie*. "What can he do with the low-fat milk that's left over, he wants to know."

I asked, "Doesn't Grand-mère keep a cow in the herd for herself so she can have milk, cream, and butter?"

"Yes," he said. "But with all the extra people in the house this summer, she didn't have any to spare when Gaston asked her to bring butter and cream for his sauces. So she dipped into the *fromagerie's* supply."

"And God save us," Casey said, patting her flat abdomen, "if anyone in Normandy runs short of butter and cream. Eating the way we do here, somehow I've still lost weight."

"Running five miles a day helps," David said, slipping his hand around her elbow.

"And so does cutting curds." She gifted him with a bright smile, the product of expensive American orthodontia.

"*Bonsoir*, you beautiful young people." Gaston came over with glasses and wine. I made it a point to stand behind Casey when she and Gaston exchanged *la bise*. He noticed, giving me another sly wink. He said, "Now we have a party! Tell me, my precious child," he said, handing a glass to Casey. "What is it about making cheese that fascinates you so? Jacques has told me you have become indispensable this summer."

"It's the chemistry involved in the process that interests me," my earnest chem-major offspring answered, deflecting what I read as a flirtatious pitch from our host. "Jacques has let me experiment a bit with the mix we feed the cows—more clover, less molasses, different varieties of grain, and so on—so that I can see the effects of diet on the finished product. After the last inspection by the European Union, he even let me experiment with pasteurized milk. The EU has something against raw milk."

"No!" Gaston feigned shock. "Cooked milk in our Camembert? The horror."

Casey laughed. "It was terrible stuff. Tasted like the mass-produced crap sold in American supermarkets."

"And you, David?" Gaston handed him a glass. "What keeps you busy while mademoiselle plays Dr. Frankenstein in the *fromagerie?*"

"I deal with the shit," he said with a beautiful grin. "Antoine and I are working on a process to sterilize the dairy waste and convert it to fertilizer slurry more efficiently."

"Tell me it isn't so, Antoine. I'm sure you can find something less aromatic to occupy the boy." Gaston traded Antoine a glass of wine for the bottle of cream. "Now we have a feast. Except…" He nodded toward the buckets of seafood still on the counter next to the sink. Antoine took this as a hint and asked how he could help. Gaston needed to clean the sole, so would anyone mind giving a hand with the shellfish? Antoine and I volunteered while Casey and David wandered off toward the herb garden below the veranda to join Grand-mère and Freddy.

At the sink, Antoine and I drained the whelks—sea snails—and piled them in the center of the large platter Gaston set out for us. Then we tackled the mussels. Antoine, who always seemed to know how to do everything, handed me a knife with a short flat blade and showed me how to pop open the mussel shells without spilling any of the juice inside and losing the taste of the sea.

As I worked side by side with this recently discovered cousin, in that idyllic place, a warm evening breeze full of the scents of lavender and rosemary ruffling my skirt against my bare legs, I was nearly overcome by a wave of happiness. I'd come through a difficult year and a half since the death of the husband I loved very much. My life working in network television was possibly coming to an end, and I wasn't as upset about that as I thought I would be. And somehow in the middle of all things, I had met Jean-Paul, opening a whole new set of possibilities. Moments like that always worry me, make me wait for the other shoe to drop, the effect of too many years spent in the *sturm und drang* of the news business. But I decided on that wonderful summer evening, to just take a deep breath and enjoy the moment.

"It's beautiful here," I said, scraping some algae from a mussel before opening it.

"Yes." Antoine paused to look out across the countryside. The sun hovered over the far horizon, painting the sea beneath bright orange. "How long can it last as it is, I wonder?"

"You sound wistful."

"I am," he said. "I love what we have here, but I don't see many in the younger generation staying around to work on the land as their parents and grandparents did."

"David is majoring in agronomy," I said. "All of this fascinates him."

Antoine nodded. "When he finishes at the university, he will teach, like me, and he will advise. Eventually he might manage a large operation. But will he stick around like his father and milk another man's cows twice a day, every day, for the rest of his life?"

"I can't really see that happening."

"Family farming is disappearing here just as it has in America," he said, pulling another mussel out of the bucket. "A few years ago, when we were still living in San Luis Obispo, Kelly and I took the children on a road trip across America to see the great farmland of the Midwest. And do you know what we found?"

"Tell me."

"Ghost towns," he said. "Mile after mile, we saw fields bursting with crops, fabulous abundance, among the most productive in the world. What we did not see were people. Young people, anyway. Empty towns, closed-up shops; nearly everyone has moved away. Big Agra leases the land it needs and brings in seasonal workers. The famous farm lifestyle—"

He thought for a moment. "What I think you would call the Norman Rockwell, *American Gothic* farm life went missing a generation ago, replaced by industrial farming."

"Are you afraid that will happen here?"

He shrugged, maybe yes, maybe no. He said, "Our family owns one of the most productive farms in Normandy. My father is in London, my brother is in Paris, your brother knows about investments, not farm management, and you are in Los Angeles. Our children are all teenagers and I have not seen any interest from them in staying. So the big question, my dear cousin, is this: When Kelly and I move back to California so that I can resume my work at the university, who will be left in our family to manage the estate?"

"When you move back?" I said. "Sounds like a decision has been made."

"I talked to Kelly yesterday," he said, looking glum. "Her mom was diagnosed with Parkinson's."

"That's a tough one," I said. His blade skidded off the edge of a mussel shell and scraped his thumb. I took the knife from him. "No sharp objects for you when your mind is elsewhere."

He nodded as he took a sip of his wine. "For the last five years, we've worked our butts off getting the estate back into shape. Now Jacques has the *fromagerie* and the herd well in hand. The cider operation is actually profitable again, though I don't have anyone in place to hand it off to when we go back to California. And what's to be done with the fields? How do we exit without everything collapsing in our wake?"

"What does Kelly say?"

"We agreed to enroll Christopher as a senior in the high school in California near her parents to establish residency for the state universities. Beginning next month, he'll live with his grandparents and go to school until we get things figured out and can join him. Lulu isn't ready to give up her friends here, so she'll be back at the village *collège* for at least the fall term. I'm looking at January, February, after we finish the distillation of the fall Calvados before we can think about leaving. June at the latest."

I looked out across the terrace to the herb garden where Grand-mère and Freddy were snipping herbs for Gaston's sauces. I said, "I don't want to be around when you tell Grand-mère."

"She knows," he said, raising a shoulder. "She's known from the beginning; we didn't plan to be here this long. Why do you think she and Aunt Isabelle went to such lengths to draw you into the family fold?"

"Me?" I had to laugh. "I know nothing about farming, and my life is six thousand miles away."

"Maggie, it's not only you that Grand-mère has her eye on. She sees David as the best hope for the future of the estate. But he is in the wrong family line to inherit Martin property. However, your Casey and my Lulu…"

I turned to see where my daughter was, and found her with David, looking out at the ocean. "You think Grand-mère is plotting a sort of dynastic union between our family and the Bretons to keep the estate functioning?"

"We'll see," he said, taking his knife back from me and picking up another mussel. "We'll see."

What Antoine said reminded me to keep a close eye on my

grandmother; she was full of tricks. I know how hard she worked to bring Jean-Paul and me together, hoping that I would follow him home to France when his appointment to Los Angeles finished so that I would be near her, forever. Her campaign had been quite successful, though how things would work out in the end for us was still a great unknown. It made perfect sense that she would now focus her machinations on my daughter and David Breton with the same goal. Gaston was not the only person I would not turn my back on while I was there.

When all the shells were open, Gaston set the platter of mussels and whelks in the middle of a large round table and summoned his guests. We ate the fresh shellfish raw, doused with various spicy sauces and washed down with a very old, rustic white wine from Burgundy; it was the color of honey. Empty shells were tossed into pails, where they soon formed precarious towers. There was a time I would have passed on raw snails, but among the things I had learned during my sojourn in France was to just eat what was put in front of me, enjoy it because it was always interesting and delicious, and not to ask a lot of questions about what it was or where it had come from, either geographically or anatomically. So far, no disasters.

The conversation was lively and fun. Over the last nine months, ever since I had learned that I belonged to this family in France, I had worked on my rusty college French, with a great tutor, Jean-Paul Bernard. And now, after a two-week immersion in the country, I found myself easily slipping between French and English and hardly noticing. Several times that night I had to remind myself that Guido, while fluent in Spanish and Italian, was left clueless about what the rest of us were talking about when everyone was speaking French. Renée Ferraro, I noticed, made sure that Guido did not feel excluded, even if that meant the two of them holding a separate conversation all of their own.

After the shellfish, there was a moment of respite. When Gaston rose from the table and tied on his big, white chef's apron to prepare the next course on the large grill at the far side of the veranda, Casey and David cleared the table. I went over to watch Gaston cook, hoping to learn something.

First, he slathered the lobster and crabs, in the shell, with butter and herbs and then cooked them over a dried apple-wood fire until the shells were brown. While they cooked, he set a large paella pan over the fire at the other end of the big grill and poured in a sauce made of fresh herbs, butter, and cream. When it was hot, he laid in the fileted sole and cooked it quickly. Then he added the crabs and lobster, gave it all a toss or two, and then to the applause and cheers of his guests, flambéed the pan with Calvados and then set the pan in the middle of the table for people to serve themselves.

As I savored every bite I vowed to join Casey on her morning run. After I mopped the last of the sauce from my plate with a piece of bread, I sat back, sated and happy. At my house, the meal would end there. But we were in Normandy, and far from finished.

Casey and David cleared the table again while Gaston poured shots of Calvados into exquisite little glasses and passed them around. We had reached the midpoint in the meal, time for the traditional *trou Normand,* or hole. A break. It was believed that alcohol opened the blood vessels of the stomach in preparation for the next round of food. So, we drank our shots, and we rested, and got ready for the next course.

The conversation turned to the ad hoc graveyard among the carrots. Antoine asked Gaston about the actual process of disinterring the remains.

"It would be so much easier if the poor bastards were American, British, or French," Gaston said, rising to check the fire in his grill. "If they were, an honor guard, a brass band, and a specialized military unit would be at the site tomorrow at dawn. A motorcade would carry away the remains and fly them to Hawaii for identification. And then someone would hand Élodie a check for the carrots that were disturbed, and we would be done with it. However, if, as Élodie assures us, they are German, the priest will ask the parish sexton to appoint some men here to do the honors. He will offer prayers for the immortal souls of the dead, up they'll come and off they'll go to Orglades to be joined again in yet another anonymous hole."

"I would sure like to expedite all that," Freddy said. "I can't wait for the lab in Nice to get back from vacation."

"There is a way," Renée said. "I spoke with Nice this afternoon. If you'll forgive the description, there is a skeleton crew in place at the forensics lab. If anyone can deliver to them proof of the nationality of the remains, then the proper authorities will be notified and you'll be finished with the problem. As soon as the day after tomorrow, perhaps."

Grand-mère caught my eye and held it. Clearly, she had something to say to me. Privately.

"No more talk of dead people," Gaston said. "Now we eat."

The entrée was served: grilled summer vegetables and pan-seared escalope of duck with *foie gras*, served with sauce Normande, which is made of fresh cream, butter and, Calvados, of course. The duck was accompanied by a lovely dry Côtes du Rhône.

Coffee, apple tart, cheese, and apple brandy followed. The cheese Freddy brought from the *fromagerie* stank up the car on the way over, but tasted rich and mellow with the delicious Calvados *hors d'age* that Gaston uncorked and poured for us with great ceremony.

We lingered. The conversation turned to the community center Freddy was building for the residents of his new development. Eventually the center would offer a year-round swimming pool, a gym with locker rooms, and a large multi-purpose room with a kitchen. At the moment, though the facility was still unfinished, the kitchen and the locker rooms were functional and were being used by the students who were working on the estate that summer. The young people were housed in a tent city on the graded site of the future tennis courts behind the community building, locating their joyful evening noise as far away from Grand-mère's house as it was possible to be while remaining on the estate.

Gaston, as the mayor, hoped that he and Freddy could work out an arrangement so that the villagers would be able to use the facilities. At least the senior citizens, the mayor said. And the youth, David added. Freddy suggested that a little help with the permit process might sway him. And so it went until the conversational string ran out. It was time to bring the evening to a close.

As we said our good-byes and walked out together to the car park, Renée offered Guido a lift, and he did not refuse. Grand-mère shooed Freddy, Casey, David and Antoine into Antoine's Mini, took me by the elbow and handed me Freddy's car keys. "I need to check something, tonight. You'll drive."

We waited until everyone else was gone. When the lights of the second car turned from the drive onto the village road, Gaston came out from around the house carrying a shovel and a flashlight.

"Will this do?" he asked.

"Assez bien, merci." Grand-mère put the shovel into the trunk and climbed into the passenger seat holding the flashlight in her lap.

Gaston leaned into her open window. "I am not sure this is wise, Élodie."

"Wise?" She shrugged. "Perhaps not. But necessary, yes. Maggie, dear, *allons-y.*"

There was no moon. We drove through the dark under a canopy of stars, the only car on the village road.

"Are you going to tell me where we're going?" I asked.

"We are going to rob a grave, my dear."

━6━

"SOMEONE IS OUT THERE, Grand-mère." I shone the flashlight into the carrot field where I had seen a faint glimmer in the sweep of our headlights when we made the turn at the end of the orchard. Just a bit of light among the carrot rows, or maybe not; there and gone too quickly for me to be confident that it had been there at all. A reflection off a scavenging rabbit's eye or a shiny leaf?

"Zut alors," Grand-mère said, aiming the flashlight into the trench where the skull had been found. "You see? It's what I was afraid of."

I did see. Someone had been there before us, digging around in the bottom of the trench with a tool no bigger than a garden trowel. Or one of Olivia's excavation tools. I looked off again into the distance where I thought I had seen a light, but there was nothing to see except carrot tops ruffled by a breeze.

"Did they find anything?" Grand-mère asked, giving my shoulder a little nudge. "Go down closer and see, please."

It was dark and creepy out in the carrot field, and even creepier down in a trench that intruded into a mass grave. But Grand-mère was so determined that I take a look that I hoisted up my skirt and did as she asked. I scooped up some of the loosened dirt at the bottom of the trench, held it up to the light and let it run between my fingers. Nothing but rocks and soil.

"What are we looking for, exactly?" I asked.

"The one man we didn't burn," she said, handing down Gaston's shovel.

"What happens if we find him?"

Above me, she was a black outline, backlit by the light streaming into the night from the headlamps of Freddy's Jag. I couldn't read her face and her only immediate response was to lift one shoulder. What did that mean?

"Just dig," she said.

And so I did. I started at the marker Pierre Dauvin had placed at the spot where the skull had landed after it fell off the ditch-digger scoop and walked back to the spot where the scoop's teeth had first bitten into the ground to bring up that last load. Between the two points, I dug, dumping the turned-up soil onto the road above. Grand-mère kicked through each load with the toe of her shoe, now and then holding something up to the lights from the car before dropping it again. When the hole I stood in was about three feet deeper than the trench, I stuck the shovel into the ground and leaned on it. Soft soil or not, the digging was hard work.

"Ça va?" Grand-mère asked.

"How far down did you put him?"

"Maybe one meter, but remember the soil builds up over time."

I wiped my face with the tail of my blouse and pulled out the shovel. My phone buzzed in my skirt pocket before I had plunged the shovel back into the dirt. I pulled it out and checked caller I.D. It was Casey, so I answered.

"What's up?" I said.

"Where are you?"

"I'm with Grand-mère."

"I thought I heard you come in, but there's no one here. It spooked me."

"Guido isn't back?"

"No. No one is here."

"Are the doors locked?"

"When did anyone around here ever lock doors?" she said. "Is Grand-mère okay?"

"Everything is just peachy, honey. We'll be home soon. I'm calling Antoine to go over and check the house."

She argued a little about the necessity of that, but agreed to open the front door and wait for Antoine to arrive. Grand-mère was talking over me, asking what was wrong, but instead of answering her when I ended Casey's call, I called Antoine and asked him to check the house. I could hear jazz playing in the background so I knew I hadn't wakened him, but I was sorry to send him out again. He did not seem put out by the request and promised to go straight over. When I put my phone away again I told Grand-mère that Casey had heard something.

"Antoine is going to see about it?" she asked.

"He is."

She nodded as she pointed at the shovel. "Please, *chérie*, just a little further down, yes?"

I dug. I hadn't gone much further before the tip of the shovel glanced off something hard. Grand-mère heard the clunk and bent forward, urging me on. Feeling a bit queasy, I poked around with the tip of the shovel to define the outlines of whatever was down there, found an edge, wedged the shovel under it and lifted.

"Ribs," I said, jumping away, feeling queasy. I had dislodged three of them, pale brown spikes now sticking up out of the black earth.

With surprising agility for an old girl, Grand-mère lowered herself into the trench and took the shovel from me. She scraped around in the dirt among the remnants of someone's rib cage. Then she got down on her knees and dug with her hands. Out of the dirt came shreds of rotted fabric, hard black lengths that looked to me like bits of an old leather belt. And buttons. Lots of brass buttons. She asked for the flashlight to examine one of her finds, seemed satisfied with it, and rose to her feet.

"*Chérie*, can we cover this back up now?"

"What did you find?"

She shook her head. "Better that you don't know."

With that, she put a hand on my shoulder for support as she climbed back out onto the road. I filled in the hole and stomped around on the dirt in my sandals to pack it down again. When I was finished, the area looked like what it was, a recent hole, filled in. And that was all right. I picked up one of the brass buttons Grand-mère had dropped, a Nazi eagle still attached to a shred of heavy fabric, and knew that in the morning when Pierre investigated he would find all the proof he needed that the remains discovered in that place were, indeed, German. Grand-mère offered me a hand out. Standing at the edge of the trench, for insurance, or maybe out of habit, I took out my phone and snapped a few photos of the site before we got into the car and drove home.

When they heard the Jag drive up, Casey and Antoine came outside.

"Holy *merde*," Antoine said when he saw how filthy we were. "Was there an accident?"

"No, no," Grand-mère said, patting his cheek on her way inside, leaving a muddy streak. "Looking for night crawlers in the carrots."

She went on upstairs without saying anything more. I wanted to follow, but my daughter held me by the arm and gave me a hard-eyed, motherly looking over.

"You need to explain yourself, missy," she said.

"Did I blow curfew?"

Antoine chortled. He leaned over and kissed Casey on the cheek, decided against getting that close to me, and said, "I'm not sure I want to know what you two were up to tonight. I'll sleep on it and maybe we'll talk tomorrow. Maybe."

"In the morning," I said, "will you please call Pierre and tell him that during the night someone was digging in the sewer trench?"

He glanced up the stairs, following the sound of Grand-mère's bedroom door closing. All he said was *"Merde."*

Casey and I stood in the open doorway and watched him until he had crossed the compound and gone back inside his house before we closed and locked our own front door.

"Seriously, Mom," Casey said, following me into the kitchen. "You and Grand-mère went digging?"

I took the button from my pocket and handed it to her. When she realized what it was, she paled and set it on the counter.

She said, "You do know that it's illegal in Europe to buy, sell, or display Nazi insignia."

"I haven't done any such thing. I merely dug around on family land and that's what popped out."

"Dear God, Mom." She reached over and felt the shred of fabric still attached to the button. After a minute, she asked, "Why?"

"I don't know," I said. "Grand-mère was looking for something."

"Did she find it?"

"I don't know what she found. There wasn't much light out there and she was not sharing. But I do know this: we weren't the only ones who went digging tonight. We'll leave it to Pierre to figure it all out. In the meantime, sweetheart, I need you to say nothing about this, to anyone. If Pierre asks you, don't lie. After all, you really don't know anything, right?"

"Except that you came home looking like you'd been wrestling in the mud."

"And maybe we were."

She picked up the shred of fabric and dangled the button in front of me. "What are you going to do with this?"

"I have no idea. I should have dug a hole and buried it."

"I'll deal with it." She slipped it into her pajama pocket.

Casey stayed close beside me while I locked the back door and went upstairs.

Though there was a hopeful band of pink rising along the eastern horizon, it was still dark when I set out for a run with Casey and David. An easy five miles, they said. On flat ground; a given because the area was entirely flat. But they were young, and fast, and competitive, so I gave up the effort to keep stay abreast of them and settled for the struggle to merely keep them in sight in front of me. After the big dinner at Gaston's the night before and some grave robbing afterward that left me muscle-sore, I woke up feeling stiff and logy. A good run usually makes me feel better, but at a pace more suitable to a forty-something cookie like me than a dash down the side of the village road with two very fit youngsters.

We all wore reflectors on our shoes and on the fronts and backs of our jerseys, but during the transition between dawn and daylight we were barely visible to cars on the road until they were right on us. As Casey and David pulled out further in front of me, I lost sight of them altogether except for a glimpse in silhouette when they went over the slight rise where the culvert at the Foullard farm driveway passed under the road.

I carried a little flashlight. When I heard cars coming I would aim its beam on the pavement at my feet so that I could be seen. At that hour of the day in a farm community lots of people were headed toward work, and I was certain that plenty of them were as sleepy when they left home as I had been.

As odds would have it, two cars approaching from different directions would pass just when they were abreast of me. There was no shoulder, so I stepped off into the sloping, grassy verge and walked until they passed, watching the ground to avoid rabbit holes. The cars passed and I went back up onto the pavement. Twenty yards up the road, the car on the far side, the one headed in the same direction I was, skidded into a U-turn, sped up and seemed to aim right at me. I raised my flashlight and aimed it at the driver's face. All I saw was a wide grin in a field of white at the same time I dropped and rolled down the embankment, stopping just before I would land in a soggy ditch. Above me, the driver bumped back into his lane, made another U-turn, and sped off. As soon as he passed me, I was on my feet and running as hard as I could; he was headed toward Casey and David.

"Hey Mom," Casey, with David close beside her, loped toward me. They had turned and met me as they headed home. "You okay? You look beat."

I bent over and tried to breathe. I managed to ask, "Did you see that guy?"

"What guy?"

"Just some idiot."

They walked beside me until I could breathe normally again. After a few minutes, we set off at an easy jog. We had left that morning through the compound gate, but returned by turning up the farm access road because Casey was curious to see where Grand-mère and I had been digging the night before. The sun was fully up by then.

We came around the corner at the end of the orchard, and stopped dead. The scene around the sewer trench looked as if the gates of hell had opened up and vomited out the charred remains of all those benighted souls my grandmother had buried so long ago. Bones lay everywhere, on the road, among the carrots, up on the hedgerow berm. Some were crushed as if a vehicle had run them over.

"Mom!" Casey was shaking. "Did you and Grand-mère do this?"

"Of course not." I put my arm around her. Thinking about the driver of the car that had run me off the road a few minutes earlier, I said, "Someone came here after we left, looking for something. Wonder if they found it."

David pulled out his phone and called Pierre Dauvin. And then he called his father. Immediately, we heard the motor of Jacques's delivery van start up and come toward us from the direction of the *fromagerie*. David jogged down the road to meet him, to stop him before he would run over any of the bones. Jacques got out of his little truck and for a moment just stared at the macabre scene before he started walking to meet us.

Apparently, Casey had already told David that Grand-mère and I had been out there digging the night before, because David retold what I told her to his father. Jacques walked around a bit, stepping over a femur to look into the trench, thinking things through. After a brief conversation with David, Jacques came over to me.

"Maggie," he said, "this worries me. It wasn't here when I drove in this morning. Whoever was here can't be far away. I want to drive you and Casey home now, before Pierre arrives. He can be very difficult to get along with until he's had time to assess a situation. David and I will take care of him until he calms down."

We protested, but he insisted. Pierre would get to us eventually, Jacques said. But later would be better.

When Jacques dropped us off in front of Grand-mère's house, he told Casey he would understand if she needed some time off from work. She said, "Pierre, the cows won't take the day off, so I won't." With that, she headed straight inside to shower and dress for work at the *fromagerie*.

Jacques asked me for more details about Grand-mère's escapade the night before. There actually wasn't very much to tell him, but I gave him all the dirty details. I also told him about the car incident that morning. The grave digging gave him pause, the car sent him reeling.

Jacques had a strong Norman accent so I couldn't always understand him, especially when he spoke fast and used local slang, as he did when he fulminated about the idiot who forced me off the road. He kept pointing to my grass-stained knees as he told me, I think, that I was lucky I wasn't crushed just like the bones in the road had been. Sometimes, he said, locals who aren't quite sober find sport in forcing runners and bikers off the road. But—and here he tapped his wrist where a watch would be if a cheesemaker wore a watch—it was the close timing of the two events that worried him.

Casey came out of the house wearing her white coveralls, with her hair tucked up inside a white cap, ready for work. Jacques waved her into the truck, gave me some apparently pithy last words of advice, kissed me on both cheeks, got in and drove them off. To avoid the road that had become a bone yard, he took the back way out of the compound to the narrow old road that passed above the orchard and the cider house, turned along the far side of the pasture and ended at the milking barn. It would be a bumpy ride.

I watched until I couldn't see them anymore, happy that Casey had not walked to work alone that morning. Worried about the trouble my grandmother and I were in, I collected Gaston's shovel from Freddy's trunk and cleaned it under a garden hose. The day was already warm, and I felt every mile I had run, trying to keep up with the kids. I leaned the shovel against the garden gate, took a drink from the hose, and headed for the house. As I went up the back steps, I nearly collided with a grim-faced Olivia on her way out after fetching the keys for the potting shed where she kept her tools from a rack of house keys inside the back door. Her only response to my greeting was a curt nod before she hurried on her way.

Grand-mère called to me as soon as she heard the door. I looked into the kitchen and found her at the big oak table that ran down the middle of the room, having croissants and coffee with Grand-mère Marie, Gaston, and Ma Mère, the abbess at the convent in the village, who wore her full black habit on that warm summer day. I wasn't surprised to see the abbess and Marie at the kitchen table so early in the day, or Gaston for that matter. The three women had been friends forever, bonded in youth, companions during the Nazi Occupation. They were inveterate, or incorrigible, matchmakers and meddlers. They had paired up Marie's daughter Louise and Grand-mère's son, my Uncle Gérard, though the union had not been a happy one. After two sons, Antoine and Bébé, the couple split up, though they never divorced. One might expect that spectacular failure to have stopped the matchmakers, but it hadn't, as I knew only too well.

From the way they were all looking at me, I thought they had been waiting for me. I steeled myself, and went into the kitchen to see what was up. I was a drippy, sweaty mess, so I didn't actually touch cheeks with anyone during the exchange of greetings.

"Gaston," I said, washing my hands at the kitchen sink and drying them on a paper towel. "Your shovel is outside. Let me know when you're leaving and I'll put it in your car."

He and the three women exchanged a look full of meaning that I couldn't read. I wasn't going to say anything about the carnage on the access road until I knew what they were up to.

Ma Mère and Grand-mère seemed to be in fine fettle, color up, posture straight. But I thought that Grand-mère Marie seemed frail that morning, and it worried me. When she picked up her bowl of *café au lait*, her hands shook. I was sorry that I had missed their earlier conversation because something definitely was brewing among them. Whatever it was had upset Grand-mère Marie. I did not suspect that any of them had taken a shovel to the trench after Grand-mère and I left.

Grand-mère poured coffee and milk for me and set it at the place beside her, handing me the basket of croissants when I sat down. The croissants were still warm. As I reached for the butter and homemade preserves, Grand-mère Marie wrapped a wedge of fresh melon in a thin slice of French ham and set it on my plate. She had known me as a baby, and lost me when I was a toddler. The way she spoke to me and fussed over me, it seemed that in her mind I was still that tyke.

After the meal Gaston fed us the night before, I thought I wouldn't eat again for a week. But suddenly I was ravenous. After

I washed down the first bite of croissant with coffee, I looked into each of the faces at the table, all of them still watching me with great intensity. I asked, "What's up?"

Grand-mère slipped an envelope under the edge of my plate. "Antoine found this on our door this morning when he came with the croissants."

The note inside was written on stationery from the village's workmen's hotel, the only hotel in town. The Gothic-looking script was an old-fashioned German hand, but the words were English. The author said that she was the daughter of a soldier who had been posted in the area during the war. While her father had not been allowed to divulge his exact location for security reasons, he had managed to send home photographs of the house where he was billeted. Sometime during the last year of the war, he went missing and the family never learned what happened to him.

A day ago, she wrote, she received a Google alert with a report that human remains, probably from World War II and probably German, had been found on a farm in Normandy, in the very area where her father had been. How happy she was when she recognized that the house in the background of the online images was the very same house that was in her father's snapshots. Her father had been very fond of the place and she would very much like to be given permission to pay a call. Perhaps someone there might help her know what happened to the dear man. The letter was signed Erika Karl, born von Streicher.

I slipped the letter back into its envelope. "This is what you were afraid would happen, Grand-mère. A survivor has shown up. Did you know anyone by that name?"

The three women nodded in unison, one forward tip of the head each. Clearly, from the grim looks on their faces they had not been fond of Herr von Streicher.

"Will you talk to the daughter?" I asked.

"No." Grand-mère cleared her throat. "Gaston believes it is time for me to talk to you about what happened here. With your cameras."

"Wonderful," I said. Concerned that she might change her mind, I said, "Today?"

She nodded.

"It will have to be this morning," I said, "because I'm off to see Jean-Paul's mother right after lunch."

"All right."

"Grand-mère Marie, Ma Mère," I said. "Will you join us?"

No, no, Marie said, her English was too terrible for her to say anything for American television. Besides, her hair was a mess and she needed to finish putting up the plums. Anyway, what could she say that Élodie wouldn't say better? No thank you, she wasn't ready to be a movie star.

Ma Mère shook her head. She would need permission from the diocese to speak on camera, but she promised to ask for the bishop's blessing in case I had questions for her later. As a caution to me, she said, "The Occupation is a painful topic for all of us who were forced to work for the men who not only took over our country, but our homes. Please remember that."

I assured her that I would go gently. We did not need all of the grim details, I told her, but what happened to them was still a story that needed to be told by the people who suffered through it. It was important that there be a record. She agreed to that. I turned to Gaston and asked him, "Are you in?"

Grand-mère Marie laughed. "He was just a baby then. What could he know?"

Gaston seemed very relieved to have an out. Besides, he said, he had town business to deal with. An American motorcycle club was coming through on Saturday after visiting the D-Day beaches. Old people, he said, bike touring. Some of them were the children of men who fought on those beaches. As mayor, he wanted to make sure that signs were put up on the road from Pérrier to direct the group into the village center so they would come and see the memorial that had been erected after the war in honor of the American G.I. liberators of 1944. The *café tabac* would fly its American flag to welcome anyone in need of refreshment, and would be very happy to sell some souvenir postcards.

Grand-mère reminded him that the baptism party for Pierre Dauvin's nephew would be on Sunday. She hoped the motorcyclists weren't planning to camp out overnight at the regional park, as they had last year. She did not want a phalanx of motorcycles to come roaring down the beach road on Sunday and scare the children and foul up traffic. Marie, however, thought it might be nice to invite the bikers. "Wouldn't the children love to see so many motorcycles? It would be like a parade. And maybe we knew some of their fathers."

As mayor and therefore the village's head cheerleader, Gaston liked the idea. My grandmother did not. "Let them spend their money at the *café tabac*," she said. Ma Mère added, "It is a party to celebrate the baby, not to remember war." And that was the end of it.

Guido came in through the back door just as that issue was settled. He looked a bit bedraggled; grizzled chin, rumpled clothes. When all eyes turned to him, he blushed.

"Good morning," I said. "Coffee?"

"I had mine, thanks. Good morning all," he said without venturing all the way into the kitchen from the mud room. The bruise on his jaw had turned several interesting shades of blue and purple. "I'm just going to grab a shower and get to work." He offered a wave in lieu of saying good-bye and turned to go up the back stairs. He made it part-way up, then came down again. "Maggie, what's the schedule for the day?"

"We're going to film a conversation with Grand-mère. I like the morning light in the kitchen, so let's set up in here, see how it looks." I turned to my grandmother. "Ready in about an hour?"

She shrugged, that was fine. I turned back to Guido. "Okay with you?"

"Yep."

"And don't forget," I said to his retreating back. "I'm leaving right after lunch, so you're sprung for the afternoon."

Marie giggled. "I think he'll find a way to occupy himself." Poor Guido hung his head and made a quick retreat.

If we were going to be filming in Grand-mère's kitchen that morning, then lunch for the workers would have to be prepared at Antoine's house, where Marie lived. Marie volunteered to supervise the women who came in to cook. The two grandmothers were working out lunch details when a thought occurred to me.

I asked, "What time did Antoine bring the croissants this morning?"

"It was just daybreak," Grand-mère said. "Half past six?"

"We got in last night after midnight," I said. "And there was no note on the door. So, when did Erika von Streicher Karl put her note on our front door?"

─7─

"PULL THE EXPOSURE BACK a couple of stops," I told Guido. "Let's desaturate the color a bit."

He did as I asked, then stepped back from his camera so that I could see the effect. Onscreen, I wanted my grandmother's story to look something like faded snapshots in a family album, its hard edges softened by time. This was an old story, after all.

Grand-mère sat at the far end of the well-scrubbed oak table that ran down the center of the big farmhouse kitchen. The microwave oven and American-size refrigerator behind her were the wrong background for a film segment about events that took place over seventy years earlier. I asked her to move a little to her right so that the appliances were out of frame. The shift was enough so that when she settled back into her chair, late morning light streaming through the windows over the ancient stone sink now touched the top of her head and picked up gold highlights in her dark brown hair. I knew she dyed her hair to cover the gray, but she had a good hairdresser so it looked perfectly natural, even in sunlight. At ninety-two, Grand-mère was still elegant, slender and straight and graceful in the way that French women seem bred to be. She looked too genteel to be the mastermind of the murder of seventeen men.

"Guido," I said, "will you sharpen the focus? The soft color makes Grand-mère look dreamy enough."

He leaned way back to better see his monitor. "Looks fine."

"Where are your glasses?" I asked him.

As his hand came up to his breast pocket, where his glasses were, he looked across the room to see whether Taylor, one of our film interns, had noticed. We would be using two cameras in this segment, and Taylor was behind one of them. She was serious about her work, and as this was her first opportunity to participate in primary filming, she was focused entirely on the image in the monitor of her lens and not on whatever Guido might be up to. Besides, I thought that something was developing between her and Zach, one of the other film interns, a man closer to her own age and experience than my old friend Guido was. I also thought that Guido, fresh from an overnight visit with the district's handsome *procureur*, and after getting a bit of a comeuppance the day before, ought to be more ready to think about something other than his next conquest.

"The focus?" I said, patting the glasses case in his pocket.

With another glance toward Taylor, he put on his glasses, made the focus adjustment, and glared at me.

Grand-mère busied her hands by picking through the colander of raspberries on the table in front of her, taking out twigs and leaves. She seemed deep in thought before she asked, "Maggie, dear, how does the settlement of your mother's estate progress?"

"Slowly," I said. "Isabelle's estate is complicated."

"You still call her Isabelle?" she asked. "You can't call my daughter, Mother?"

"I never knew her, Grand-mère. To me, Mother is the woman who raised me. And Isabelle is Isabelle."

The small lift of her left shoulder showed both acknowledgment of what was to her a sad truth and her resignation to it. "If money is a problem until the estate is settled—"

"I'm fine, thank you." I checked Taylor's camera and got a thumbs-up from Guido about sound levels on the synchronized sound recorder. It was time for me to take the chair on Grand-mère's left so that I faced her across the corner of the table. Guido's camera had me in profile, Taylor caught me full face, the opposite of their camera angles on Grand-mère. After I had settled into my seat, there was a little rearranging of key lights behind us to separate us visually from the background. When I was assured that both Guido and Taylor were ready to begin, I turned and gave my grandmother a smile that I prayed did not look mercenary. "As long as I meet my film deadline, I'll be solvent."

"Well then." She set the berries aside and folded her red-stained hands on the table in front of her. So far, the cameras hadn't seemed to bother Grand-mère as we walked around the property, talking about the estate's history, its people, and its various enterprises. Indeed, she seemed to enjoy the attention and the constant companionship. But this conversation about the men buried under the carrots was on a different plane altogether, and I knew I needed to proceed with caution.

"Grand-mère," I said, "anytime you want to stop, or if there's something that is too painful to talk about, promise me you'll let me know."

Her cheeks colored. "And then what? You pack your cameras and go home, perhaps to lose your job?"

"No," I said, smoothing a stray strand of her hair. "Nothing as dire as that. I'm sure we can come up with something that will make the network happy. Discovery of the skull alone, with some spooky background music and light effects, could be turned into something more if we need it to."

She smiled at the thought, and relaxed some. The von Streicher letter had upset both her and Marie, robbed them of some of their normal resilience. Until Grand-mère told me she wanted to talk on camera about how all those men came to be buried where they were, I was ready to scrap the piece rather than cause her further pain. I admired her fortitude in going ahead with it, but I wasn't sure that we should. Maybe she sensed my qualms, because she caught my hand, and after a few breaths she squared her shoulders, looked at Guido's camera lens, and nodded. "I am ready to tell my story now, as it should be told. Will there be a drum roll or some trumpets to start us off?"

"Artillery fire in the background would be appropriate." I checked again with Guido and Taylor; in sync, in focus, we had speed and we were ready. To Grand-mère, I said, "For this segment of the film, the first thing we'll see is a black screen. Slowly, a title crawls across from the right: OCCUPIED NORMANDY, FEBRUARY 25, 1944. And then your story begins."

"But that isn't where the story begins, *chérie*," she said.

"It's your story, Grand-mère." The cameras were rolling. "Where does it begin?"

"It was so very long ago." Absently, she touched the little pouch of soft flesh under her chin. "And I was so young. Just fifteen I think when the war began. Still in school."

"In the village school here?" I asked when her pause stretched long.

"No. In Paris still, with my parents. When the Germans arrived in 1940, they swept in on us like a biblical plague. Overnight, we went from being a free people to subjects living under tyranny. Papa thought I would be better off here in Normandy with friends. Better food than in Paris and fewer troops for the father of a young daughter to worry about. As I have told you, my father, your great-grandfather, was a cheese broker. He knew most all of the *fromagers* in France. The good ones, anyway. So for safekeeping, he brought me to this village to board with his old friend, Giles Martin."

"My other great-grandfather," I said.

"Eventually he was, yes."

"Is that how you met my grandfather?"

"Oh, no. I knew Henri from childhood. Our families used to pass summer holidays together in Anneville-sur-Mer, where you visited when you were here last fall. You remember?" She searched my face, always hoping for a profound connection I doubt was there. Though the land had been in my family for centuries, everything and everyone here was new to me. Knowing that seemed to fill her with regret. "Of course, we had only a simple cottage then. Your mother took it down to build the modern pavilion that's there now." She smiled. "A big improvement over the old, I admit. Indoor plumbing and Wi-Fi; what would your grandfather have said about that?"

"Did your families expect you and Henri to marry?" I asked, nudging her back toward the topic.

She gave me a little Gallic shrug, meaning, perhaps. "They were not unhappy or surprised when it happened, yes? It was no secret that I was always in love with Henri, though he was several years older and seemed to think I was a little pest when we were children. But he wasn't here when I arrived. As soon as the war began, he and his brother enlisted. By the time I arrived, Henri was already a prisoner of the Germans somewhere in Poland. And his brother had perished."

Henri was in Poland? I jotted down a question to ask her later. "Tell me about your life during the Occupation," I said.

"Ah, well." She gazed off across the kitchen, her eyes lighting on the old stone sink and the row of jars on the counter that she had sterilized for her next batch of preserves.

"Was it life?" she said. "It felt like a bad dream I could not wake from. One day I was a schoolgirl, and the next I was a forced laborer, working on the farm of my parents' dear friends, growing food for German bellies, but not our own. Certainly we ate better here than my family did in Paris; they nearly starved before the war was over. But until you have lost your freedom to simply walk about, to read a book of your choosing, to live life on your own terms, you can't know how cruel the Occupation was. I think I could tolerate hunger better than the oppression."

I poured her a glass of water from the pitcher on the table. She wrapped her hands around the glass, but did not lift it to her lips. After a moment, she continued.

"To begin, we were a world of women, children, and old men. And, of course, the Boche. Many of our men, the ones like Henri who had gone off to fight, were now prisoners of the Germans. Others left the country or went into hiding. Some joined the *Résistance*. But the rest of them, oh my dear, it was terrible. During that first summer, any remaining able-bodied men, older boys, and some of the young women were swept up by the STO, the *Service du Travail Obligatoire*, and taken away to work in German labor camps. They were slaves, Maggie. And many of them starved before the war was over.

"I suppose that those of us left to work here were the lucky ones," she said. "If we had known what horrors the Nazis imposed on so many millions of people, we would not have complained about our plight. My father had been wrong: There was no safe place for anyone, anywhere."

She dropped her eyes to her stained hands. After a long pause, I put my hand over hers.

"Can you talk about the Germans posted here?" I asked.

Again, a little shrug as she turned her focus toward me. "Arrogant, of course. And cruel. They walked around with an insufferable swagger. They had been trained to believe that they were a superior order of men, and that we were nothing. But—" She leaned forward, pinching her thumb and index finger together and holding them up to me. "But they were tiny men. What is that word your daughter used? Such a good one. Ah, yes, pissant. Pissant low-level functionaries in Germany before the war: clerks, accountants, that sort of thing. And they were pissant functionaries during that big war: little men with little jobs in this little place. Most of the soldiers posted here were too old or too unfit for combat duty. They weren't suited for anything grander than keeping an eye on a bunch of farm girls."

"But there were combat troops in Normandy," I said.

"*Bien sûr*. There were Waffen-SS combat troops all along the coast, the Atlantic Wall they called it. But many of those men were not German."

"SS, but not Germans?" I asked.

"Not all. Maybe not most. The Waffen-SS conscripted men from all of the areas that Germany conquered and annexed. Czechs and Austrians, Turks and Poles were put into uniform and folded into the German war effort as forced laborers of another sort. We had very little in this village to entertain or interest them, so we saw little of those troops until the rout after D-Day. When the time came, they couldn't surrender to the Allies fast enough."

"Interesting," I said. "At some point, soldiers commandeered this house. Tell me about that."

"What can I say?" A little shrug as she gathered her thoughts. "In the summer of 1940 a platoon of soldiers, seventeen men in all, moved into this house because of its size and location. From here, they oversaw production and shipment of food from the farms of five villages. It was a large area, and a very valuable one; people have to eat. The officer in charge was Major Horst von Streicher, a petty tyrant of the first order. Before the war, he was headmaster of a boys' school. I suppose that bossing around little boys was good training for commanding us, but it taught him nothing about making cheese and cider or growing crops."

"Surely," I said, thinking of my German friends and colleagues, many whom I admired, "there must have been some kind or generous men among the Occupation forces."

"A benign cancer is a cancer just the same, *non?*" Her left shoulder rose in a dismissive shrug. "But I must tell you that our experience here was not the same as the experience of some others. This estate became a work camp for those of us who were assigned here. But in the villages and elsewhere, only one or two soldiers would move into a house with a family. If those people did as they were told, they could otherwise ignore the foreigners living among them and eating at their table. It was not a good situation, but it could be borne."

"Sometimes friendships of a sort must have developed," I said.

"Yes, they did. But not here."

I said, "Major von Streicher's daughter left a note on your door this morning asking you to speak with her. If you sat down with her, what would you tell her about her father?"

Grand-mère shook her head. "I have nothing to tell her that a child should want to hear about her father. He has been dead for over seventy years now, so she is not young. But she is still his child. No, I will not speak with her. But I will tell you, my dear, in front of these cameras, what happened to us."

"Go ahead." I said.

She began telling her story in calm, measured tones, but became more emotional, more angry, as her narrative unfolded.

"By the autumn harvest of 1940, there were only eight of us women left to do all the work of the estate," she said. "Every day, we rose before the sun to milk the cows and start the day's batch of cheese. We plowed and planted and harvested using horses—big Percherons—because there was no petrol for the tractors. After the harvest, we made cider and distilled brandy, and put up preserves. And every day, we had to clean up after those *putains de salauds*, do their laundry, and prepare three meals for them. The soldiers ate like pigs and drank like fools and complained that we had no beer, no Champagne, no eggs for their breakfast after they ate all of the laying chickens."

"How were you treated?" I asked.

"I can't say that we were ever treated well," she said. "But when the Germans arrived in 1940 as victors, they were generally disciplined, more so than the English and American soldiers who came during the *Libération*. For those men it was, *oh là*, French girls! No, the Germans had strict rules against fraternization, and initially they held themselves aloof from us civilians, which was fine with us. But by the summer of 1943, when the war began to go badly for Germany, everything changed. I think that when the men here realized that their fatherland would lose the war, again, and that they would soon go back to their miserable pre-war lives, they didn't give a damn about discipline anymore."

I asked, "What did they do?"

"They drank," she said. "The worse the war news became, the more they drank. We had always served them cider with dinner and brandy after. But now they refused the cider and demanded brandy with their meal. They got drunk. And when they were drunk, no female was safe. We started watering down the brandy, to slow them, but it didn't work. All we could do was to set out their daily ration on the table with their meal and go lock ourselves into our quarters."

"Where were your quarters?"

"The women workers slept in a loft in the cider house," she said. "We kept the doors locked, of course, not only for our safety but to keep the men from stealing brandy that was stored in barrels on the ground floor. On Christmas night—it was 1943—a group of soldiers broke in looking for more brandy. As drunk as they were, some managed to get up the ladder to the loft. They fell in among us, grabbing anyone they could catch. We were young girls, virgins, and the men did not care. After that night, it became a regular war for us, trying to stay safe from them."

"Did you complain to Major von Streicher?"

"We didn't dare," she said. "He had already taken a village girl, a child of fifteen, into his bed as his regular victim. No, instead, we went to the village priest. But the priest asked us to do what we could to take care of ourselves without involving the church."

Grand-mère held up a finger. "Wait before you pass judgment on the priest, *chérie*. By that time, there were people in hiding all over the parish, maybe a dozen in the cellars of the convent alone, and more in the rectory. The priest was afraid that a complaint to von Streicher, who was not a just man, would bring scrutiny on the church that might imperil every one of us. Even the blessed women of the convent would not be safe if their cellars were searched."

"Who were all those people in hiding?"

A little shrug. "All sorts. From time to time, people escaped from Nazi labor and prisoner-of-war camps. Those who managed to get home had to be hidden or they would be shot. There were people from the *Résistance*, a family of Jews that had hoped to find sanctuary among the English on the Channel Islands until the Germans occupied there in June of 1940 as well. There were spies and pilots: English intelligence used the open fields of Normandy to land small planes and gliders that brought in and took out strategic information and people. Sometimes they were shot down, sometimes they crash landed, other times they had to wait for pick-up. Those men and women needed to be hidden until they could get out again."

A sudden thought came to her that made her smile. "One day we found a wounded English pilot in the orchard and hid him in the cider house loft for some weeks until he was well enough to be taken to the sisters at the convent. Can you imagine what the Germans would have done to us if they had caught us hiding him?"

"I assume the flier was gone from the loft before that particular Christmas night," I said.

She wagged her head, maybe yes, maybe no. "But we agreed with the priest."

"Is that when you began hatching your plan?"

"Yes. We talked and argued about what to do. Some of the girls were too afraid to act, afraid of repercussions. The Nazis were known to exact punishment for any infraction on whole villages or on family members who were prisoners of war. So whatever we did, we risked putting many other people in peril."

"But you did act."

She nodded. "On New Year's Day of 1944 we learned that the Russians had chased the Germans out of Ukraine and were in Poland. As the Red Army marched across Poland headed toward Berlin, whenever they came upon a German prisoner-of-war camp or a concentration camp, they opened the gates and released the prisoners."

"Ah." I looked at the note I had jotted earlier; she had told Pierre Dauvin that my grandfather set the cider house on fire. "When did Henri come home?"

"Early that February," she said. "He was nothing more than a skeleton when he arrived. Of course, he had to go into hiding. If the Germans spotted him, they would shoot him, and probably all of us. We made a nest for him in the drying room of the *fromagerie* so that we could keep him warm and feed him regularly. We skimmed cream off the milk before we made cheese to fatten him up. For three weeks he rested and healed."

"And plotted?"

She smiled as she nodded, perhaps remembering Henri, her late husband. My grandfather.

"During the winter months on the estate," she said, "as we do to this day, besides making cheese every day, we distill brandy from the apple cider that we put up in the fall to ferment. And we prune the apple trees in the orchard. While he was resting, Henri helped out by sharpening our pruning knives." She reached into a drawer, pulled out a knife that was no more than five inches long when it was folded, and demonstrated opening it as she spoke. "You see, the blade is curved; the tip is very sharp. When it is folded it can be carried in a pocket."

"You keep one in the kitchen?"

A little shrug as she folded the knife back up. "Yes, of course. It is perfect for trimming vegetables."

To get back on topic, I asked, "What was happening in the war at that time?"

"The Allies were bombing German cities by then," she said. "At the same time, here in Normandy, the *Résistance* cut telephone and telegraph lines to disrupt communication," she said. "It was time for us to act."

Grand-mère took a sip of water, preparing herself. "Henri showed us how to use the pruning knife to sever the carotid artery in a man's neck by using nearly the same twist of the wrist we used to cut little sucker limbs off tree branches and trunks.

"One night, we told the soldiers that we would be celebrating

the first pouring of the first batch of brandy from the big *chartenais*."
She looked up. "What would you call it? I don't know the word in
English."

Taylor, our intern, pulled out her mobile, tapped the screen, and
then announced, "It's an alembic pot used in the double distillation
of brandy."

"Youth comes to the rescue," I said, giving her a thumbs-up. "A
chartenais is a still."

Grand-mère smiled at Taylor. "Thank you, child. You'll have to
show me how to do that."

I think that we all needed that little break. When she was ready
to resume, Grand-mère sat up taller in her chair.

I said, "You invited the soldiers to a celebration."

"Yes," she said. "It was nonsense, of course. They had been there
for three previous winters and there had been no such celebration. But
a party is a party, yes? We told them that all the women of the village
would come that night for a feast in the cider house. There would be
good food and plenty to drink. Of course, we never gave them food,
so they got very drunk, indeed, on empty bellies. Through it all, there
was a gramophone playing, men shouting and singing; lots of noise.
As we knew they would, the *cochons* went after the women. When a
soldier made advances, the object of his intentions would invite him
into a dark corner, and then out would come her knife. As Henri
promised, it was quick, and it was quiet."

"None of the men put up a fight?"

"*Oui,*" she said with a little shrug. "But there was always a second girl standing watch in case her friend needed help. Don't forget
the work we had been doing. The women were very strong, and the
Germans underestimated us; that was our advantage."

"You participated in this?"

"*Bien sûr*, of course. It was my job to bring the knives. I hid
them in a basket under some bread and cheese."

"You're telling me that a handful of women killed all seventeen
of the men?"

"I think there were eight of us that night, so we were outnum-
bered by the Boche," she said. "But we did not need to slit every

throat. Some of the men got, how shall I say? Dead drunk. We left them where they fell. On a signal, a fanfare was played on the gramophone and the men who were still standing were told that the feast was coming. We herded them to tables set up a back corner, separated from the doors by racks of brandy barrels. When they were seated, devouring bread and cheese, we ceremonially removed the bungs from some brandy barrels, the lights went out, the barrels were tipped over to spill, and the women escaped through the coal chute. Henri and our wounded pilot had barred the cider house doors by then. Once the women were safe, Henri—" She searched for the right words. "Henri flambéed the Germans."

"Using brandy as fuel, he set the cider house on fire?" I said. "And the men inside perished."

"Exactly. We helped them get accustomed to the fires of hell right away, yes?"

"An entire platoon went missing," I said. "Someone in the German command must have come looking for them."

"*Bien sûr,*" Grand-mère said. "An arrogant bastard named Klemm, *Oberst* Klemm, the colonel, arrived with some men from Cherbourg about a week later; remember that the communication lines were down. By the time they arrived the burned ruins of the cider house were gone, replaced by a hay mow. And the men were in the field under the winter turnips. We were questioned, of course. But to the Germans, we were a bunch of ignorant milkmaids and farm girls. What did we know? Only that the soldiers said they had been given orders. They packed their things and left."

"And that satisfied Klemm?" I asked.

"Germany was under siege, and there was a lot of chaos. Many soldiers were going AWOL by then." She shrugged. "Klemm looked around a little bit, but there was nothing to find except for some very old brandy von Streicher had been hoarding in his room. Klemm took that and left."

I leaned closer to her. "What did you do with the soldiers' personal effects?"

"Everything was handed over to the *Résistance*. You can imagine how valuable it was for them to have authentic German uniforms, papers, even underwear and toiletries, when they sent agents to infiltrate German lines. And, of course, the weapons were very welcome."

She started to say something else, but looked from Guido to Taylor and asked me to have them turn off their cameras. I made the signal for them to cut, and when the red lights above their lenses went dark, I turned to her.

"Are you tired, Grand-mère?"

"Yes, a little. But I want to tell you something that I do not want to say in front of the cameras."

"Do you want me and Taylor to leave?" Guido asked.

"That isn't necessary. It's just this: I believe that the skull Freddy dug up belonged to von Streicher. He was the only man who was not inside the cider house when it was set on fire."

"Where was he?" I asked.

"He never left the house," she said. "When I took the knives to the cider house I was told that von Streicher was still up here, with the child he forced into his bed every night. He kept a hoard of food and drink in his room, so he was having his own little feast."

"What did you do?"

"I found him in the salon, and I dispatched him."

"By yourself?"

"*Oui*. And then I went back to the cider house to help my friends."

When I remembered to breathe, I said to Guido, "That's enough for now. Let's pack up."

Grand-mère watched Guido and Taylor put away the cameras and sound recorder, turn off the key lights, and fold the reflectors.

"Lordy, Grand-mère," I said, rising to kiss her cheek.

She caught my hand; she looked tired. *"Fini?"*

"With this segment, I think so. If there's anything you want us to cut out, or if there's something you want to add, we can do that later. It's an amazing story. Terrible, but amazing."

"Well then." She pushed her chair back and rose from the table. "I'll just go see how Marie is getting along with lunch."

On her way out, she turned to me and said, "When you go

for tea with Veronique Bernard this afternoon, I hope you consider wearing that lovely mauve dress. It will travel well. And the color suits you. In case you agree, I had it pressed, and your ecru sandals cleaned. They are in your room."

With that, she went out the door. I still had not told her that someone else had gone digging in the enemy's grave. She would learn about it soon enough.

Guido, Taylor and I took the equipment out to our little studio to put away. Right off, I wanted to get a first look at what we had captured. Even as Grand-mère spoke to me, I was mentally editing the piece, as I usually do. I knew we had something interesting.

Our little studio was, indeed, little. There was just room for Guido, Taylor and me to squeeze in. When we opened the door and found the other three interns, Zachary, Devon, and Miller, lounging about, I sent two of them off with cameras to check on activity at the trench and to film whatever they could get away with. Pierre Dauvin was out there, and by now he knew that someone had been digging around. He had yet to come to the house asking questions, but I knew he would get to it. Soon. So, before he did, I asked the third intern, Miller, to please wash Freddy's car, making sure to vacuum the mud left by the shovel out of the trunk.

While Guido stowed cords and cameras and plugged battery packs into chargers, Taylor took care of the intern's primary duty: she tossed out the cold coffee dregs in the *cafetière* and started water heating for a new pot. I downloaded the morning's footage onto a digital editor and pulled up the footage from the day before. For the first look, I split the images on the monitor into six screens and ran the indoor and outdoor footage simultaneously. Among us, we had captured the skull's tumble off the scoop from four angles. Grand-mère we filmed from two.

"Take a look, you guys," I said, pushing my stool back so that they could see what we had. "I like the visual contrast between the soft light of Grand-mère's narrative this morning with the footage taken at the trench yesterday in bright sun. What do you think?"

We talked about various directions we might take the film, but I was too distracted to give the conversation much brain power. I kept looking at the time. There was still about an hour before lunch, when everything would come to a halt. Immediately after lunch, I was heading out to Villerville to meet Jean-Paul's mother and I probably wouldn't be back until after dinner. That was too long to go without knowing what Pierre Dauvin was up to. Or how much trouble Grand-mère and I might be in.

I told Guido and Taylor about the bones on the road. They were intrigued. When I said, "Let's close up and go outside," Guido immediately grabbed a couple of small video cameras and headed for the door. Taylor asked if it would be all right if she stayed behind to catalogue the footage from the last couple of days, and of course it was.

Guido and I took a couple of bicycles from the collection beside the potting shed and rode off down the graveled farm road. After a few bone-jarring minutes, I said, "You and Renée Ferraro seemed to hit it off last night."

He smiled. "She's interesting. We're going to some sort of community concert this weekend."

"You mean, like a date?"

"Don't tease me," he said. "But, yeah, like a date."

"Good for you." I reached across and patted his shoulder.

"She's a cougar," he said. "She's years older than me."

"Enjoy it. She might teach you something new."

He chuckled to himself. "Trust me, she already has."

Pierre Dauvin wouldn't let any of us near the dig site. Zachary, trying for an aerial shot, had borrowed a twelve-foot ladder from the orchard, lugged it up onto the three-foot-high root-ball of the hedgerow along the road, and had somehow wedged the ladder in among the prickly hawthorn. He sat perched atop the ladder while little Devon, who stood maybe five-one and weighed all of ninety-five pounds, tried to steady this precarious installation so that Zach could shoot over the heads of the *gendarmes* milling around the road near the trench.

"What are you getting?" I asked Zach, leaning my bike against the rise of the hedgerow.

"Come up and see," he said.

"No thanks. You're young, you'll heal faster than I would. But don't fall, okay?"

He laughed, and Devon told him not to shake the ladder.

"Seriously," I said, "what do you see?"

"There are cops and guys in blue jumpsuits. And bones every-where. They take pictures of the bones *in situ*, then they scoop them up and dump them onto a tarp."

"Have they found anything?"

"Other than bones?" he asked. "Not much that I can see. Except they made a couple of plaster casts of tire tracks or footprints or something."

"You're getting good footage?"

"Can we just say I'm getting footage?"

I complimented my interns on their resourcefulness and after asking Zach again not to fall off his perch, I left them to it. Giving Dauvin and his men a wide berth, I climbed over the hedgerow and down into the orchard. I walked to the end and climbed back over onto the access road. The night before, at just that spot where the road turned, I thought that the headlights of Freddy's car had bounced off something shiny. I scanned the carrot field, trying to figure out where that something might have been, if there had been anything at all.

A week before harvest, the feathery tops of the carrots stood near-ly two feet tall. The furrows between rows were maybe eight inches deep. Even a good-sized person could crouch down or lie down and hide himself out there, especially at night. Walking between rows, I headed off toward that ephemeral sighting.

The tide was out. A stiff breeze off the Channel whipped the carrot tops, first one way, and then the other, brushing them against my bare legs. I pushed a stray strand of windblown hair behind my ear, and when I looked back in the direction I had come, I could see Pierre Dauvin up on the road, watching me. I waved, he waved back. When I turned again to continue forward, out of the corner of my eye I saw a bit of pale blue among the vastness of deep green crop. The wind shifted and that bit of blue was gone again, but I headed in the direction I had seen it. Again I stopped to get my bearings, and there it was, no more than six feet further along and one furrow over. Blue jeans. Faded blue jeans left in a heap in the middle of a furrow, in the middle of a carrot field. It seemed odd.

I pushed my way toward the jeans out of curiosity. But as I drew closer, my view less obstructed, I saw not only jeans, but also a T-shirt and a spill of long blond hair, and I knew who was lying there. I called out to her, "Solange!" There was no response.

Her tee shirt rose and fell with the breeze, and maybe as she breathed, though from the angle of her head and the red mass at her temple, I doubted that she did. Afraid to move her, I knelt, felt for a pulse, found none, saw pupils fixed and dilated. Saw a triangle-shaped wound on her temple and the congealed blood that had flowed out into the soil. Worst of all, the day was warm and already the stench of death hovered around her.

─8─

"HOW DID YOU KNOW where to look for the girl?" Dauvin loomed over me as I sat in the middle of the field with my head between my knees.

"I wasn't looking for Solange," I said, risking to sit upright without keeling over again. "We wanted a better camera angle on what you were doing."

"Pffh, c'est des conneries."

His words were unfamiliar to me, but from his tone I understood what they meant. He knew I was lying. Dauvin squatted beside me, took my chin in his hand and looked into my eyes with genuine concern. *"Ça va?"*

"Yes, I'm okay," I said. "It was just, she's so young, Pierre. What happened to her?"

He shrugged. "We'll wait for the doctor to tell us. Now, how did you know she was here?"

"I didn't," I said. "That is, I didn't know that anyone was out here. But I was looking for something. Before I tell you why, though, I need to remind you that whatever you discover in the process could involve not only my grandmother, but yours."

"Oh là." He shook his head. "Those women; what can we do about those old women?"

"Love them?" I said.

He smiled an upside down French smile and offered a hand to help me to my feet. "Can you walk on your own?"

"Of course," I said, sounding more certain than I felt. Seeing that beautiful young woman getting zipped into a body bag and lifted onto a stretcher had knocked my legs right out from under me. Solange was only a few years older than my Casey, and in that moment I could imagine the pain I would feel if she were my own dear girl being taken away. I asked, "Who calls the parents?"

"Someone will go to their home as soon as we have an address. Who here would know that?"

I told him that Solange's professor, Olivia, could probably help him, and that Olivia was staying at Freddy's house. No scandal, I told him, just a matter of convenience. As far as I knew, anyway.

There was no way I could avoid telling Pierre what Grand-mère and I had done the night before. And so I did, from finding little spade marks in the dirt made by someone who had been in the trench before me to using a borrowed shovel and digging up skeletal remains. I had no answer to his big question: Why? Because I did not know.

"When we drove up last night," I told him, "I thought I saw something out in the field. Just a quick flash in the car lights."

"You think it was the girl?" he asked.

"I didn't know what it was. I still don't. But I was curious, so I came out here for a look."

"Curious," he said, nodding toward the road. "Like them?"

They were all there, the two grandmothers, my cousin Antoine and my brother Freddy, Jacques and his wife Julie, the various students, estate workers, people from the village. All of them waiting for news. It was a small town. Everything that happened was everyone's business. Or so they thought.

I stopped walking toward the group and reached for Pierre's arm. He turned and looked at me expectantly. I said, "Last night, when I saw that someone had been digging before we arrived, I wondered if the light I had seen came from out in the field. Had we scared some-one off? Were we being watched? It worried me that someone might go back there after we left."

"You admit you came here last night with a shovel, but you claim that this mess was not your doing?"

I took out my phone, opened the picture file, pulled up an image, and handed it to him. "I took this last night after we finished, in case anyone had questions."

He was good at keeping a cop's poker face, but I saw his eye-brows go up. After studying the picture, he forwarded it, and then he pocketed my phone. "Were you in the trench again after you took the picture?"

"No. We got into the car and left."

"Is the time stamp on your phone correct?"

"It is. The time is set by satellite."

"You drove your grandmother back to the house," he said. "Can you be certain that she did not come back later?"

I shrugged. "She was exhausted when we got home. She went straight to her room. I heard her shower—the old house has noisy pipes—and I assumed she went right to bed after."

"And you?"

"Same. Shower, and straight to bed. Grave digging is hard, dirty work, Pierre."

"Can anyone corroborate the time you returned home?"

"Antoine, and my daughter."

"Family, so reliable as witnesses." He managed a little smile. "There will be more questions. But for now, as your police say, don't leave Dodge."

"Oh, hell." I had forgotten for the moment about tea in Viller-ville that afternoon. I checked my watch. There was just time to clean up, grab a bite, and make the drive, but in the circumstance I could not imagine being charming over jam and crumpets, or whatever the French serve at tea. Surely Jean-Paul's mother would understand. "Pierre, I need to borrow my phone to make a call."

He took my elbow and we started walking again. "Your grand-mother carries a phone. I'm sure she'll let you use it."

When I explained to Grand-mère why I wanted to borrow her phone, she said, "Absolutely not. Veronique Bernard is expecting you. You'll go, as arranged."

"Pierre," I said, catching his eye. "I am leaving Dodge, but I'll be back tonight."

He shook his head. But Grand-mère shook a finger at him. She had worked too hard setting things up to allow the death of a young stranger to interfere with her plans for me. Clearly, Dauvin understood what he was up against, and with some caveats, he relented and agreed that I could travel as far as Villerville as long as I would return by evening.

"You will give me a number where you can be reached at all times," he said.

"I would," I answered. "But you have my phone."

"Madame Martin," he said to Grand-mère. "The loan of your telephone, please." And to me, he said as he handed me her phone, "You will surrender your passport to me, Madame MacGowen, before you go anywhere."

⸺9⸺

GRAND-MÈRE WAS RIGHT. The mauve dress traveled well. I was clueless about what the French etiquette was for visiting a lover's mother for the first time, so I simply did my best to follow my grandmother's cues. If I had been a very young woman setting out to beard a future mother-in-law in her den, I would have been fraught with nerves as I headed toward this tea party. But as I was neither very young nor engaged to the beloved son, and in context with the events of the rest of the day, this meeting didn't amount to very much. I chose to interpret Mme Bernard's invitation as a gracious gesture born out of curiosity about the woman who was spending so much time with her son and heir. Heir of what, I had no clue, except for good brains, good looks, and good manners. And that was legacy enough for me.

I would have been happier if Jean-Paul were joining us, not because I needed hand-holding, as welcome as that would have been

just then, but because he was so lovely to have around. He was, however, unable to get away from whatever it was that he was involved
with in Lille until Sunday. He was still officially the French consul
general to Los Angeles until the first of September. He was using his
holiday month to explore possibilities for his next thing, and tying
up the ends of his obligations to the appointment.

My own professional future was just as uncertain as his. When
Guido and I finished the film we were working on, we would also
finish our contract with the television network that had been our
professional home for the last decade. And after that? I had no clue.

The drive to Villerville would have been a good time for me
to ponder things, both current and future, but as I drove along the
highway in Freddy's freshly washed Jaguar, trying to stay out of the
way of the usual French speed demons took about all the concentration I could muster. Just the same, the drive was a welcome diversion
after the grim events of the morning.

It was a beautiful summer day. The countryside I drove through,
farms and ancient villages, looked like photos from a travel brochure.
After about an hour, I left the main highway and its lush green farmland to wend my way through picturesque fishing villages along the
Route du Littoral, the coast road that runs along high chalk bluffs
overlooking the English Channel, or as it is called in France, *La
Manche*.

All along the road, there were signs for turn-offs to the D-Day
landing beaches. The week before, I had taken Casey for her first
visit to the beaches and the American military cemetery at Colville-
sur-Mer. She had been very moved by the experience, and remarked
that the gauntlet of shops offering authentic battlefield souvenirs we
passed through along the access roads to the battle sites was tacky.
They were junk shops, with yards in front littered with burned-out
jeeps and parts of downed aircraft and promising uniforms, patches,
and other bits of war detritus inside. The surprise to both of us had
been the number of cars parked in front of those shops.

So far, I had made good time. As I was so close, I decided that I
might spend a few minutes having a look at one of those stores, hoping to get some idea what might be valuable enough for someone to
pillage a grave to acquire. Or, possibly, to kill a young woman over.

I pulled into the rutted dirt parking area in front of a shop offering BEST PRICE, BEST SELECTION and went inside. There were only a
few shoppers. One corner of the store was filled with racks of old uniforms from various Allied nations; they were generally moth-eaten
and low-priced. Glass display cases held insignia, buttons, medals,
and other small items. Nothing I saw was German.

A young man with gold eyebrow studs and tattoos vining up his
neck over his bald head, came in through a door behind the glass
cases carrying a large piece of olive-drab-colored metal, a scrap off
some sort of machinery.

"Here it is, Harry, the flange I told you about." His accent was
British.

"Let's have a shufti, then." A man who had been squatting to
look at the bottom shelves of a display of camouflage nets stood
with much creaking of joints and walked over to the counter. He
wore typical summer tourist togs, a Hawaiian-print shirt, shorts and
flip-flops, a camouflage of another sort. But I recognized him. On
Thursday, he had been among the crowd hoping to see something
more than blue police tape when word got out that Freddy's excavator dug up a skull.

Harry, who also had a British accent, examined the piece of scrap
and said, "Aye, B-17 all right. I'll take this, then. I have a bloke always looking for B-17 parts. Vincent, you hiding any more bits back
there, letting them go a few at a time, trying to get a good price from
me?"

Before the clerk, or maybe owner of the establishment, could
defend himself, a tiny woman with sunflower yellow hair came out
from behind the uniform racks.

"Don't pay Harry any mind, Vincent," she said. "Someone once
told him he was funny and he's believed it ever since."

I must have chuckled loudly enough for her to hear me, because
she turned toward me. She stared for a moment, and then came
toward me.

"Look, Harry," she said, eyeing me from top to bottom. "She's
that American film star was pointed out to us at that farm yesterday.
You remember."

"I am American," I said. "But I'm not a film star."

"So you say, but that's what everyone was gossiping about, pointing you out where you stood with that old lady." She wagged a finger at me. "Mind, I don't recognize you, but that's what everyone was saying."

Enough of that, I decided, and turned to Harry. "I recognize you. You were trampling my grandmother's carrots."

He guffawed. "Big farm like that, what's a few carrots more or less? No need to call the coppers."

"It wasn't that you trampled the carrots," I said. "It's that you weren't wearing EU-approved footwear when you did it."

He roared with laughter and she wagged that finger at me again.

"Now that's clever," she said. "Takes talent to come up with wit that quick, doesn't it Harry?"

"Why were you out there yesterday?" I asked Harry. "Did you hope to find something?"

"Me and Ruthie were over here junking in the shops, looking for this and that, when we got a Google alert, snaps of the skull and all that. You never know what the farmers in Normandy might turn up, so we went over to that village to have a look."

"Are you a dealer?" I asked.

With a shrug, he said, "I keep my eye out for a few collectors, sure. But I wouldn't say I'm a dealer. Not like Vincent here."

"I understand that it's illegal to sell or display Nazi artifacts anywhere in Continental Europe." I was looking at Vincent. "But is there a market for it?"

"Not much of one in Europe," he said. "But there are collectors, sure. Most of the blokes looking for Jerry artifacts are abroad."

"Skinheads?" I asked. "White supremacists or neo-Nazis?"

"Not that lot," Harry said. "They want new shit, you know? All custom made, spit and polish, that's what they want. No, the collectors are historians. Hobby historians, I call them. They want the authentic stuff, put it up on your shelf in the lounge for the neighbors to see and for the missus to dust."

"How do they get it if it's illegal to buy or sell?"

The two men exchanged a glance, but it was Ruthie who spoke. "In England it's legal to sell Nazi artifacts online. Not on this side of the Channel, mind you, and not in shops. But online is all right."

Out of curiosity, I asked, "What are buyers looking for?"

"Bits and bobs," Harry said again, apparently as specific an answer as he wanted to give.

"Curios, oddities," Vincent added. "Now weapons, that's a different matter. You find something in good condition and you'll get a nice payday out of it. Feller we know recently sold a Mauser, pristine condition, for what, Harry? Thirty-five, forty thousand quid I think Artie got for that, didn't he, Harry?"

Harry held up his hands, didn't know or wouldn't say. He turned his attention to a shoebox full of old photos on the counter.

"You know good and well what Artie got for it, Harry." Ruthie nudged his shoulder. "The sale was all over the Net, so it's no secret."

"Interesting," I said, because it was.

"Tell the truth now." I had Harry's attention again. He took a step closer to me, all smiles gone. "You found something in the ground out there, didn't you? Something more than just an old skull. You've come here wanting to know how you can unload it and how much you can get for it, haven't you?"

"No." I saw menace in his eyes but did not let my gaze falter from his florid face when what I truly wanted to do was get the hell out of there. Clearly, this whim of mine to check out a junk shop was not the best idea I'd had in a day already marked with not-so-great ideas. "All that has been found at my grandmother's farm is a pit full of bones. Last night that pit was looted and a young girl was murdered. For the safety of my family, I want some idea who that might have been."

"Murdered?" Ruthie gripped Harry's arm, but he seemed not to notice. "Did you hear that?"

"Film business not so good, is it?" Harry said with a smirk, entirely disregarding what I had said. "Need to make a little quick cash, do you? You tell me what you have and we'll talk numbers."

"Shut up, Harry," Ruthie said. "No call for that."

It was time for me to go. I went over to the counter, wrote my mobile number on the back of one of Vincent's cards, and handed it to him. "I would appreciate a call if you hear anything."

"Right you are." He slipped the card into his cash drawer.

Ruthie was still telling off Harry when I walked out. I had not only learned the going price for a pristine Mauser, but also something about the sleazy market for Nazi relics. The scary part of that was, some of them knew exactly where to find me and the people I hold dear.

I needed to make up some time. Along the coast road, as I navigated my way through the traffic roundabouts the French put in at intersections instead of stop signs or signal lights, I took some pride in not slowing as I approached and not being run over by cars coming at me from all directions at *haute vitesse*, meaning crazy speed.

The country roads don't cross at tidy right angles, so turnoffs can come close together. The signage with multiple arrows can be confusing for the uninitiated, like me, to sort out at top speed. A turn or a straightaway can be missed in the blink of an eye. By about the fifth roundabout I was certain that I was lost. The GPS on the console spoke in such rapid French that I had no idea what it was telling me. Just as I hit a wall of beach traffic near Deauville and started looking for a place to pull over to ask for help, I saw the sign for Villerville and aimed the Jag in the direction I hoped the arrow was pointing.

Jean-Paul had given me very detailed instructions for finding his mother's beach cottage after I turned off the *Route du Littoral* because there were no street numbers to follow. Before I reached the village of Villerville, I was to look for a greengrocer, Lemarchand Ludovic, and turn left immediately after, heading toward the water. The street name was Chemin de Devaleux, but he didn't remember there ever being a sign to tell me that. Another left turn, he said, and then watch for a pyramid-shaped red-tile roof peeking above the road on the water side.

The red-tiled pyramid, I discovered, was the cap on a tall square tower at one end of a massive half-timbered confection. Though the house stood high above a beautiful white, sandy beach, this was not my idea of a beach cottage. More like a small hotel or a mini-castle. The driveway down to the house had been cut out of the sheer face of a cliff, a long, steep descent that ended in a loop with a rose garden at its center and a sheer drop-off into the water if I missed the turn.

As I parked next to the house and got out of the car, a woman emerged from among the roses carrying a basket of freshly cut flowers.

Wearing wide palazzo pants and a loose, sleeveless silk blouse, she seemed to float as if borne on the wind as she walked toward me. Somehow, the white hair framing her unlined face made her appear younger than I knew she had to be as the mother of a fifty-year-old man. Jean-Paul had gray at his temples and on the points of his chin in the morning before he shaved. Someday, would his hair be as white as his mother's? Would I still be around to find out?

Mme Bernard set her basket of roses on the front steps and pulled off her gardening gloves. "You are Jean-Paul's Maggie," she said, offering me her hand as she presented her cheeks for *la bise.* "Welcome."

"At last we meet," I said, handing her the basket Grand-mère and Marie had packed for me to bring.

She lifted the starched napkin on top for a look. "How perfect, my dear. Élodie's preserves. And her cheese. Please thank your grandmother." By then she had hooked her hand around my arm and steered me up the front steps into a long, cool entry hall. "I'll write her a note. Do come through. I thought we might relax on the veranda. The view from there is so lovely."

Inside, despite its size and apparent grandeur, the house was indeed pure beach cottage. I saw comfortable furniture, raffia mats on scuffed oak floors, shelves crammed with books and old board games; a place for family to relax. A set of tall French doors on the far side of the main salon opened onto a broad lawn with a swimming pool overlooking the sea in its middle.

It was a warm day, and the pool looked very inviting. I love to swim. Gliding through water is as close to flying as I can get without sprouting wings. But this was not the time. My hostess showed me to a table under a bright red canopy with a magnificent view of a wide sandy beach, reachable from the lawn by a long switchback staircase. We were hardly settled before a young woman I guessed to be the maid came out with tea and a plate of exquisite little pastries, a bowl of fresh berries, little rounds of toasted baguette, a crumbly, smelly cheese and fig jam. Mme Bernard gave the woman some rapid instructions that I thought had to do with the flowers she had left on the front steps when we came in.

We sipped tea and worked our way through the conversational preliminaries, a gentle version of the third degree. My husband, Mike Flint, had died about a year and a half earlier. Jean-Paul's wife, Marian, had been gone for over three years. I knew that the sudden loss of his wife from an aneurysm had left Jean-Paul and his teenage son, Dominic, reeling.

"They were children together," Mme Bernard said, watching my face for a reaction. "My son was so much unprepared to lose Marian. I wonder if women aren't able to manage loss more easily than men."

"I couldn't say," I said. "But I do know this: Mike and I, and Jean-Paul and Marian were very happy. If either Mike or Marian were still alive, Jean-Paul and I could be nothing more than friends. But I also believe that if they had not died and the four of us had met, we would all be great friends."

She laughed softly as she poured more tea into my cup. "Jean-Paul said very much the same thing. I am delighted he has found such a friend as you. And do forgive me if I am meddling, but mothers do, you know. Our efforts may be misguided from time to time, but it is second nature for us, yes?"

"I'm certainly guilty of it," I said. "Or so my daughter tells me."

"Yes, but sometimes when we meddle on behalf of our children, we do the correct thing. Not always, but sometimes." Her gaze shifted to a ferry in the distance, possibly crossing the Channel from England headed toward Le Havre to the east of us. After a pause, she said, "I saw a familiar name in the news last night that reminds me I was a meddling mother. Someone I believe you've met."

"Oh?" I waited for a shoe to drop.

"Pierre Dauvin." She sat forward in her chair and rested her chin on tented fingers. "He is, I believe, currently the *capitaine* in charge of the *gendarmerie* in your grandmother's district. Is he a Martin relation?"

"Probably, somewhere along the way," I said. "It seems to me that everyone in the village is a cousin to some degree. Or is married to a cousin. Was Pierre's name in the news because of the bones that were found at my grandmother's?"

"A skull, yes?" The way she said "a skull" sounded dismissive, as if that discovery were incidental to having seen a familiar name.

"How do you know Pierre?" I asked. The topic had been meddling in the lives of our children. The man was a policeman. I could think of many possibilities for where she might be headed.

"Pierre was just a boy," she said. "About sixteen, I think. The same age as my daughter, Karine. She was always a sensitive girl, a romantic. Over a summer holiday, she went to China with a group from our parish. This was in the mid-eighties, just as China was emerging. The group did some touring, and because it was a church-sponsored trip, they visited an orphanage run by an order of nuns. Karine had never seen such poverty; all those precious little children who needed care. By the time she came home, she had decided God was calling her to become a nun to go off and save all the little children of the world. My husband and I didn't know quite how to handle her sudden religious fervor because it was so unlike her."

"What did you do?"

"I believe you know that my late husband was a great friend of your Uncle Gérard."

"Yes," I said. "It was because of my uncle that Jean-Paul and I met."

"Well, your uncle suggested that we put Karine in the hands of the abbess at the convent in your grandmother's village and let Ma Mère take care of her. So we did." She furrowed her brow. "Ma Mère, the abbess, is a Martin cousin, is she not?"

"Family connections get complicated very quickly," I said. "Ma Mère's sister Marie, whom everyone calls Grand-mère Marie, is my Uncle Gérard's mother-in-law."

"I knew there was a connection." She put a fat strawberry on her plate absently. "Well, Ma Mère did not have Karine spend her time on her knees praying. Instead, she sent her off into the village as a volunteer to work in the school, and in the clinic, and so on. And she met a boy."

"Pierre Dauvin?" I asked.

'Yes, Pierre," she said with a knowing smile. "And soon she was as in love with Pierre as she had been in love with God's work a

month earlier. But they were just babies, so it was impossible. Ma
Mère suggested to us that what Karine needed was to see the world,
to have some adventures so that she could burn off some of that pas-
sionate energy, and also discover what her true path in life might be.
And so we left poor Jean-Paul to his studies, and my husband and
I took Karine on a grand tour. A safari in Africa, a visit to Machu
Picchu, a hike to the bottom of the Grand Canyon; it was glorious
for the three of us."

"And she forgot about Pierre?"

"No." Suddenly she grew serious. "Young people are capable of
intense and abiding love. I believe that there was a very special bond
between those two. But it was your grandmother who advised us to
keep Karine away. She never said why, but she assured us there was
good reason. When we returned from our adventures, we sent Karine
to school in Scotland. It was there that she fell in love with painting
and found her calling."

I made a mental note to grill my grandmother as soon as I got
home about why she warned Mme Bernard away from Pierre.

"And how is Pierre?" she asked out of more than simple curiosity.

"Busy," I said, searching for neutral words to describe what he
was busy with. "One of the students working *chez* Martin this summer had an accident overnight and he's looking into it."

"A local girl?"

"No," I said. "She was studying archeology in Paris, *l'école du
Louvre*. I don't know anything more about her."

"She was badly hurt?"

I said, "Unfortunately."

"*Quel dommage,*" she *tsk*'d, sounding sincere. And then she
moved on to other topics

We talked about my work for a while, the strange world of television production. And about Mom and my dad, and even a bit
about Isabelle, whom she had known through Uncle Gérard. She
told me about her husband, who never quite recovered from the
effects of tuberculosis he picked up in a German forced labor camp
when he was a teenager during the war. She made sure to tell me that
she was too young to remember anything about the war, though the

experiences her parents suffered through during that awful time still lay over their entire generation, what's left of it, like a black pall. And would until the last who remembered had perished. I knew from listening to my grandmother that, sadly, what she said was true.

The sun moved lower in the western sky and I began looking for the right moment to take my leave. We had met. I liked her. I hoped she approved of me. I hadn't spilled anything on my mauve dress. We had established that she was not above meddling, but I wasn't worried that she had anything to meddle with where I was concerned. Jean-Paul and I were friends and lovers, but, so far, that was as far as it went. And we were not children.

I was just about to mention that I had a long drive ahead, when the curtains at the open French doors moved aside and Jean-Paul himself walked through. My stomach did the usual happy flip that happens whenever I catch sight of him, but I thought that he looked especially handsome that afternoon. He was tanned and fit, wearing a perfectly tailored suit perfectly; he looked as comfortable as he would if he were wearing old shorts and sneakers instead. I knew he had been in meetings all morning, but his white dress shirt was still crisp and his tie still had a perfect knot.

"Ah, here you are," he said, draping his suit coat over the back of the chair next to me as he leaned over to kiss his mother first, and then me. Before he sat, he scooted the chair closer to mine. Taking my hand, he asked, "Have we solved all the problems of the world yet?"

"Not a one," his mother said, obviously delighted to see him. The maid appeared with a teacup and a fresh pot of tea, which she set in front of him. As Mme Bernard passed her son the plates of fruit and cheese, she said, "So, have you surprised us to prevent us from telling each other tales about you?"

"Too late for that, yes?" He laughed as he loosened his tie and opened the collar button of his dress shirt. "No. I decided that there was nothing happening in my meeting that could be nearly as interesting as seeing the two of you. So I fled."

"You'll stay for dinner?" Mme Bernard asked him. She turned to me. "Maggie?"

Before I could say anything, Jean-Paul answered for both of us. "Maggie has a long drive home, *Maman*. Unless she is prepared to spend the night…"

"Another time, I would love to," I said. "I enjoyed having this afternoon off from my work, but I do need to get back." I did not add, or else Pierre Dauvin would send out a search party.

Mme Bernard did not seem disappointed, but she was gracious about hiding any relief she may have felt. "You will come back, Maggie. Soon I hope. And you, my son?"

"I will have to be happy with simply seeing your sweet face, *Maman*, before I leave as well. A friend dropped me off on his way to join his family in Deauville for the weekend. I need to be in Paris early tomorrow. So, Maggie, do you mind driving me to the train station in Caen? It's on your way."

"If I can find the station," I said. "I'll probably miss it and have to keep you."

"Nothing would make me happier," he said, squeezing my hand.

Good-byes were brief. On our way back through the house, the maid handed Mme Bernard Grand-mère's basket, now full of roses with the stems wrapped for travel.

"Thank Élodie for me," she said. "Both for the lovely gifts and for sharing her lovely granddaughter."

At the front door there was a farewell round of *les bises*. I gave Jean-Paul the car keys, and as he opened my door for me, I saw a very familiar overnight bag on the floor of the back seat.

"Am I really dropping you at Caen?" I asked as he pulled out onto the road.

"Yes," he said. "On Sunday night."

"So," I said, "your meetings today were boring?"

"*Au contraire*. Generally, quite interesting. I was invited to a Euro Zone summit to talk about counterfeit labels."

Part of Jean-Paul's role as consul general to Los Angeles had been promoting and protecting French trade with the United States. A consistent headache was the flow of cheap knockoffs of expensive French designer goods out of Asia and into the ports of the American West Coast. Jean-Paul had worked in tandem with American

Customs, Homeland Security, the French government and various French trade associations to identify counterfeit labels and keep them out of the marketplace. Just for research, we went to quite a few swap meets on weekends, looking for fakes. And always found them.

"There was a bit of a *contretemps* at the meeting," he said, "when one of the German delegates overheard one of ours, a hard-assed old rightist left over from the Sarkozy era, saying that it was time for Germany to pay for the cleanup of their own trash. This remark came about when a press release was distributed affirming that the remains found on your family estate yesterday are, in fact, German military."

"He said, trash?"

"Close enough."

"Just how deep do anti-German feelings still run in France?" I asked.

"I think it's a generational issue," he said with a shrug as he dodged an oncoming car making an unsafe lane change around a slower one, a road boulder going only maybe eighty miles per. "For the people who remember the war, those feelings are as profound as their memories are long. But younger people don't seem to share the animosity; the issues are not theirs. I suspect that the German response to the sort of insult that the French delegate lobbed is a matter of generation also. An older German in such a meeting would know that he is still expected to wear his nation's guilt like a hair shirt, and he would have kept his mouth shut. It was a young man who made an issue of the comment."

"How did this dust-up end?"

"To smooth the waters," he said, reaching for my hand, "I was asked by the committee to speak with the mayor of your village about perhaps making sure that the remains are treated with dignity."

I was surprised. Very. "Do you know Gaston Carnôt?"

"Is he the mayor?" When I said he was, he shrugged. "Not yet."

"Tell the truth, Monsieur Bernard," I said, seeing a wicked gleam in his big brown eyes. "You volunteered for this little job, didn't you?"

He laughed. "Why would I do that?"

"Maybe you'll change your mind when I tell you what's been going on." I told him about Solange. And about the night before, and the bones this morning. He listened, as he always does, with great interest, asking questions from time to time. When I finished, he pressed my hand against his lips and then rested it on his knee.

"My dear, my dear." What followed promised to become something lovely, but my telephone rang. Grand-mère's phone, actually. If it had been mine I would have ignored it. But most probably this call was either for her or from her and needed to be picked up. I asked Jean-Paul's forbearance, and answered.

There was some "um" and "ah" on the line before a familiar voice said, "Maggie?"

"Guido?"

"Jesus, I thought I was calling your grandmother. Hell, Mag, I thought they'd hooked you up, too."

"Who?"

"That damn Dauvin. I was in the studio, working, minding my own business, when he barged in and hauled me away, brought me down to the police station."

"Why?"

"Solange," he said. "At least I think that's why. I can't understand most of what they're saying. But they did let me make a phone call. First I called you, but Dauvin answered your phone so I thought he had you in a cell, too. So I called Renée, and she told me to fuck off. Last resort, I called your grandmother, but got you."

"I have her phone, and, obviously, Dauvin has mine. After last night, Renée is in an awkward position with anything that involves you. But surely she'd give you the name of a local lawyer."

"The thing is, someone told Dauvin that I had spent the night with her. So, he calls her and asks if she can alibi me during the time frame they think Solange was killed. And she says, no."

"Why? Was she saving face?"

"For what? Maggie, I didn't spend the whole night with her."

"You left Gaston's with Renée."

"Sure. But she's like a guy, Maggie. She had her way with me, said thank you very much, and took me home right after."

"When did you get in?"

"Around midnight. A little after. I was kind of upset about the whole thing. So after I got home I went out to the studio and worked for a couple of hours. When I tried to go inside later, though, the doors were all locked."

"Did you ring the bell?"

"No. I thought you were still mad at me so you locked me out."

"Oh, hell, Guido," I said. "I'm sorry. It wasn't intentional. I thought you were out for the night with Renée. Casey heard something that frightened her, and that's why we locked the doors."

"What did she hear?"

"Doors. Or, a door. But there was no one in the house."

"If it was around midnight, she probably heard me going out."

"Where did you sleep?"

"In the studio. On the floor. On the cold, cold stone floor."

"It was warm last night, Guido," I said. "But I am sorry. Did you explain what happened to Dauvin?"

"Why bother? It's not a very good alibi is it?"

"No," I agreed. "What have you told him?"

"Nothing. *Nada. Rien.* Zilch."

"Keep it that way," I said. "I'll try to get someone over there."

When I ended the call, I filled in Jean-Paul on the details, though he had figured out most of it from what he overheard. He said, "I'll make a call."

He did. He gave whoever was on the other end a quick summary and asked to have someone go look after Guido right away. He said *bon* and *merci* a few times, and hung up. By then we were on the toll road, flowing with traffic at a conservative ninety miles an hour. I checked the dash clock; we were still almost an hour from home.

I asked, "How long do you think it will take for your friend to get to Guido?"

"Not long. He's local. He'll be there before we are."

We were back on village roads, no more than fifteen minutes from Guido's cell in the *gendarme* barracks when Jean-Paul's phone buzzed. After saying hello, he mostly listened. There was more *bon* and *merci* and the call ended.

"So?" I asked.

"It looks like your Guido will be the guest of the district *gendarmes* at least for the near future. My friend tells me that Guido has formally engaged the local *avocat*—lawyer—he sent over, and that he is in good hands. On advice, Guido has declined to give a statement, and he will request that the district *procureur* be recused from all matters relating to his case on account of extreme prejudice."

"That was fast," I said.

He shook his head. "Except for the issue with the *procureur*, his *avocat* could have taken care of all that without necessarily speaking with Guido. Guido is with the lawyer now."

"Why are they focusing on Guido?" I asked.

"First, he's an outsider, and locals always prefer to pick on the outsider rather than one of their own. Next, someone of stature, a professor apparently, told the *gendarmes* that Guido had sexually harassed the young victim. Guido bears evidence that he had been in a recent fight. And, he has no alibi."

"All of that can be explained," I said. "But I doubt the explanations will make Guido look very good."

"There was a fight?"

"The father of one of the young *fromagerie* workers took a shot at him."

"Ah, yes. Guido was doing what Guido does. But what happened with the local *procureur*?"

"That's *procuress*," I said. "Or would you say *procuratrix*?"

"Neither. I think you'd just say angry woman and Guido being Guido."

"When can we get him out?"

Jean-Paul lifted a shoulder, making my heart sink. "We'll see. In the meantime, don't worry. Guido will be fine. The food, I was told, comes from a very good café in the village except on market day, and any cellmates will probably be local drunks or petty thieves, not hardened criminals. It is not a high-crime area. Your ambassador has been informed, so there isn't much more to do. Perhaps you should contact your employer before news gets out."

"It's four A.M. in Los Angeles. I'll call when the sun is up."

But I took out Grand-mère's phone and sent our producer a text: GUIDO'S IN THE SLAM. TALK LATER.

"Not the first time I've sent that message," I said, pocketing the phone. But it was the first time that I was afraid he might not get out again. Pierre Dauvin wouldn't let us speak with Guido on Friday night, but he gave permission for us to bring a bag of toiletries and some fresh clothes on Saturday morning.

After a week apart, I had Jean-Paul within an arm's reach, and the interlude with his mother had been pleasant enough. But the rest of the day had been a nightmare. I wanted it to be over. We stopped at a favorite little restaurant in the village of Pirou for dinner, but I could not tell you what was put in front of me to eat. I apologized to Jean-Paul for being such miserable company. Before the cheese, he asked for the check and we drove home. That night, for the first time since we began sharing a bed, we did not make love, and nothing was said about it.

Maybe I slept, but I couldn't be sure. Jean-Paul held me in his arms and snored softly against my neck. I had been at Grand-mère's long enough to be familiar with the night sounds. The old house creaked as it cooled after a warm day; breezes ruffled through the trees outside. Sometimes I could hear the lowing of cows in the near pasture and the big Percheron horses snuffling at each other in the meadow beyond. I tried to lie still so that I wouldn't waken Jean-Paul, but I was so on edge that every sound seemed amplified. When I heard water from somewhere in the house rattling through the pipes, I waited to hear a bedroom door close. Surely, Casey or Grand-mère had gotten up to use a bathroom or get a drink of water. But only silence followed.

Unable to be still any longer, I disentangled myself from Jean-Paul, took the flashlight out of the bedside drawer, and ventured into the hall. First I listened at Casey's door. When I heard nothing, I opened the door enough to see the mound she made under her duvet. Grand-mère's room was at the end of the hall. I put my ear against the cold wood and heard her heavy, regular breathing.

Standing at the top of the stairs, I peered down into the darkness below. All was still, except for my imagination.

"*Psst*, Maggie."

I jumped even as I recognized Jean-Paul's whisper.

"Is there something?" he asked, putting his arm around my shoulders and looking down the stairs.

I shook my head. "Old houses creak, old pipes rattle."

"You weren't sleeping."

"Too restless."

He took the flashlight from my hand and turned it on. "We'll just go have a look around, all right? For your peace of mind."

We went downstairs, turned on the lights, looked in every room, checked every door, every window, every tap. Everything seemed to be as it should be.

"All right?" Jean-Paul asked. "Will you be able to sleep now?"

"We'll see," I said. "We'll see."

─ 10 ─

SATURDAY WAS MARKET day in the village. While there was a big Champion supermarket nearby in Créances where one could buy packages of toilet paper large enough to fill the backseats of the generally tiny French cars, most locals and an impressive number of summer visitors preferred to stock up on meat, cheese, and produce at the Saturday market. Except for morning croissants and maybe *croque monsieur* at the *tabac*, local cafés and restaurants did not serve food on market day. When Pierre Dauvin gave us permission to see Guido, he asked us to pick up lunch not only for Guido but also for Jaqueline Cartier, who would be on duty at the *gendarmerie* and unable to get away.

Traffic headed into the village would be heavy from all directions, and parking would be worse than usual. It was a beautiful, clear and warm day, so Jean-Paul and I decided to ride bikes into town. From the bike jumble behind the potting shed, we choose two that had inflated tires and front baskets and headed out. We stopped first at the kitchen garden to tell Grand-mère that we were leaving. She was picking peas.

"Grand-mère," I said, nodding in the direction we had come.

"Are you aware there's a weeping woman sitting against the wall beside the garden gate?"

Grand-mère peeked out from around the pea frames. "Is she still there?"

"Let me guess," I said. "Could she be Fraulein von Streicher and you've refused to speak with her?"

"If I won't speak with her, how would I know who she is?" Grand-mère dumped a colander full of freshly picked peapods into the big pail at her feet. "Aren't the peas lovely? I think the fertilizer slurry David put on the soil has made a great improvement. We'll have them for dinner tonight. I think there will enough more by Monday to put up in the freezer."

Jean-Paul set the bike down to pluck a pea off the vine. He squeezed the pod open and with his thumb pushed the fresh little peas into his mouth.

"Perfect," he said, chewing happily.

I asked Grand-mère, "Do you want us to ask her to move along? Perhaps see if she needs transportation?"

"She'll only come back," Grand-mère said. "No, it'll get hot where she's sitting soon enough, and she'll go of her own accord. So, where are you children off to?"

"Dauvin is letting Maggie take lunch and a bag of toiletries to Guido," Jean-Paul told her. "We're hoping we'll be able to speak with him."

Grand-mère stopped picking peas and turned to me. "You've been so worried, dear. How is Guido holding up?"

"I spoke with him this morning. He had a rough night," I told her. "But he has a good lawyer, and the American consul is coming to speak with him this afternoon. We'll see."

Jean-Paul said, "They're holding him under *garde à vue*, so they have only three days to bring charges. He could be out by Monday."

When they let Guido out, if they let him out, I wondered how long they could prevent him from returning to the States. When Olivia first made an issue of Guido's attentions to Solange, I considered sending him straight home rather than having to deal with the inevitable fallout. As long as I've known him, Guido's existence has been a constant muddle of broken hearts, his and theirs. The drama gets tiresome. But he is also tremendously talented in technical areas where I am not. Professionally, we were always a good team. Except when his love life intruded. Damn and blast, Guido, I fumed to myself. Damn and blast.

Jean-Paul pulled me into his arms. With my face against his chest, I started breathing normally again. He said, "It's too early to worry so much."

"Do you really have to leave tomorrow?" I asked.

"We'll see. I wish I could stay until you get tired of me."

"That will never happen," I said.

Grand-mère, the devil, had a happy smile on her face as she watched us. "Since you're going into the village, will you run a little errand for me?"

"Before I say yes," I said, "promise me that shovels won't be involved."

"No, no. Not this time." She tapped my cheek for being saucy. "But if you would, I have a small package to deliver to Ma Mère at the convent. Marie repaired the gown Pierre's nephew will wear for his baptism tomorrow; the garment is very delicate."

"We'll be careful with it," I said, walking my bike beside her as we headed toward the house. Out of the blue, I asked her, "Grand-mère, is Pierre related to us?"

"Let me think how." She handed the pail of peas to Jean-Paul and looked off into the distance for a moment. "Ma Mère and Marie are sisters. Their brother married a woman whose brother, Dauvin, married Pierre's grandmother."

"If I followed that," I said, "Pierre is my cousin Antoine's second cousin by marriage, but he isn't related to you or me. Not by blood, anyway."

"If you want to split hairs," she said, "there is no blood relation between Antoine and Pierre, either. Pierre's grandfather died during the war and his grandmother married Dauvin later. Why, is it important?"

"No," I said. "Jean-Paul's mother asked that question yesterday and I didn't know the answer. Something else she said made me wonder if you had some sort of issue with Pierre when he was a teenager."

"Pierre was a lovely boy." Her answer was brusque. Clearly, there was something she was not saying. And she quickly changed the subject. "Tomorrow is Pierre's nephew's turn to wear the baptism gown. So, do get it to Ma Mère straight away. And don't forget, there will be a party for the baby at the beach after church."

"Do we take gifts for the baby?" I asked, holding the back door for her.

"No, we take food." She picked up a canvas shopping bag from the kitchen table and gave it to me. Inside, I could see a tissue paper-wrapped parcel. "And while you're at the market, if you don't mind, would you stop at Armand the butcher's stall? He usually parks his trailer in the forecourt of the church, under the old oak tree. You'll know him by the smoke he puts out. For market-day lunches Armand cooks lovely *saucissons* over driftwood on a big brazier. Very smelly, and very delicious. Guido will be delighted if that's what you take him to eat. Would you please ask Armand to add about two kilos of shaved ham to the platter he is putting together for the party? Tell him that Freddy will pick up the platter on his way to the beach tomorrow."

"Anything else?" I asked.

"No, dear," she said. "Except, will you see if that woman is still sitting there?"

I went out through the garden gate and took a look. The woman was no longer against the wall where we'd seen her earlier. Would she be back? Probably.

With the baptismal gown in the basket of my bike and Guido's duffel of essentials in Jean-Paul's, we started on our way toward the village, a distance of about five miles from the estate. I wanted to avoid whatever was going on around the sewer-trench gravesite, so we went out through the front gate instead of shortcutting along the farm access road.

Traffic on the village road was heavy, but it moved right along. Gaston had warned us about the American motorcycle club that was coming through the area that Saturday. We met them head-on as we approached town and were nearly blown off the road. The riders weren't rude or aggressive, but the sheer number of them seemed to take up all the available air and pavement. At the first opportunity, we turned off onto a narrow side road and came into the village behind the convent. I was familiar enough with the layout of the building to remember a walkway that led from the convent's back gate into the close, the walled garden at the center of the massive sandstone edifice.

The convent looked ancient, Romanesque with a later Gothic addition. But the entire structure was actually built postwar. The original building was leveled by Allied bombs after D-Day and rebuilt later to appear as much like the original as possible. During the rebuilding, modern plumbing and wiring were added as part of the nation's general facility upgrade during *le Grande Trente*, the thirty-year period of postwar modernization. But the character of the architecture and the place of the convent in its village remained intact.

We left the bikes and Guido's bag in the close and made our way along the labyrinthine interior corridors to the abbess's office.

"Here you are," Ma Mère said, rising from her desk when we tapped on her open door. "Élodie called to say you were on your way. Monsieur Bernard, how lovely to see you again."

"And you, Ma Mère." He bowed slightly as he took the hand she offered.

After *la bise*, I set the shopping bag on her desk and she took out the tissue-wrapped bundle.

"Perhaps you haven't seen the gown, my dear." Carefully, she laid open the tissue to reveal a delicate silk garment trimmed in exquisite handmade lace. The fabric carried the patina of age, the brightness of the original white mellowed to the tones of a string of old pearls. I was afraid to touch it.

I said, "It's beautiful."

"You couldn't possibly remember, of course. But you wore the same gown when your mother presented you to the Church for holy baptism, just as she had when Élodie handed Isabelle to the priest at the font. Can you imagine ever being so small?"

I asked, "Does every child in the parish wear the gown?"

"Oh, no, dear." Gently, she folded the tissue back over the garment. "A small group of women made the lace and sewed the gown for the presentation of a very special child. Since then, all of their children, and their children, have worn it."

"It's very old?" I asked.

She smiled as she tucked in a stray ribbon. "The silk came from an American parachute, my dear."

"Retrieved in 1944?" I asked.

She nodded once as her hands disappeared into the sleeves of her habit. "It doesn't seem like very long ago at all. And forever ago at the same time."

A young nun with a sweet Asian face entered the office from a side door and stood there silently.

"May I offer you coffee?" Ma Mère asked us. "Or perhaps lemonade?"

"Thank you," Jean-Paul said. "But another time, I think. We have been sent on errands."

Without a word, the little nun disappeared back through the door. We took that as our cue and said our good-byes. As she saw us out, the abbess turned her attention to Jean-Paul.

"How is Karine?" she asked him.

"My sister?" He seemed taken aback by the question. "You know Karine?"

Ma Mère dropped her head in a little nod. "When she was still a girl, she spent the better part of a summer with us."

The memory tumblers suddenly seemed to align for him. "I didn't realize this is where my parents sent her. I was away at school at the time, buried in the *prépas*, and so most of the world passed me by."

"Karine is well?"

"Yes, she'll be pleased to hear you asked about her," he said. "She and her husband have two children, a boy and a girl, though they're hardly children anymore. Her son will sit for his *baccalauréat* in May. Karine teaches painting and sometimes exhibits her work."

"And she is happy?"

"Karine is Karine, as happy as she decides to be."

Ma Mère ushered us to the door and waved us on our way. We collected Guido's bag from the bike basket, and leaving the bikes where they were, went out to join the market day crowd.

The village square was an irregular quadrant bordered on one side by the vast stone convent, a lovely Romanesque parish church

opposite, with the *mairie*, where Gaston presided over town business, and the *gendarme* barracks on either side between them. A tall
plaster cameo with the profile of Marianne, the symbol of the French
hearth and home, embellished the front of the *mairie*. She seemed to
face down the large French national *tricolore* waving from the top of
the *gendarmerie*, the local headquarters of the national police; the yin
and yang of French officialdom.

On Saturdays, the generally quiet square teemed with activity.
Vendors walked among the crowds offering samples of their wares to
lure buyers to the stalls lining the streets, sometimes on both sides.
The sweet, earthy smells of fresh produce combined with the heavier
scents of cheeses and meats, of seafood fresh from the water, and the
smoke from what we would call barbecues in America all blended
into one delicious gastronomic mélange. It was lunchtime, and I was
hungry.

Armand's meat stall was easy to find. We just looked for the
densest plume of smoke and walked toward it. Armand, it turned
out, had a strong Bretagne accent that I couldn't manage with my
emergent ability with French, so Jean-Paul took over. He gave the
butcher Grand-mère's instructions and ordered *saucissons en croûte*
for four people for our lunch. Armand slashed a long baguette from
end to end, slathered the bread with homemade brown mustard
and local sweet butter, and then laid long, thick grilled pork sausages straight off the fire into the slit. With three quick hacks of his
big knife, he had four sandwiches on his cutting board. These he
wrapped in white paper and stacked into my canvas market bag.

During all of this, Jean-Paul and Armand kept up a conversation about pig slaughtering and the onerous burden of the European
Union food processing regulations on small artisanal producers. I
couldn't always follow what they were saying, so my attention drifted
off to the crowd and the festival atmosphere of an active market day
in summer. Two of the cheese stalls were covered with butcher paper
and closed, which seemed unusual at the height of the day. There
was a stir of some sort at a bakery stall and out of curiosity I turned
to see what was up.

A tall, fair, raw-boned woman, probably in her late seventies, seemed to stumble into the road in front of the baker's stall as if she had been pushed. When she found her footing and straightened up again, I recognized her. Here was the weeping woman, Erika von Streicher Karl, herself.

After brushing off her skirt and taking a deep breath, she looked around the square, seemed to find what she was looking for, and marched down the middle of the street until she came to a stop at the flower stall of ancient Mme Cartier, our family's cheesemaker's maternal grandmother. Mme Cartier was roughly Grand-mère's age, somewhere north of ninety. Her hips bothered her, so she sat among her buckets of bright, fresh flowers in a folding canvas chair. Erika came up beside her, startling the old dear by thrusting a sheaf of papers under her nose. Mme Cartier took the papers because she truly had no alternative, perched some reading glasses onto her nose, and took a look at what she'd been given. She was two stalls over, and the crowd was noisy, so I couldn't hear what she said when she'd had a look. But I understood the hand that flashed up and slapped the German woman soundly across the face. Then she ripped the papers into shreds and spat on them as the wind made the bits dance around her feet.

The breeze wafted the shreds toward us. One of the fragments collided with my leg. I peeled it off, and to my profound dismay, saw the uniformed chest of a man with the same eagle- and swastika-embossed buttons running down the front of his tunic that I had un-earthed from the carrot-field grave Thursday night. Obviously, Erika had been showing around a set of old photographs that had been scanned into a computer and printed onto plain paper. I handed the fragment to Jean-Paul and scurried around, trying to scoop up as many of the rest of the bits as I could.

Erika saw what I was doing and made a beeline toward us. She held out her hand to me, and said, "Please." She wanted the torn scraps. I wadded them, walked over to Armand's brazier and used his long fork to push them into the coals until they caught fire. Erika followed me, protesting. "All I want," she started, but I grabbed her by the elbow and marched her away, into an alcove at the side of the church where we were out of view of the crowd.

"What the hell do you think you're doing?" I demanded, steamed by her brazenness.

"My father was here in the war," she said in heavily accented English. "He was such a fine man. I hoped to find someone who might remember him. He was lost during the war, you see. Missing in action."

"Oh, there are people around here who remember him all right. But not as a fine man. Dear God, woman, he was the invader. The occupier."

"Well, yes." Her arms went out to the side. "But there was an accord signed; we became allies, the French and the Germans. We were on the same side."

"Where the hell did you study history?" I said.

She sniffed at that. "My mother told me all that I needed to know because in school we did not talk very much about that time."

"That's clear," I said. "The uniform your father wore is still in-flammatory. Hell, if someone today walked down a street anywhere in Europe wearing your father's Nazi uniform, he would be arrested. Don't you understand that?"

"I understand this: My father was just another man caught up in world events, like the men here. That does not make him a criminal. So, why won't anyone talk to me?"

"If you had to come looking for people who knew your father, couldn't you have found some pictures of him in civilian clothes?"

"I thought people would recognize him more easily if they saw him in photos taken here, as he looked when he was here."

I had to turn away from her. She was either crazy or stupid and I had no idea what to do next, other than maybe slapping her other cheek, which I did not do, though sorely tempted. Jean-Paul was standing nearby, making sure that things with Erika didn't get out of hand. I gave him a little wave and he started toward us.

I turned to her. "Exactly what is it that you hope to gain here?"

"You have to understand," she said. "I was very young when my father went away to war. I don't have many memories of him, except that he was very tall and very kind. He made a good life for his family. I remember our beautiful house and the gardens, a maid and a nanny. We had music lessons. And then, after the war, the Russians came, and everything was different. We lost our home, our position, all of our comforts. My mother, my brother and I had to share a single room. There was no toilet, no water. My mother went to work cleaning the train station. A woman of refinement, she had to scrub away the scum left by lesser people. It was a terrible humiliation for all of us."

"You really should go to the library and check out a couple of books about what your father and men like him did during the war," I said, stepping away from her and taking Jean-Paul's arm for support.

She was so lost in her own reverie that I doubt she heard what I said.

"You live *chez* Martin," she said. "I've seen you there."

"That is my family's home."

"And the old woman there?"

"She is my grandmother," I said.

"Why won't she speak to me?"

"She doesn't remember your father the same way you do. What she could tell you about him she believes no child would want to hear."

"But she remembers him?"

"As clearly as the woman who slapped your face does."

Her gaze shifted off toward Mme Cartier's flower stall before it came back to me. "Does she know how my father died?"

I lifted a shoulder. "Perhaps."

"Is my father among the remains found on her farm?"

"You would need a DNA test to determine that." I squeezed Jean-Paul's arm. "Right now, I have other things to do. I recommend that you go away and leave these people alone before someone does something that gets them into trouble."

She seemed to deflate. "Yes, all right. But I beg of you, please ask your grandmother to give me just a moment of her time."

"I will," I said, turning away. "But I'm warning you, if she agrees to talk to you, you won't be happy with you what you hear."

"Maybe yes, maybe no. Whether she speaks to me or not, one way or another I will learn what I have come to learn." With that, she headed off toward the small car park behind the *mairie*.

━II━

I EXPECTED TO FIND Guido behind bars in some dark recess of the *gendarmerie* playing mournful tunes on a harmonica. Instead, he was sitting at a table in the day room playing cards with his keeper, Jacqueline Cartier. I knew from experience that Jacqueline had very limited English, and that Guido's French was nearly non-existent. Yet somehow they managed to communicate well enough to be keeping up a spirited game of blackjack. I found it ironic that Guido, the suspected sex-maniac killer, had been left in the sole custody of that lovely young woman.

"Cozy," I said, looking around. The long room apparently was a combination meeting and break space. There were basic kitchen facilities along one side, a narrow cot at the end, walls covered with announcement boards, and rows of tables and chairs in the middle. "Not what I expected."

Guido chuckled as he set his cards aside. "A couple of the cheese vendors got into a scrap out in the market. As I understand it, the guy from Pont l'Évêque objected to the guy from Créances labelling his stinky cheese as a Pont l'Évêque because Créances is outside the correct *terroir*. The Créances guy said he wasn't breaking any law. Cue the stand-up slugfest, enter *gendarmes* stage right. Pierre hauled them in and locked them in separate cells until they cool off. Because there are only two holding cells, he put me out here to wait for you. Hey Jean-Paul, how's things?"

"Interesting," Jean-Paul said, offering his hand. "But when you and Maggie are around, things generally are interesting."

To Guido I said, "I'm impressed that you managed to get all the details of that little dust-up. Have you been studying French under your covers at night?"

He laughed. "No, Renée came by to apologize and she explained it all to me."

"Did she now?" I said, setting the shopping bags on the end of the table. "Fancy that."

"Yeah." He blushed a bit. "My lawyer explained to her that it wasn't me who said I'd been with her all night, when I wasn't. She told me she overreacted."

Jean-Paul set the bag of toiletries and fresh clothes in front of Guido. I'd tucked in a couple of paperbacks, in English. Before Guido could touch the bag, Jacqueline took it over to the next table and gave the contents a thorough inspection. As Guido watched her, Jean-Paul and I unpacked the shopping bags. Besides the sausage sandwiches, we had bought fruit, some ripe tomatoes, cheese, Greek olives, extra bread and cold cuts for Guido's dinner, and bottles of beer and water. By the time we had emptied our bags, there was quite a feast spread out on the table.

Jacqueline zipped Guido's bag closed and set it on the cot. At our invitation, she helped herself to food and drink, and then excused herself. She carried her lunch to the far end of the room and sat down to eat, alone. I understood that she was giving us some privacy to talk with Guido, though the language issues alone would have kept her from following most of our conversation. Jean-Paul gathered his lunch and went to join her. He did this, I knew, not to give me and Guido privacy, but to find out anything he could from Jacqueline.

Guido and I ate while we talked. He told me that his lawyer told him that the working theory of the crime until, or unless, there was new information, was that Guido came back from his assignation with Renée sexually frustrated, a supposition apparently based on the experiences with *madame le procureur* of more than one man in town. Guido had then demanded sex from Solange. When she turned him down, he took that prize which she would not give him willingly. The struggle that ensued turned deadly.

When I saw Solange's body it was fully clothed, her garments intact. I asked, "Was there evidence of a sexual assault?"

"They haven't done an autopsy yet," he said with a shrug, though his expression was grim. "So far, it's all just theory. Except the part where they locked me up; that's real enough."

"Guido," I said, putting my hand on his arm. "Did you ever have sex with Solange?"

"Hell no," he said with convincing force. "Jeez, Maggie, people had it all wrong about who was the aggressor there."

"She came on to you?"

"Yes, but not the way you're thinking. That girl was something else. Driven, hyper-motivated I guess you'd say. She had this idea that I should follow her around with a camera so that when she made some huge archeological discovery everything would be recorded. I was then to make a commercial-quality documentary about her which she would show when she presented her doctoral dissertation, or something, and she'd become an instant superstar."

"What did you tell her?" I asked.

"First I said no, didn't have the time. Then I said, forget it. After that I told her to quit nagging me about it. If she wanted to be the star of her own show she could go hire her own film crew."

"Did she stop asking after that?"

"I wish, but no. One time, she got mad enough when I told her I wouldn't do as she wanted that she launched herself at me, fangs and claws drawn. I was fighting her off when Olivia, the old bat, walked in. She assumed that her precious student was defending herself from me, like I was some predator."

"Did you explain to Olivia?"

"I tried." Guido set his sandwich aside, leaned back in his chair and let out a long, pent-up sigh. "There was something weird between those two, Maggie. Sometimes I thought it was sexual. But I think it had more to do with jealousy. Solange had asked me not to mention the film thing to Olivia, or this big discovery she said she was working on. She told me that Olivia was always trying to hold her back, and that Olivia would take all the glory for whatever Solange found."

"I know from being around my dad that the relationship between a mentor professor and protégé student can get very complex," I said. Isabelle, my biological mother, had been one of my father's bright graduate students. "The relationship can be sexual, competitive, possessive, loving, and full of jealousy all at the same time."

"How is the old battle-axe?"

"Olivia?" I shrugged, trying to remember when I had seen her last. After I found Solange, Grand-mère bundled me off right away to visit Jean-Paul's mother. Jean-Paul and I got home late last night after trying, and failing, to see Guido. That morning, because we had left by the front gate instead of using the farm road, we hadn't seen anyone. I said, "I don't know. But she must be very upset. I think everyone is."

He covered my hand with his. "Finding Solange like that must have been damned awful for you, Maggie. How are you doing?"

"I keep thinking about her parents," I said, fighting back an unexpected rush of tears. "I can't imagine getting that call."

"Yeah." His head dropped. "Damn. Solange."

That name seemed to descend over the room like a black pall. All conversation ceased. In that gap in time and reality, fighting back one of those random bursts of panic that sometimes hit parents, I wondered where my beloved daughter might be at that moment; an active imagination can be a curse.

For something to do, I started gathering up the remains of lunch and wrapping the leftover cheese and fruit for Guido to have with his dinner later. Jean-Paul and Jacqueline were doing the same. The rustling of wrappings that filled the space where conversation had been was interrupted by voices at the reception desk out front. And then that very dear daughter, Casey, and her seemingly constant companion, David Breton, were shown in by the *gendarme* on desk duty.

There was a great happy exchange of *les bises* all around, as if these newcomers had swept something dark from the air. Jacqueline was David's first cousin. They engaged in some good-natured teasing that ended when he took over polishing off her half-finished sandwich. Casey co-opted the remains of mine.

"Hey, Jean-Paul," she said, positioning the sandwich for a first bite. There was a shopping bag hanging from her arm. "When did you get here?"

"Last night," he said. "How's the cheese business?"

"It's interesting," she said.

He nodded toward her bag. "Did you bring us some?"

"Oh!" She held the bag out to Guido. "I baked you a cake."

"With a file in it?" Guido asked.

"Of course." She finally took a bite of the sandwich.

Guido opened the bag and took out a small bakery box. Jacqueline took the box from him, opened the lid, carefully looked over the contents, and then, with a shrug, put the box back on the table in front of Guido. David explained to her the joke about the prisoner, the cake, and the file. She shrugged again and said, "But it's a fruit tart." Jokes don't always translate.

"Casey," I said, "have you seen Olivia?"

She nodded, swallowed. "She took her students back out to the dig by that old stone wall in the pasture that Grand-mère showed her. The students were hoping for a day off, but she insisted. In fact, she was pretty intense about it. Antoine said she needs the distraction. Frankly, she's a mess about Solange."

"How are the other kids taking it?"

Casey shrugged and raised her palms in a perfect French expression meaning, who can say? "Everyone's upset by what happened to her, of course. I mean, she's dead. So I hate to say this, but Solange wasn't very popular. Full of herself, you know. A diva. Everyone in the student camp was assigned cleanup duties. But she somehow managed to disappear whenever it was her turn to scrub johns or take out the trash or whatever. Pissed everybody off. I hear it was even worse out in the field with the other archeologists."

"How so?"

"You know who Raffi is?"

I shook my head.

"The cute one. Black curly hair, long eyelashes."

"Hey!" David interjected, pointing at his own chest.

She glanced at him. "You're cute, David. But you have to admit, Raffi is damn cute, too."

"*Pffh,*" he said and took another bite of Jacqueline's sandwich.

"So," she said, turning back to me. "Raffi said that the other day, out at the wall dig, he had something in his sieve that looked like a bit of a stone tool, and Solange came right over and took it from him. And then she commandeered his dig site."

"What did he do?"

"What could he do? He said it was pointless to say anything to Olivia because she would only say, as she always did, that archeology is a collaborative undertaking. He said that from then on he just made sure that Solange didn't get anywhere near where he was working."

"I'd noticed that she tended to sit alone at lunch," I said.

"Yes, and not by her own choice," David said.

"Other than this Raffi," Jean-Paul said in French for, I thought, the benefit of Jacqueline, "was anyone especially angry with Solange?"

Casey and David exchanged glances and shrugs. Referring to the two of them, David said, "We hang out with the students sometimes, but because we live with our families and not in the camp we aren't involved in their housekeeping issues. And we don't work with them, either. All that Casey and I know is what the others tell us. I never saw anything between Solange and the rest except some sniping. Did you, Casey?"

She shook her head. "You should ask Antoine. The agriculture students tell him everything."

I made a mental note to speak with my cousin Antoine, and my film interns. None of them had mentioned issues with the other students they were bivouacked with. Certainly I couldn't remember any of them mentioning Solange. But we did not sit around and gossip.

Pierre Dauvin walked in during the ensuing lull in the conversation. Looking at the remains of our lunch, he said, "Quite a picnic here."

"We were just leaving," Casey said. She kissed Guido's cheek and warned him to be careful when he bit into his cake. When she leaned in to kiss me, she whispered, "We'll wait for you outside. I want to talk to you." The two young people swept out as suddenly as they had swept in.

Pierre asked Jacqueline about the state of the scrappy cheese vendors who were cooling off in the lockup. She pointed to her ear: We could hear snores coming from the back somewhere. Pierre nodded and went off down a hallway toward the noise. He was back a few minutes later, guiding one of the two cheesemongers by the arm as he gave him instructions to immediately clear out his stall and go straight home. Next week, the man was told, he should park his stand on the far side of the square. And for the sake of peace he should refrain from labelling his cheese something it was not by custom entitled to be called.

"*Bon? D'accord?*"

"*Oui, bon.*" Sure, fine. The dejected man slouched out with his hands thrust deep into his pockets. The snoring in the back continued. I wondered how many times that morning before the cheese dust-up, the man remaining in the lockup had rested his elbow on the copper-topped bar at the *café tabac* and knocked back quick *petits blancs* until he had summoned sufficient liquid courage to accost his competitor.

Pierre went over to the cot at the end of the room, picked up Guido's duffel, took a quick look inside, and announced that picnic time was over and it was time for Guido to reclaim his cell. Jacqueline stowed the food for Guido's dinner in the refrigerator, ran a quick sponge over the tables, and then quickly left through the front.

"Don't worry, my friend," Jean-Paul told Guido as he shook his hand. "This will be straightened out soon enough."

I gave my old partner a hug and told him that Lana, our executive producer at the network, sent her best wishes. He said, "I doubt that's what she said, Mag. But thanks for coming and cheering me up."

"I put a French phrase book in your duffel," I said. "Might come in handy."

He laughed. As he turned away to follow Pierre, he said, "You know where to find me."

Pierre handed me my mobile phone. "Your mother called," he said.

As Jean-Paul and I walked out, I scrolled through a day's worth of accumulated messages in my phone. Only one number, one with a French exchange, was unfamiliar. I showed it to Jean-Paul. He didn't recognize it either. I hit Connect and waited for someone to pick up on the other end. I got a message: "It's Vincent. Try me later." I left my name and put the phone away.

"It was the war salvage dealer I told you about," I told Jean-Paul. "Love to know what he has to say."

When we emerged back out into the bright sunshine of early afternoon, Casey and David rose from their seats on the shaded front steps of the *mairie* across the square, brushed off the bottoms of their shorts and walked toward us. The market vendors were closing up their stalls and preparing to leave. A few straggling shoppers lingered to chat or to bargain for any leftovers.

At old Mme Cartier's flower stall, Jacqueline Cartier and the young nun we had seen in Ma Mère's office that morning were putting all of the unsold blooms into a single bucket. Later, those flowers would be arranged and placed on the church altar for Sunday services. Armand the meat vendor collected the rest of the buckets and poured their water over the smoldering coals in his brazier. Then he wiped the buckets dry, stacked them, and put them into the back of his truck. He locked the brazier onto the side of the trailer on which he displayed his cheese, and then connected the trailer to the truck. When this was finished, he walked over to Mme Cartier and helped her from her chair. With Jacqueline following them, carrying her great-grandmother's folded chair, Armand boosted the lady into his front seat. While he finished cleaning up his stall site, Jacqueline leaned against the truck's passenger door and chatted with the woman resting inside.

"That is so sweet," Casey said, a dreamy look in her eyes as Armand drove off with elderly Mme Cartier. "I love these people."

"Was there something you wanted to talk to us about?" I asked her, interrupting her reverie.

"Yeah." Again she exchanged pointed glances with David before she spoke. "Mom, all of Solange's things are still in her tent. It's kind of creeping everyone out, if you know what I mean."

"Have the *gendarmes* looked through her tent?"

"Yes. Pierre told us he's finished with it."

"Her parents will pack it up when they get here."

"That's the thing," she said. "They aren't coming. I don't know where they are, but wherever it is they can't just rush over. They told Olivia that they have arranged for Solange to be cremated and for the ashes to be sent to them. They gave her an address to send personal effects. Olivia went into the tent to start packing it, and fainted dead away. The *pompiers* had to come and revive her. She can't do it."

I looked from Casey to David, and then at Jean-Paul. Jean-Paul smiled his upside-down smile and shrugged. He said, "A task for *Maman*, I believe."

"Why me?" I asked my daughter.

"What Jean-Paul said. It's a mom thing. We all talked it over and decided that if Solange's mom can't be here, someone's mom should do it for her."

"I could argue the logic of that, but never mind. I'll do it. I hardly knew the girl, so I doubt I'll faint. But it's still a pretty tall request."

"Thanks, Mom." She leaned in and kissed my cheek.

"When would be a good time to do this?"

"Tonight we're all going down to the beach at Anneville-sur-Mer to play volleyball and have a barbecue and generally chill. No one will be in the camp."

"Good time to pack up the ghosts," I said. "Now, beat it, you two, before I change my mind."

Jean-Paul needed to speak with Gaston, the mayor, to pass along a request that there be some decorum during the removal of the German remains from Grand-mère's field. We found *M. le maire* near the fountain in front of the convent, scolding a vendor about having left a mess behind the week before. The offender was threatened with a fine or, worse, banishment from the Saturday market, if it happened again. The dear nuns had cleaned up after him last week, Gaston told him. Because the vendor had caused them such an inconvenience, Gaston suggested he should go right inside now, ask Ma Mère for forgiveness and drop a tithe of his day's proceeds into the mission box as atonement. *"D'accord?"*

"Oui, oui," the man agreed with obvious resignation, pronouncing the affirmative "hway, hway," and not "we, we," as I'd been taught. As he slouched away into the maze of the convent, Gaston came toward us. I made the introductions, and Jean-Paul stated his case.

"Dommage," Gaston said with a deep shrug accompanied by raised palms. "It is finished. Too late for the marching band and twenty-one-gun salute, *non*? The remains are in the hands of the undertaker in Pérrier, awaiting instructions from the German *Volksbund* about where to plant them next."

"Will there be any attempts at identification?" I asked.

The shrug again. "Except for one man, the remains were so badly charred that identification would be nearly impossible. And certainly it would be very costly and time-consuming. Whether the Germans choose to undertake such an onerous and probably fruitless task is up to them."

"What about that one set of remains?"

"I have only one answer, my dear Maggie." He leaned toward me. "I don't give a damn."

I looked up at Jean-Paul. "Mission accomplished? Can you tell the angry German delegate at your meeting that you plighted his case?"

He hesitated before he nodded. "If it continues to be an issue for the man, I'll suggest that he propose that the European Union adopt a protocol for the handling of international remains found inside member nations."

"Bah!" Gaston groused. "Just what we need. Another way for the EU to interfere with local authorities."

"What do you suggest?" Jean-Paul asked.

"Will your Boche friend be appeased if I ask the priest to say a prayer of forgiveness for those who trespass against us during mass tomorrow?"

Jean-Paul smiled as he looped his hand around my elbow. "Yes. Perfect. Thank you."

We started taking our leave, but Gaston stopped us.

"Maggie," he said, "that woman you spoke with at the market this morning, who was she?"

"Erika von Streicher Karl."

"I thought it might be," he said with a scowl. "What, exactly, does she want?"

I held up my palms. "I know what she says she wants, but I have to believe she's looking for something more than merely finding out what happened to her father. Gaston, she told me about the beautiful life her family had until the war ended and the Russians came in. She said the Russians took away everything, so apparently they lived in the Eastern Sector somewhere. As she talked, I got the feeling that she expects to find something here that will give her back the comfortable life that she lost."

"She knows something?" Jean-Paul asked.

"Or she's just crazy. I don't know. But she is certainly driven."

"Do you think she could be dangerous?" Gaston asked.

"I think she should be more careful," I said. "If not, someone is likely to take a crack at her."

"I'll ask Pierre to keep an eye on her."

Gaston made me promise to bring Jean-Paul to dinner at his house very soon. We said our good-byes and set off to retrieve our bikes from the convent close.

"Did you learn anything from Jacqueline Cartier at lunch?" I asked.

"Enough that I gathered you don't need to worry very much about charges against Guido," he said. "He had a big contusion on his face when he was brought in that seemed to support the notion that there had been a struggle with the girl, Solange, before she died. Guido's lawyer told Dauvin that he should ask the father of one of the *fromagerie* workers what he knows about how Guido got that contusion. The man, Monsieur Bontemps, has gone fishing. He will be brought in for questioning tonight when his boat comes in on the tide. If his story matches Guido's, there will be only the problem of an alibi to deal with."

"Was there a struggle?" I asked as I kicked back my bike's kickstand. I didn't remember seeing anything other than the great gash in Solange's head. But I hadn't stayed to examine her.

"Apparently," he said. "Agent Cartier wouldn't go into detail. She said they expect a medical report Monday or Tuesday."

"Guido can last that long," I said.

"What now?" Jean-Paul asked as we wheeled into the lane.

"I'm taking you home for a nap," I said.

"To sleep?"

"Eventually," I said, kissing the underside of his chin. "Maybe we'll get around to sleep."

— 12 —

WE COULD HEAR the drone of Freddy's trench-digging equipment in the distance as soon as we turned off the byway onto the village road. Jean-Paul wanted to say hello and to see where all the fuss about the remains had been, so we bumped over the culvert at the end of the estate's access road and made our way around the end of the orchard.

Wisely, this time Freddy had left the operation of the excavator to its owner and was walking along beside the progressing sewer trench, giving instructions that it seemed to me were being mostly ignored. We could see the patch of fresh, packed black soil among the vast bright green of the carrots in the field where the grave had been excavated, and then filled in.

Jean-Paul and I leaned the old bikes against the root-ball berm of the hedgerow and started across the road. Freddy met us halfway. After greetings were taken care of, he told us that Pierre had cleared him to continue digging his sewer line. He was several days behind schedule because of the inconvenient discovery of the skull, and its friends, but he was hopeful that if he and his crew worked through the weekend they would be ready when the plumbers came to lay the sewer pipes next week.

"Surely you're taking time off tomorrow for the baptism events," I said.

"Can't escape them," he said with a resigned lift of his shoulders. "But the crew can continue without me for a few hours."

The very good news he had to give me was that as soon as the sewer line was in and connected, Freddy would be ready to fill the year-round saltwater pool at the development's community center. It would take a few days to condition the water, but very soon the pool would be ready to use. The day had grown very warm and the thought of plunging into a pool and swimming to exhaustion was enormously appealing to me.

"Two weeks," he said. "Three at the most. Right now the locker room facilities and the kitchen the students are using are on a temporary septic diversion that is giving me all sorts of grief. I'll be relieved when the entire facility is finally connected to the sewer."

We listened while Freddy laid out his plans for getting his village ready to open for viewing by potential buyers. Indeed, the project had been a life saver for him that summer, the season of his divorce, among other personal problems.

The equipment operator summoned him, so we said our goodbyes and went to collect our bikes. I was ready for that nap.

"Maggie?" I heard my cousin Antoine call out from the other side of the hedgerow, somewhere out in the orchard. "Is that Jean-Paul with you?"

We climbed the berm and found a gap amid the hawthorn that was wide enough to pass through without getting too badly scratched. Antoine was perched on the lower rungs of a ladder under an apple tree a few rows in, talking with a couple that, by their dress, open gestures, and relaxed posture had to be Americans. Antoine waved for us to join them.

"Maggie, Jean-Paul," he said as we approached. "Meet Henry and Paulette Matson, the Count and Countess of Rutland."

Jean-Paul's eyebrow rose, meaning he was dubious. But what the heck? I offered my hand to the woman. I said, "I've never met a count and countess before."

She took my hand in both of hers and laughed a big, happy, open American laugh; the count had a playful sparkle in his eyes. They were an attractive pair. He was tall and sturdy-looking, with a crop of sandy curls atop his head. And she was petite, with sweet, delicate features. Her hair, at least at the moment, was in the red spectrum, short and perfectly cut to frame a heart-shaped face. They were in that wide zone the Americans call middle age, casually dressed in obviously high-end summer clothes.

Jean-Paul said, "You're American?"

"I'm Canadian, originally," Paulette, the countess, said. "But yes, we're Yanks from California."

"Are you allowed titles in America?" he asked.

"Oh, absolutely," the count said. "It's a capitalist nation. We paid good money for the title, so we're going to use it. At least, for the duration of our vacation."

"Oh, Henry." She put her hand on his arm and looked up into his face adoringly. "It is fun, isn't it?"

"You bought the title?" I asked.

"I found it for sale online," Count Henry said. "I'd asked Paulette what she wanted for our anniversary this year, and said she'd always wanted to be Lady Paulette. So I went looking, and found a posting by the Count of Rutland offering legal rights to the title. I thought, hell, if Zsa Zsa Gabor's husband, who started out as an auto mechanic or something, can lay out a little cash and become a prince, then why not us?"

"Henry, tell them the John Wayne story."

He chuckled. "It seems that when John Wayne went to Harvard to collect a Hasty Pudding Award, one of the preppies looked at his hair and asked, 'Is that your real hair?' Or something close to that. The Duke said, 'It sure is, kid. It's real hair. I paid a lot of money for it, so now it's mine.' Our title is as real as his hair was."

Jean-Paul laughed. "Why not?"

"What brings Your Grace to our humble orchard?" I asked.

Paulette grew more serious. "When Henry bought the title, we had no idea where Rutland is. The only place we could find with that name is one of the tiniest counties in England. It does have a castle, but it's the tiniest castle I think I've ever seen. We already had plans to come across to look for vine stock for our vineyard."

"And some goats," Henry interjected. "Paulette wants to make goat cheese."

She patted his arm. "So we decided that since we were coming over we might as well stop in England for a few days and have a look at our county for ourselves, do a little research, just for the fun of it. Well, there was no record of any kind in England of the man we bought the title from. And there was no record of the Count, or Earl, of Rutland at all. It was about then that the investiture papers caught up with us."

"The papers were very elaborate, very ornate," Henry said.

"About what you would expect. Except, they were in German. So, I got back in touch with the old guy I bought the title from, the now former-count, and he told me that his Rutland is in Germany, near the Polish border. We thought, we're already on this side of the pond so we might as well go take a look there, too. The old guy agreed to meet us, so we flew over to Dresden from London."

"Does he live in a castle?" I asked.

"I don't know what he lives in," Henry said, propping a foot on Antoine's ladder. "We met him in a beer hall."

"He was convincing," Paulette said. "If you wanted him to be. He was straight and tall, and he wore a beautiful suit. Even if it was a bit frayed at the cuffs and shiny at the butt, it was perfectly tailored. And he had a monocle."

"The monocle would be enough for me," I said.

"I wish I'd thought so, and left it right there," Paulette said. "But we asked some questions and he told us his big sad story. You can probably guess what it was. His family was very old and very la-di-da for centuries. And then the war came, and the Soviets came in afterward. The family was trapped behind the Iron Curtain, and all was lost."

"Except for his pride and pretensions," Henry said. "For entertainment value alone, I thought we'd made a good buy. And Paulette is right, at that juncture we should have paid for the guy's lunch and stopped asking questions."

"Why?" I asked.

"If you set out to buy a fantasy," she said, "you have to be careful not to let reality intrude."

"I made the mistake of asking him why he was selling his title," Henry said. "He told us that ever since the reunification of Germany twenty-some years ago, he's been trying to reclaim the old family land. It's come up for sale, but he's just a bit short on cash."

"He tried to hit Henry up for a loan," Paulette said.

"Yeah. He said it would be a short-term thing, that he was just about to come into some real capital."

"*Quelle surprise*, eh?" Jean-Paul said with an ironic chuckle.

Paulette answered him in Canadian-accented French: "No surprise at all."

"Do you think he is genuine?" I asked.

"A genuine fraud or a genuine count?" Henry asked with a chuckle. "We asked about the ancestry we had just bought into. He didn't have much to say, except that his sainted father went missing in action during the last war and nothing has been the same since."

Though I suspected I knew what the answer would be, I asked, "Did he tell you where his father went missing?"

Paulette pointed to the soil under her feet. "Right here. When he told us his father was an officer in the German army stationed in Normandy, I looked him in the eye and asked him if his father was a Nazi. He denied it."

"If the man was among the Occupation forces stationed here," I said, "he wore the swastika."

"Of course he did," she said. She kept her eyes on me to the point that I became uncomfortable. "We have no illusions about the man. He said something to us that was so strange, that when Henry saw the news about the German remains found on a farm in this same village where the father went MIA, we got a car and drove over from Burgundy to see if we could find out anything about the count."

Antoine rose from his ladder perch. "The remains found here were charred beyond recognition. No one will ever know the identities of those men."

"That's fine with us," Henry said. "I have a feeling that the sins of the father who was posted here during the war have come to rest on the son. Maybe there is some karmic justice about that."

"What, you believe in karma now, Henry?" Paulette asked with a little chuckle. He grinned and kissed the top of her head.

"What did he say that was so strange?" I asked.

Paulette took a breath. "He told us that if he had the money, he would go to Normandy and search for his father's remains, even if he had to use his bare hands to find him. He said that if he could locate his father's grave, he knew his fortunes would turn around."

"Magical thinking?" Jean-Paul said.

"Wonder what he meant?" I said.

"It's a puzzle." Henry reached up and plucked a ripe *Binet Rouge* apple from a branch over his head and took a bite. Immediately, he spit the bitter fruit into his hand. "What the hell?"

"It's a cider apple," Antoine said. "Not meant for eating."

Paulette was still eyeing me. "You're American, right?"

"I am," I said.

"But you live here?"

"This is my family's estate. I'm just visiting."

"You know how sometimes when you're traveling you see some-one and you persuade yourself you know that person? Well I know I've met you." She aimed a manicured fingernail at Jean-Paul. "I believe that you and I met at a fund-raiser for the Long Beach Sym-phony last year. Aren't you the consul general for Los Angeles?"

"For two more weeks, I am," Jean-Paul said with a little bow. He was absolutely handsome, but he didn't look very ambassadorial at the moment in his well-worn khaki shorts, T-shirt, and scuffed sneakers, his unshaven face glistening from the heat of the day.

"I knew it." She tilted her head and studied me again. "Has any-one told you that if you put on makeup and did your hair you'd look just like Maggie MacGowen? You know who she is, does those investigative film specials for television."

"I've heard people say that," I said. Antoine and Jean-Paul were trying not to laugh, and mostly failing. I reached my hand toward her. "Hi, I'm Maggie MacGowen."

"Well, damn." She laughed that big American laugh again. "What are you doing here?"

"Visiting my family," I said again.

Henry was peering down his nose at me. "I read about this. You're making a film about getting to know the family you only recently learned that you were part of."

"Guilty as charged."

"You haven't run into our count, have you?" she asked with an airy laugh.

"Not unless he was bones," I said. "Does the Count of Rutland have a name?"

"Von Streicher," Henry said. "Horst von Streicher."

From our reactions, they knew something was terribly wrong.

"Your count was here," I said. "Major von Streicher had command of a German platoon that was billeted at my grandparents' home. He may have been dear to his family, but he was detested by the people here."

"Jeez, Henry, you'd expect a count to be at least a general. But a lowly major?"

Antoine said, "His daughter says he was a schoolmaster."

"Daughter?" Paulette took a step toward Antoine. "The count has a sister? You know this person?"

"We've run into her," Jean-Paul said. "She's been lurking around, trying to find out what she can about her father's tenure here."

I asked, "Is there any chance your count will find the funds to actually come looking for his papa?"

Henry laughed. "It's high season along this coast right now. Good luck to him finding a place to stay, and paying for it. We lucked out last minute and found a room in a private home because of a cancellation. It's pretty cute, but it's costing us almost as much as the George Cinq in Paris would. If the count is dependent on the money we gave him for those fancy investiture papers, he'll have to sleep rough. Don't tell my beautiful wife, but the title came cheap."

"Maybe he's already sold the title to three other people since we saw him," Paulette said. "Wouldn't put it past him."

Jean-Paul wrapped his arm around me and I leaned my head against his shoulder. I was sorry that the great joy these people had been having as the ersatz Count and Countess of Rutland, even if only for a summer, had been burst. Paulette was right, if you buy into a fantasy you have to be careful about letting reality intrude. Both of the von Streicher siblings seemed to be living out a fantasy of another sort. I could tell them with some certainty that their father's remains had been unearthed. And I could tell them how he died. But I had a feeling that the bones were only part of what they were after. What was the rest?

Paulette was telling Antoine about the room they had found in the village.

"It's in a darling old stone house. And the owners are the sweetest couple. They have a brand new baby and a toddler. The husband told us that normally they serve breakfast to their guests, but right now they have their hands full. And we don't mind at all, do we, Henry?"

He shook his head, but his attention had wandered off toward the cows crossing the far pasture, on their way to the milking barn. The conversation turned to cheese making, one of Paulette's passions; she wanted to make goat cheese at their Hawaiian ranch. Antoine suggested a tour of the *fromagerie*, which they eagerly accepted. Jean-Paul and I excused ourselves, said the polite good-byes, fetched our bikes, and rode home. For a lovely long nap. And it was lovely.

The sky had turned gray, threatening rain, by the time we left the house again that evening, headed for the student camp to pack up Solange's personal effects. This time we borrowed Grand-mère's big Range Rover and drove the short distance up the village road to the still-unpaved road into Freddy's housing development.

Along the western coast of the Cotentin Peninsula, because of the tidal patterns, land accretes, or builds up over time. Three centuries ago, the village road had run along the shoreline. Now it is at least three-fifths of a mile inland. The original, and still legal, deed to my family's estate defined the western extent of their land as the mean high tide line. What that meant for us, and particularly for Freddy, was that the wide strip of accreted land on the far side of the village road was ours, a gift from the sea. If that land were drained and further saltwater intrusion stopped, then the soil could be sufficiently amended to become fertile farmland. But the process would be expensive and the family had no need for more arable land. So it had been left alone, a long, wide barren tidal plain. Until Freddy decided that he could build an ocean-view community on it.

The engineering of Freddy's development was complicated and innovative. Already the eco-friendly infrastructure, architecture, and use of natural elements in the landscaping had drawn attention. The idea of a planned community for seniors who would bring their pension incomes into an area of under-employment and de-population, and that would integrate their needs with services already existing, and under-utilized, with a traditional village had been embraced in the form of public subsidies, environmental advisors, and tax breaks that made it possible for Freddy to begin construction a full year earlier than he had hoped. It wasn't a large-scale project, but it was, still, an enormous undertaking for a man whose background was in finance, and not development. Freddy did have the considerable experience and support of our Uncle Gérard, who was a builder, and Gérard's English second wife, whose expertise was marketing. And a significant amount of capital from my share of Isabelle's estate when it was finally settled. But overall, the project was Freddy's baby.

We parked near the future tennis courts, where the student tents were lined up in rows separated by alleyways that the students had named: Atlantic Coast Highway, Rue de Carotte, and Way Off Broadway. I gave Jean-Paul a quick tour of the development, from the cluster of home sites built around a wide and winding parkland, to the community center that was, actually, near the center of the development. When it was completed, the center would have a year-round pool, a gym and fitness studio, locker rooms, meeting rooms, a wide covered veranda for outdoor dining and events, and a commercial-grade kitchen. At the moment, the facility had bare concrete floors and unpainted sheetrock walls, but it had been set up to accommodate the students for the duration of their summer courses. The plumbing in the locker rooms worked, there were dining tables and chairs, sofas and easy chairs and a wide-screen television set up in the larger of the meeting rooms. The kitchen was fully functional. Their housekeeping was a bit spotty, but altogether the students had made good use of the place.

Solange's tent was in the middle of the camp's three rows, at the end nearest the locker rooms. After they finished their search, the *gendarmes* had sealed the tent entrance, a flimsy wood panel, with blue police tape and a warning note. I had called Pierre Dauvin to make sure that it was all right for us to go inside, and he had given us formal permission with the caveat that if we found anything that he had missed during his search, we were to let him know immediately.

The tent, like the others, had a wood floor, wooden sides halfway up, and canvas above. When we first went inside, the closed-up space was hot and stuffy. We propped open the door and tied up the canvas window flaps to let in the evening breeze off the ocean. And then we stopped to take a look around. There were a narrow iron-frame bed, a small dresser, a coat rack, a desk, and a chair all crammed into twelve-feet square. The only light was provided by two reading lamps and a bare fluorescent bulb hanging by its cord from the center support beam. We had brought some green plastic trash bags and a few boxes, but set them aside when we found a carry-on suitcase and a large canvas duffel under the bed. Jean-Paul took the duffel and began to unpack the desk, and I started on the dresser.

I found the sorts of clothing one would expect a young woman to have brought for a summer of archeological work. In the top drawer of the dresser there was a week's worth of utilitarian white cotton underwear and socks that had taken on the particular dinginess that I would call college-dorm gray. The camp had no public laundry facility because the houses under construction would each have their own laundry hookups. So I suspected that Solange had hand-washed her clothes, probably with shampoo or hand soap, rather than using the coin laundromat in the village. The second drawer of the dresser held T-shirts, shorts, and jeans, a swimsuit, and a couple of sweaters. A cotton skirt and blouse for dressy events like dates and dinners out hung from pegs on the coat rack.

After the clothes were packed, there was still plenty of room in the suitcase. I found a muslin laundry bag hanging from a nail driven into a wooden side support. Thinking that the few clothes inside should be laundered before they were sent to the parents, I lifted the bag off the nail to take home. The bag felt oddly heavy, and when I set it atop the dresser, there was a metallic clank. I opened it, and dumped it. Dirty Ts, underwear, a muddy pair of shorts. And a filthy white sock with a bulge in the toe. I reached into the sock.

"Look at this, Jean-Paul." On my palm, I held a beautiful gold pocket watch I had pulled out of the sock. It was covered with dirt, but I could still see the elaborately etched filigree on the cover, swirls of twining leaves and flowers embellished with gemstones. The watch looked very old. And it looked very expensive. I used a cleaner sock to wipe off the layer of grit embedded in the etched grooves until it shone. Jean-Paul took the watch from my hand for a closer look.

"My grandfather had one of these big old watches," he said. "He wore it hanging from a jeweled fob on the outside of his vest. A symbol, I think, of a man's status. Or a gift from a father with high expectations for a son."

He pressed the winding stem and the lid popped up to show the jeweled clock face. There was engraving inside the lid. Jean-Paul handed the watch back to me so that I could see what had been written there.

Something, probably a name, had been crudely scratched off and another name, equally crudely, scratched under the first. I couldn't read the original, but the second was abundantly clear: H. VON STREICHER.

"Where the hell did Solange get this?" I said, turning the watch over, looking for markings. "And where the hell did von Streicher get it?"

"The count?" Jean-Paul asked with a wry grin. "Obviously, he stole it. To the victor belongs the spoils, yes?"

He took out his phone and snapped a picture of the watch. Then he turned it over and took a second picture of the jeweler's mark embossed in the watch body near the hinge. He copied the engraved number inside the back cover into a text line, and sent it off into the ether with the photos.

"Who did you send that to?" I asked.

He shrugged and gave me the sort of enigmatic answer I had come to expect from him. "A friend."

Jean-Paul had gone to one of France's elite *grandes-écoles* where, it seemed, he became friends with a very tight circle of men who were now the core of the upper echelons of the French bureaucracy. Whatever the situation he ran up against, he always had a friend he could call for information, advice, or a bail-out. He was certainly handy to have around whenever I found myself in a pickle.

He took another clean sock out of the bag, put the watch into it, and gave it back to me. I dropped it into the front pocket of my linen shorts, feeling it drag down the light fabric. There was no mystery about how Major von Streicher acquired it. As Jean-Paul said, he stole it. But as we continued packing the tent, with every step I felt the weight of the watch against my leg, setting off a new round of speculation about how the thing happened to land in Solange's laundry bag.

In a corner, behind the coat rack, I found a bucket of tools marked as the property of the department of antiquities research, *l'école du Louvre*. I set them beside the door to return to Olivia. Jean-Paul put a stack of books that belonged to the university library next to the tools. On top of the stack was a library-bound monograph by Olivia Boulez with the word *Viducasses* in the title. There was a sticky note on the cover with my name written on it.

"What is that?" Jean-Paul asked when he glanced over and saw me thumbing through the slender volume.

"Solange was going to lend me an article about the early Celts in the area." I set the book back onto the stack.

"What about this?" He handed me the notebook that Solange always carried with her. Inside, I saw her meticulous sketches and notes, some of which I had seen when she was trying to persuade Pierre Dauvin that she could be useful to his investigation. The question was, did the notebook belong to the university project she was working on? Or was it personal property that should go to her family?

I propped the notebook against the bucket of tools. "I'll ask Olivia, her professor, and Raffi, who is one of the other graduate students."

Personal books, shoes, and toiletries filled the rest of the case. I zipped it up and set it beside the door. Jean-Paul pulled a wafer-thin laptop out of the top desk drawer, along with the usual accumulation of pens and paperclips and rubber bands that people dump into desk drawers. I spotted a new flash drive, still in its packaging, among the clutter. I opened the computer, woke it from sleep mode, took the flash drive out of its wrappings and put it into one of the computer's drive ports. A few clicks, and the computer files were downloading to the removable drive.

Jean-Paul looked over my shoulder. All he said was *"Oui?"*

"I don't know what it is yet," I said, "but I'm sure I have a very good reason to take a look at Solange's files."

He chuckled. "Elementary spycraft; never hand over information until you know what it is."

I cupped his chin in my hand and looked into his deep brown eyes. "And what, exactly, do you know about spycraft?"

"As I have said before—"

"I know, if you told me you'd have to kill me."

He kissed me. Things were just getting interesting when his mobile phone rang. He stepped back and took the call, said, *"Bon"* and *"merci,"* affirmed to the caller that his son, Dominic, was fine and yes, Dom was beginning his university preparation studies in September, and how happy he was that the caller's wife had recovered from whatever ailed her. Lunch next week would be grand, and good-bye.

"So?" I said.

"The watch was made at the Paris workshop of Breguet in 1935. It was ordered by a national association of cheesemakers and engraved for presentation to one Giles Martin."

"My great-grandfather," I said.

"So it would seem that this von Streicher stole or appropriated your great-grandfather's watch for his own use."

"The bastard," I said.

"Peut-être," he said, maybe so. "But how did it come into the possession of this young woman?"

"I just may have an answer," I said. I had puzzled my way through that same question until a possibility came to me. "But first I need to talk to my grandmother."

A shadow crossed the door and we looked over. Two of my interns, Taylor and Zach, were hovering there, peeking in through the open door. I introduced them to Jean-Paul, and said, "I thought you'd be at the beach with the others."

"We were," Zach said. "But Raffi—you know who he is?—Raffi got there late. He told us that he'd waited in the camp until you arrived because he wanted to make sure someone was here, looking after things. He said he saw that old woman who's been hanging around the estate for the last few days walking around the construction site. You know, we all have stuff like cameras and tools and computers in our tents. The doors lock, but they aren't really secure. Still, we never had to worry about anyone messing with our stuff until all those people showed up after the bones were found. We didn't know how long you would be here, so Taylor and I came back to make sure someone was around in case that woman, or anyone else, came into the camp."

"Has anything gone missing?" Jean-Paul asked.

Taylor held up her palms. "A couple of the kids thought that someone had gone through their things. And that woman makes people worry. She's seriously weird. She walked right up to Raffi when he was at his dig site out in the pasture and wanted to know what he'd found. Solange had said she did the same thing to her."

I said, "Then it's a good idea to keep an eye out. I'll talk to Freddy and Antoine and see if we can set up some security here."

Taylor and Zach exchanged a telling look.

I looked from one to the other, and said, "Yes?"

Zach pointed to the tops of the temporary light poles Freddy had erected at the ends of the alleys between tents. There were video surveillance cameras atop every pole.

"When did you put those in?" I asked.

"Thursday," Zach said. "That's when someone went into Raffi's tent. We pooled our money and bought the system at an electronics store in Pérrier."

"Who monitors the cameras?"

Taylor held up her mobile phone. "Anyone who wants to. Zach set it up so that the cameras feed to a Cloud account. All of us have access to it. You know, we didn't want anyone to think Big Brother was watching them."

I heard Jean-Paul chuckle softly as he put an arm around me. I looked up at him and said, "Talk about spycraft."

"Does Pierre Dauvin know about the cameras?" Jean-Paul asked.

Again, Zach and Taylor checked with each other before either spoke. She said, "Why would he?"

"Solange," I said.

She thought about that for a moment. "I guess that because Solange didn't die here in camp, we just didn't think there was anything to say. Is that wrong?"

"I don't know, Taylor," I said. "But I would love to see what you captured on Thursday night into Friday morning. And the *gendarmes* probably would, too."

"Just go here." Zach took a pencil out of Solange's collection, and a note pad. He wrote down the access information for the Cloud account and handed it to me. "It's a fairly primitive system; cheap. The images aren't very sharp, and we set the cameras to capture only fifteen frames a minute. But the images are date- and time-stamped so you can scroll through and find what you want to see."

"You amaze me," I said, patting him on the back. "You endlessly amaze me."

"Film is my life." He shrugged. And then he asked, with a hopeful gleam in his eye, "If you find something on the tape, think it could be used in the documentary?"

"Possibly," I said. "Let's get a look at it first."

The two youths sat on the edge of the cot while we finished packing, chatting amiably with Jean-Paul about their ambitions as filmmakers. He asked questions that were both pointed and supportive, and I was impressed by how well, and how realistically, they understood what they faced. The film industry is a tough business. It chews up and spits out legions of talented people every year. But there are always more waiting, hoping to replace their soon-forgotten predecessors.

Taylor and Zach helped us load Solange's things into the car. We said our good-byes before Jean-Paul and I went back into the tent. We stripped the bed, folded the linens, and rolled up the thin Ikea mattress. After a last check under and behind all of the furniture, we went out, locking the door behind us. Before we got into the car, I looked around until I saw Zach and Taylor sitting on the covered veranda, drinking beer and gazing off toward the rapidly approaching tide.

"Do they have good film career prospects?" Jean-Paul asked as we drove out onto the village road.

I held up my palms. "They're serious about their work. Taylor has a natural eye for light and composition, so I can see her making a career in some aspect of filmography. Zach? He's tenacious. I'd say the odds are about equal that one day he'll either run a production company or be a career barista. Or, he'll teach. Time will tell."

"As a warning, do you tell them about your own struggles to get your foot in the door?"

"No," I said. "I didn't put my foot in the door. The door opened and I fell through. The struggles came afterward, trying to stay in the business and trying to make a sufficient living so I could take care of Casey. It has never been easy, and I have been very clear with them about that."

"And now that you're at the end of a contract, you're at a career crossroads," he said. "Which road will you take?"

"Jean-Paul," I said, laughing, though facing the end of my network job wasn't at all funny. In fact, it was damn scary. "I have been at this juncture many times before. Which road? Hell if I know. And it isn't as easy as being at a crossroads. It's more like I'm driving my life into one of your cockamamie traffic roundabouts. Five roads converge at odd angles, a jumble of arrows point who knows where, except some of them surely lead over the edge into the abyss. Which way to go?" I could only shrug.

"How many of those arrows point in my direction?" he asked quietly, taking my hand and resting it on his leg.

"Tonight?" I leaned my head on his shoulder. "All of them do. We'll figure out the rest later, yes?"

He brought my hand to his lips. "Yes."

I heard a car approaching from behind and expected it to pass. When it didn't I turned around at the same moment that Jean-Paul looked into the rearview mirror. There was a little green Toyota hanging too close to our bumper. Jean-Paul tapped the brake pedal. I saw the red brake lights reflect off the Toyotas windshield. For another beat, the Toyota rode our bumper before the driver gave the wheel a sharp turn and sped past us, narrowly missing an oncoming car. Out of habit, because I do what I do, I had my phone in my hand and snapped a shot of the back of the Toyota as it careened into the lane in front of us. The driver tapped his brakes to flash us with his rear lights, and sped on.

I looked at the image I'd captured.

"Get the registration?" Jean-Paul asked.

"Yes," I said, showing him. "German."

—13—

WE PARKED GRAND-MÈRE'S CAR under the carport at the side of the house and headed for my little studio in back where we could safely lock up Solange's things. On the way, we ran into Olivia outside the potting shed where she and her students had been storing their equipment. She was cleaning tools under a garden hose.

"Glad you're here," I said, holding out the bucket of tools we found in Solange's tent. "I believe these belong to your project."

Looking a bit fierce, she turned off the hose, took the bucket from me, and demanded, "Why did you take these?"

"I didn't," I said. "We found them among Solange's things in her tent."

"She knew better than to keep them," she scolded, maybe as a bluff to hide her feelings. Clearly, the death of her student had affected her deeply. Her hands shook as she looked through the bucket as if checking the contents against a list. Tears filled her eyes and her voice quavered when she said, "There is a mattock missing."

"A mattock?" I asked.

"It's a double-headed tool on a wooden handle about so long," she said, holding her hands about three feet apart. "A pick on one side of the head, an adze on the other."

I looked at Jean-Paul. He shook his head. I said, "We saw nothing like that in her tent."

Jean-Paul held out the stack of library books. "Perhaps you know what should be done with these."

Olivia took the books from him, read the spines, saw the bound monograph she had written on the top. Hugging the stack against her chest, tears welling in her eyes, she said, "Thank you. I'll take care of them."

I said, "I am sorry, Olivia. You and Solange seemed to be quite close."

She seemed surprised by that. "Not at all. Before she enrolled in my summer course, I only knew Solange by reputation, as the faculty generally know about all the students doing graduate work in their field. No, we were not close. I was warned that, though she was brilliant, I needed to keep a close eye on her, so maybe I spent more time with her than with the others."

"Why did she need watching?" I asked as a prompt to explain.

"Ah." She raised her palms as she thought for a moment about an answer. "I think that in America you would call her a maverick. Archeology, you know, is a destructive discipline. Many times, in the process of studying a civilization, we dismantle its fragile remains. If we are not exacting in our work, we can obliterate that which we set out to study, not only for ourselves but for those who come after us. Think of the carelessness of the Carter expeditions in Egypt and the destruction of the tombs of the pharaohs. My God, Carter's team used mummies for fire wood."

"Was Solange careless?" I asked, shuddering at the image that flashed behind my eyes.

"She could be rash. You saw, I believe, how quickly she was ready to abandon the study that was the *raison d'être* of the summer course and shift to something altogether uncharted when the German remains were discovered," she said. "I asked the *gendarmes* to take care during the disinterment because the archeology of modern warfare is, indeed, uncharted territory and I did not want the evidence to be destroyed should such a study mature. But our purpose this summer is to try to establish whether the Viducasses, a tribe of the Celts, had established settlements on this coast. If we found Roman or Viking remains, they could be evidence that there were earlier settlements that had been conquered and built over. I was in no way willing to set the prescribed work aside and head off in a new direction just because the appearance of a skull—a modern skull—seemed sexier at the moment."

"But Solange was ready to go in that direction?" I asked.

She raised the bucket of tools. "It would appear that she was, yes?"

Jean-Paul had been listening quietly, as he tended to do. He asked, "By what criteria did you select the students for field work this summer?"

"Applicants submitted an essay, samples of their research papers, and recommendations from the faculty."

"Her work satisfied you?"

"Oh, yes. Her written work was outstanding, as were her recommendations, though I was given several private cautions to keep tight reins on her," Olivia said. "I found her essay to be quite poignant. She wrote that she had great interest in the ancient people and civilizations of this region because she has deep family roots in the area. Though her family has migrated away, she still feels a cultural connection."

"Did she explain what those roots were?" I asked.

Olivia shook her head. "Nothing specific."

Jean-Paul asked, "Have you contacted her family?"

"Yes, through our consulate in Ecuador. The family sent instructions for the disposition of the remains, as I know you heard, but apparently they are unable, or unwilling, to travel here."

"Very sad," I said. "Very sad, indeed."

"I am desolated," she said.

We again offered our condolences, and turned to leave.

"Maggie," she said. When I turned back she gestured toward the house. "How old is your grandmother's house?

"You would have to ask her," I said. "I know that the original structure has been remodeled and rehabilitated and added on to several times. If you walk through you can see where changes have been made, random odd steps up or down and places where the ceiling isn't always the same height. Why? Are you interested in old houses?"

She smiled. "I'm an archeologist. Everything old interests me."

"Grand-mère can tell you more."

"Of course." She nodded and went back to her tool washing.

When we were out of earshot, I turned to Jean-Paul. "You didn't give her Solange's notebook."

"Nor did you," he said. "I'm sure you want a moment to look it over first."

I asked him, "Do you know what a mattock looks like?"

He lifted a shoulder. "Yes."

With my thumbs and index fingers I made a triangle roughly

the size and shape of the hole I had seen in Solange's head. "Could a mattock make a wound shaped like this?"

"It could. You have an idea I think."

"I hate to say this, but we need to talk to Pierre Dauvin."

"Now?"

"Later. Tomorrow, maybe," I said. "We'll see him at church, at the baptism of his nephew."

I unlocked the studio and showed Jean-Paul inside. Against the back wall were metal lockers with sturdy locks where we secured equipment when it wasn't in use. By shuffling things around a bit we made space for Solange's duffel and suitcase and locked them in, keeping the notebook to take inside to look through later. After I gave Jean-Paul the nickel tour, though the space was so small a nickel would be over-payment, I booted one of the computers on the counter along the side and opened the raw footage from the interview with my grandmother about the night the women slit the Germans' throats.

Jean-Paul watched the interview without speaking, concentrating, as he does, on every word and gesture. After Grand-mère waved for the cameras to cut and the screen went black, Jean-Paul said, "Remind me never to turn my back on your grandmother."

"Just don't cross her," I said. "Or her friends."

"They were lucky there were no Nazi reprisals."

"I think the women timed the attack well." I closed the program and reached for the power button, but he touched my hand to stop me.

"These computers are connected to the Internet?" he asked.

"Isabelle turned the entire estate into a Wi-Fi hotspot," I said, jotting down the access code for him. "Wherever we go within the property, we can connect to the Internet."

"So, while we're here with these computers," he said, "we might have a look at the tapes from the security cameras, yes?"

I went to the Cloud site Zach had given us, downloaded the footage onto an external memory drive plugged into the computer, and then when it was finished, exited the site.

Zach was correct about the quality. The cameras only captured images at four-second intervals, so everything had a jerky, stop-action look. Because the cameras were shooting down from atop poles, everyone was foreshortened. During daylight, we could see the faces of people who approached the camera position until they were a few yards from the light poles. But once they were near the poles, because of the camera angle, all we could see was the tops of their heads. If you knew the people well enough, you would be able to figure out from the clothing, relative size, coloring, posture, or gender who you might be seeing. Otherwise, not. And after dark, images tended to be white blobs unless they were hit with a light source, from an open window, maybe. If we needed to know who came and who went after dark, we would need help from the denizens of the camp.

On Thursday afternoon when the security system was first installed, everyone, it seemed, walked up to the cameras and mugged for them, self-conscious maybe about their comings and goings being recorded. It didn't take long, however, before they went about their business without thinking about the watchful eyes atop the light posts.

Late in the afternoon, the students began filtering in from their assigned work, looking as if they'd had long days. Most of them went first to their tents, gathered clean clothes and toiletries, and headed toward the locker rooms for showers. Later they reappeared, freshly washed and combed. Things were dropped off again at tents, and then, alone or in little groups, they wandered off toward the community center where they would prepare dinner and perhaps relax for the evening. There was a constant coming and going until about eleven o'clock, when most seemed to settle in for the night. I made a mental note to forget that Taylor and Zach went into the same tent, and stayed there.

At about half-past midnight, a small blond woman wearing shorts entered the frame at the community center end of Rue de Carotte, and entered Solange's tent with a key. Shortly afterward, a figure, just a bright splotch on the monitor, walked into the far end of the same alley, stopped, seemed to listen or watch for a moment, and then walked back out of camera range. There weren't enough visual clues for us to learn anything about who that second person was, except that he or she had been there.

At one A.M., Taylor came out of Zach's tent and walked toward the locker rooms. She returned about five minutes later, apparently having made a last bathroom visit of the night. We scrolled ahead, watching for images of people. At two A.M., the door to Solange's tent opened again. The small blond woman, now wearing jeans, came out and looked around. At one point, she lifted her face, confirming to us that she was Solange. She walked toward the community center, and out of frame.

I froze her image just when she looked up. "Meet Solange, the young woman who died."

"She's carrying something," he said. "Could it be a mattock?"

I leaned in for a closer look, then enlarged the image. Whatever she was carrying was about three feet long. A digging tool? A murder weapon?

Jean-Paul sat back and touched my arm. "What time on Friday morning did you find her?"

I pointed to the time stamp in the bottom corner. "About eight hours after this shot. When I found her, she had already been dead for a while."

He asked me to scroll back to the blur that had appeared at the far end of the alley shortly after midnight. "Can you enhance this?"

I pulled the image up as far as I could, but it quickly dissolved into a disorganized mess of pixels. I told him, "We don't have enhancement software here."

"May I send this to a friend?" he asked.

"Of course you may." He already had his mobile phone out. I watched him type in the Cloud account access code and a request to enhance the blur that showed up at hour 00:38. And a note to say hello to Lise and the boys.

There was a knock at the studio door. I opened it and found Freddy standing there.

"Grand-mère has announced dinner," he said with a little bow. "Your presence is requested."

"We're coming." I shut down the program and removed the flash drive, which I locked up in a cupboard. Freddy waited for us, making small talk.

"That couple that Antoine was talking to," he said. "Paulette and Henry Matson. He introduced them to me. They're really very interesting."

"Did they tell you about the count and countess of Rutland?" I asked.

He shook his head. "Henry is a developer. He's worked on some very large projects. Very knowledgeable. Paulette was quite engaged in the idea that we're building around the agricultural functions of the estate as a way to maintain them."

"She wants to make cheese," I said.

"Let's be careful that she doesn't steal our Jacques away from us. A good *fromager* is difficult to find."

Jean-Paul asked, "Does Jacques have a vested interest in your *fromagerie?*"

"In a way," Freddy said. "But it's a very complicated relationship."

I did my best to explain. For several centuries, the Martin estate supported a cluster of tenant families, including the Bretons, the forebears of Jacques the current cheesemaker, as his father and grandfather had been. During World War I, faced with a labor shortage, my great-grandfather, Giles Martin, brought in the first tractors and other motorized farm equipment. One by one, the tenant families moved away, replaced by more efficient machinery. By the end of the Second World War, only one tenant family remained, the Bretons. Because they were cheesemakers and not farmers, they could not be replaced by machinery.

The Bretons still lived in a pretty cottage that belonged to the estate, over on the far side of the carrot field. But the Bretons could no longer be called tenants. In acknowledgment of Jacques's innovations in cheese making and his work modernizing the *fromagerie* as well as developing the dairy herd, Antoine had set up a profit-sharing plan with him for as long as he remained *chez* Martin.

Complicating the relationship, Jacques married the girl next door, Julie Foullard. When he did, she also became family. The Foullard estate, currently under the guardianship of Julie's grandmother, Grand-mère Marie Foullard, was a substantial land-holding that wrapped around one end of the Martin estate. Marie's daughter, Louise Foullard, married my uncle, Gérard Martin, making my cousin Antoine a first cousin of Julie, and Jacques a cousin by marriage, a distinction no one paid much mind to.

After the deaths of her husband and both of her adult children, Marie had handed over management of the Foullard property to Antoine and Jacques, jointly. They grew alfalfa and pastured cows on the land, and sold the milk they produced to the Martin *fromagerie*.

"Should I draw a chart?" I asked Jean-Paul.

He laughed. "Sounds to me like a perfectly straightforward arrangement, very typical for the French. Later, when we have time, I'll try to chart my own family for you. Trust me, it will be as complex as yours."

"All I want to know is, who gets the beach house at Villerville?"

"Altogether, six cousins in my mother's line," he said. "*Merde*, won't that be fun to straighten out?"

The dinner crowd on Saturday night was the usual group: Antoine, Freddy, his summer houseguest Olivia, the two grandmothers, Casey, me, and now Jean-Paul. Because it was Saturday, the village ladies did not come in to prepare the evening meal, as they did on weekdays, and so the grandmothers put together their version of a simple supper. For the first course, Grand-mère Marie made a delicious cold cucumber soup from vegetables picked that morning in the kitchen garden. The second course was my grandmother's adaption of Venetian spaghetti *alle vongole*: linguine pasta tossed with olive oil and garlic, fresh garden peas and little carpetshell clams gathered from the tidal basin beyond Anneville-sur-Mer less than two hours earlier. Instead of shaved parmesan, the dish was garnished with a pungent, aged local cheese that was a perfect foil for the garlic. Both courses, naturally, were accompanied by fresh bread and homemade sweet butter, a red *vin ordinaire* and Antoine's cider. After the cheese and port were finished, a plate of Marie's shortbreads topped with dollops of Grand-mère's raspberry preserves was passed with the coffee.

"Jean-Paul," Grand-mère said, taking his arm after the meal, "your mother will think we aren't feeding you well."

"My mother would only be sorry that she wasn't here to dine with us," he said, walking Grand-mère toward the arrangement of easy chairs grouped in front of the fireplace at the far end of the salon. I waited for her to settle into a chair before I brought her footstool over to her. I knew her knees were bothering her.

Antoine had taken his grandmother, Marie, back to his house, where she now lived. After a little television, he would help her settle in for the night, and then probably go to bed himself. Because this was Jean-Paul's first evening with us, not counting the short night before, he could relax as a guest, with me and Grand-mère. That left Casey, Freddy, and Olivia to clean up after the meal. The three of them kept up a lively conversation about the relative virtues of French and American universities as they cleared the table and then moved the discussion into the kitchen.

When Jean-Paul and I were alone with Grand-mère, and after I was confident that she wasn't overly tired, I pulled my chair closer to hers and leaned forward. She put a hand on my knee and said, "Is there something?"

"I want to ask you about Thursday night," I said, easing into the subject that lay heavily on my mind. "If you don't mind."

"Yes, dear?"

"After dinner at Gaston's, when you and I went out and dug up those remains, I thought you found something in the earth." I took Giles Martin's beautiful watch from my pocket and held it out to her. "But now I think you put something in."

She took the watch, turned it over in her hands, popped the lid, and winced at the crude signature scratched inside. "You are so like your mother; nothing gets past you."

"This looks like an important family piece to me," I said, touching the shiny gold surface. "Why did you bury it?"

She shrugged. "I knew it would be found and returned to me. And I knew that it would show that *cochon* von Streicher for what he was, a thief and a rapist. Like the Hun who spawned him, he went into every home in the five villages he had command over and looted them of anything precious, including peace of mind. He said he was appropriating property for the Reich, for the war effort. But like so many of the Nazis who stole great treasures, he kept what he took for his own pleasure. This watch had made Giles Martin so proud. When that Nazi hung it on his tunic and swaggered around wearing it where everyone who knew Giles could see it, he might as well have cut off that wonderful man's balls and hung them from his brass buttons as a symbol of the emasculation of our people."

Jean-Paul sat on the arm of her chair and put a tender hand on her shoulder. She reached up and covered it with her own. Looking up into his brown eyes, she said, "Did Maggie tell you what we did to the Germans?"

"She did."

"I will tell you this: I slit von Streicher's throat before I shot him through the heart with his own gun. And then I ripped Giles's watch from his chest and left him to die."

"My dear lady." Jean-Paul kissed the top of her head.

"Did you give the watch back to Giles?" I asked.

"Oh, yes," she said, nodding. "After D-Day, when he was able to come home, more dead than alive, I gave him his watch and the keys to his house. When he saw how von Streicher had defaced the watch, he put it in a drawer, and that's where it stayed."

"Until Thursday," I said.

"Was I wrong to do that, Maggie?"

"That isn't for me to say, Grand-mère. But I think you may have helped to find a killer."

"The killer of that child?" she asked, brow furrowed.

"We found the watch in Solange's tent. I suspect she saw us digging around that night, went in after us, and found the watch. It's possible that someone else was out there, also."

"You were worried that we weren't alone."

"I didn't see anything, really," I said. "I was just spooked."

Jean-Paul cleared his throat. "Madame Martin, you returned the watch to Giles, but what happened to everything else that von Streicher stole?"

"Ah, yes." She sighed deeply and gazed off across the room. "There was so much brought into this house for his pleasure. Furniture and jewelry, old clocks—von Streicher seemed to like clocks especially—a few paintings, treasures even from the church reliquary. We had no great châteaux around here, and no fine museums for him to loot. There was nothing of great value to be found, except to the people from whom possessions were taken. After we dispatched the Germans, Henri and I hid von Streicher's hoard in the basement, walled it in to keep it safe for the rightful owners. The intention was to return what we could when our people came back after the war. And we did. Or we tried."

"Tried?" I said.

"People came back very changed, if they came back at all," she said. "Thousands did not return. If I remember, something like four hundred towns and villages were destroyed by the Allied bombings over Normandy during the *Libération*. Whole families were wiped out. It was a horror."

I went over to the sideboard and poured each of us a small glass of claret. Grand-mère smiled gamely, let her hand linger on mine when I reached a glass toward her. After a sip, she continued.

"We had suffered tremendously under the Germans," she said. "But at the end of the war, when we learned about the death camps in the east, when we saw what the Germans had done to so many millions of people, our deprivations, even the people we lost, were diminished in comparison. What the Nazis stole from the Jews was life itself. And from us?" She stroked the watch glimmering on the arm of her chair. "Things that had seemed important to us, after we saw—" She held out the watch. "Many of us felt shame for having cared so much for such as this. We survived. So many hadn't."

"Are you saying that people didn't want their things returned?" I asked.

"Of course they did."

"How did you find the owners?" I asked.

"Through the church, because the priest knew everyone, and their circumstances. Sometimes he brought people here for furnishings when they had nothing. Did it matter that they were not the original owners? We thought not."

"Everything was claimed, then?" I asked.

"There are still a few things." Grand-mère pointed down, toward the floor under her big chair. "Most of what is left is old pieces that are too large for modern homes."

"Who knows it's there?" I asked.

"At one time, everyone in the region. After the Nazis were gone, what was here was not a secret. People came and looked to claim what was theirs or to help identify the owners. But, after a while, they stopped coming, so Henri locked the door to the basement, and what was left is still there."

Casey came through from the kitchen, rolling down her sleeves. "What are you three whispering about?"

"Probably you," Grand-mère said with an impish grin. "How is your love life, dear?"

"Hah!" Casey said with a wide smile. "I just finished washing dishes and you guys are out here dirtying more glasses. Unfair. Mom, Jean-Paul, it's your turn tomorrow. You just wait."

"I thought we'd go out for dinner tomorrow," Jean-Paul said.

"We'll be eating party leftovers." Grand-mère set her empty glass aside and rose from her chair. "If you children will excuse me, I believe it's time for bed."

I took her arm and walked with her upstairs.

"Do you know what you need to know now, Maggie?" she asked as she opened her bedroom door.

"Parts," I said. "There are still some missing bits. I should talk to Pierre. I thought I would corner him tomorrow."

"No, dear. Tomorrow should be such a happy day. Pierre will be busy with family." She pulled out her mobile and looked at the time. "He has evening duty on Saturdays. He will be at the *gendarmerie* until midnight, unless he's out arresting drunken tourists. Now would be a better time."

I helped her turn down her bed and kissed her good night. When I went back downstairs Freddy was just closing the door after Olivia. He poured himself a glass of claret and took a seat next to Jean-Paul and Casey.

"How is Olivia?" I asked, joining them. "She seemed subdued at dinner."

"The Solange tragedy has been a shock, of course," Freddy said.

"But Olivia's okay, I think. She doesn't talk about it. But then, I doubt I'm the one she'd confide in."

"Is all well *chez* Freddy?" I asked.

"Sure," he said with a shrug. "Olivia does what she does, and I have my stuff, and sometimes we pass in the hallway. That's about it."

"Roommates," Casey said.

"Housemates," he corrected. "Anyway, as soon as I finish this drink, I'm going home to bed. Quite a day, huh?"

I caught Jean-Paul's eye. "If Freddy will lend us his car, would you like to take a little drive?"

He hesitated, obviously keeping questions to himself for the moment, but said, "If you wish."

Freddy reached into his pocket for his keys, which he handed to Jean-Paul.

"Another favor, Freddy?" I said. When he turned to me, I asked if he wasn't too tired, would he please keep Casey company until we got back? I thought we wouldn't be gone for more than an hour.

"I need a baby-sitter?" she said with a puzzled half smile.

"No. I just don't want to leave you and Grand-mère alone tonight."

Freddy turned to her. "Feel like watching a movie?"

She said, "Sure." And headed off with her uncle toward the small salon where the television was.

"Where are we going?" Jean-Paul asked as I locked the front door behind us.

"To talk to Pierre Dauvin at the *gendarmerie*."

I was edgy during the short drive, watching the cars on the road around us. When nothing unusual happened, I was a little bit surprised.

Pierre took us into his office, a utilitarian space just big enough for his desk, a row of filing cabinets, and two guest chairs.

"You're worried about your friend Guido?" he asked as he showed us to seats.

"Yes," I said. "But that isn't why we're here. This time, anyway."

I gave him the access code for the security cameras at the student camp, explained what it was, and asked him to go to the Cloud site and scroll from just after midnight Friday morning, focusing on 00:38 and 02:04 hours. He pulled up the site and frowned as he watched Solange go into her tent, noticed the amorphous figure at the end of the alley not long after. And then saw Solange, changed into jeans, emerge again less than two hours later.

Jean-Paul had gone around behind the desk to watch the images on the computer monitor over Pierre's shoulder. The second time Solange appeared, Jean-Paul asked him to freeze the image. He pointed out that she was carrying something long and slender.

Pierre looked from Jean-Paul to me. "You know what she's carrying?"

Jean-Paul nodded to me, my question to answer. I said, "We don't know anything. Except, we found a bucket of tools in her tent that belong to the university, the sort of tools archeologists use. Did you see them when you searched the tent?"

He nodded. "We examined them."

"We returned the tools to Solange's professor, Olivia Boulez," I said. "She said that a tool called a mattock is missing."

With a swipe of his finger, Pierre moved the active screen on his monitor off to one side, went to Google and brought up images of various versions of mattocks. While scrolling through the images, he asked me, "Did you see such a tool when you discovered her body?"

"No, I didn't. If the tool was there, it was under her. I certainly did not move her."

He took a pad of paper from his top desk drawer and jotted a note. "Anything else?"

"Yes. We also found my great-grandfather's pocket watch in the tent."

"Where?" There was a challenge in his voice. Obviously, he'd missed it.

"In the girl's laundry bag, along with some dirty shorts very similar to the ones she was wearing when she went into her tent around midnight."

"And how do you suppose your great-grandfather's watch came to be in her laundry bag?"

"You know that my grandmother and I dug up some of the remains Thursday night," I said. When he nodded, I said, "Grand-mère put the watch into the ground among the bones. I wonder if Solange saw us, waited until we left, dug where we had, and found the watch. Remember, I told you someone had been digging at that place before us."

"I'm afraid to ask why Madame Martin did what you say she did, so I will leave that for later," he said. "Now, Sherlock Holmes, why don't you tell me what you think happened that night?"

I shrugged, got another nod from Jean-Paul, and told Pierre what I thought. "I wonder if Grand-mère and I interrupted Solange's first attempt to dig in the area where the skull was found. Then she lay in wait in the carrot field, watching us. When we were gone, she dug where we had, found the watch, a lot of brass buttons probably, and bones. She went back to her tent, hid the watch, changed into fresh, perhaps warmer, clothes, picked up a better digging tool than she'd had with her originally, and went back out to dig again. Did that figure captured by the security camera watch her? Follow her? Have nothing at all to do with Solange? I leave that to you. But sometime later, and I think not very much later, someone bashed in her head with a tool shaped like this." Again, with thumbs and index fingers I made a triangle about the size of the hole I had seen in Solange's head. "And it killed her."

"Do you enjoy playing at detective?" Pierre asked, flipping his pen onto the note pad, clearly miffed.

"You know what I do for a living, Pierre," I said. "I'm not always playing."

"We aren't in Hollywood, madame. I would appreciate if you left the investigation to the *police nationale*."

"Bon, d'accord," I said, doing my best imitation of a French dis-missive shrug. I rose from my chair. "If you have any interest at all in the young woman's dirty clothes, do have your people come and collect them before the ladies do the Monday laundry."

Pierre dropped his face into his hands and shook his head as if exasperated. He took a hand away to glance at Jean-Paul. "My sym-pathy, monsieur."

Jean-Paul's mobile chirped. He pulled it out, looked at the screen, opened the text, glanced at it, and then handed the mobile to Pierre.

"What is this?"

"I sent the image captured at 00:38 to a friend at D.G.S.E. to see if it could be enhanced."

"You think this was a terrorist attack?" Pierre huffed with some heat.

"Of course not. But I have a friend who is assigned there and I knew he had the technical capability to enhance the image. Anyway, here is his report."

Pierre read aloud: "Person of unknown gender or coloring, stands between five-and-a-half and six feet tall, average build. Posture indicates European origin."

"Sorry," Jean-Paul said. "That's all he could determine. But it does eliminate some, yes?"

Pierre gave the mobile back. He nailed first me, then Jean-Paul with a narrow-eyed glare. "Anything else?"

"Not at the moment," I said.

"*Bon. Merci bien, madame et monsieur.*" He rose from his chair, opened his office door and gestured for us to pass through it. "*Et passez une bonne nuit.*"

"*À demain,*" I said, until tomorrow. He did not seem very thrilled at the prospect.

As we walked back to Freddy's car, I said, "You didn't say anything about the car that nearly ran us off the road this afternoon."

"No," Jean-Paul said, taking my hand. "I also didn't mention that when we drove out of the compound gate this evening, the same car was parked across the road, no more than ten meters away."

━14━

NEITHER OF US could settle down enough to sleep. Part of the frisson in the room came from the physical pleasure of being in the same bed again, spent and naked, after nearly a month apart, and at the same time feeling sad that tomorrow he would have to leave again. For how long this time? There was no answer.

"You aren't sleeping," he said, stroking my back. "Want to go down and check all the water taps again?"

"No. I'd rather go for a run."

He glanced over my shoulder at the bedside clock. "How about I read you a story?"

"Not a scary one," I said. "No ogres under the bridge, all right? I hate monsters hiding under things, especially when I can't sleep."

"No promises," he said, disentangling himself from the sheets as he got up from the bed. "I haven't read this book yet."

He opened the armoire and pulled out Solange's notebook. "I would like to take a look at this, and there might not be another chance before I have to leave."

"All right." I got up and pulled on the first pajama bottoms and T-shirt I found, both parts his. "But downstairs, okay? There's a bottle of Antoine's oldest brandy in the sideboard. I think it's time we opened it."

Jean-Paul pulled out two chairs at the end of the big dining table while I poured two short brandies into wide-bottomed snifters and carried them over. I asked, "What do you know about archeology?"

"Nothing," he said. He swirled the brandy to warm it in his hand before he took his first sip. "But I know what I like, and I think this brandy is exceptional."

"It's Antoine's, the first distillation he made after he came back to the estate from California," I said. "*Hors d'age*, old stuff."

"Speaking of *hors d'age*," he said, opening Solange's notebook on the table between us. "Let's see what the young archeologist has to tell us."

Solange kept meticulous notes illustrated with very detailed pencil drawings. While most of her sketches illustrated the process of setting up a dig site and recording what was found, Solange had also illustrated the ordinary, daily life of the estate. The first series showed the potting shed that Olivia was using to store the tools of her trade. Besides the shed itself, an old stone building with a climbing rose covering one end, there were studies drawn of the tools arranged along the walls and on the scarred wooden potting bench, from big shovels and hoes to the finest dental picks and paintbrushes.

There were several pages of what appeared to be lecture notes about setting up an archeological dig site, and then sketches of the process as it was undertaken. Before the excavation began, the area was mapped, grids were set according to map coordinates, core samples were taken of the earth, and so on. In the margins there were a few random drawings of little objects, fragments of some sort; they weren't labeled.

On another page, there was a series of little thumbnail sketches, each of them numbered. She had drawn the student camp, Grand-mère's stone pile of a house, a detail of the compound's stone wall, Antoine's students among the trees in the apple orchard, the *fromagerie*, the kitchen garden and the garden gate, the old wall out in the pasture where Grand-mère had sent Olivia and her students when the *gendarmes* shooed them away from the skull discovery site. On the facing page, she had made a map of the estate with a key that located where each of those sketches belonged. The only random drawing was something that looked like a broken obelisk in the margin near the old wall. At the base of this very small sketch were the letters *FeR*, but it wasn't given a location on the map.

"She was a good draftsman," Jean-Paul said.

"Some of these are frameable." I turned the page and found a sketch of the Volvo excavator next to Freddy's sewer trench, with a recognizable Freddy at the controls. "Can you decipher what she wrote here?"

Jean-Paul leaned closer, read, shrugged. "There are some academic references to published articles about the Viducasses, and some notes about Viducasse relics found in the area of Vieux-la-Romaine." He looked up at me. "Do you know where Vieux is?"

"South and east of here, I think. Near Caen? We saw the road signs on our drive in from Paris."

He nodded. "Apparently that was the chief settlement of these people your archeology professor is interested in. Rome conquered the Viducasses, in fact all of Normandy, in the first century. Solange believed that if either the Romans or the Viducasses were in this area as well, they would not have left anything that is recoverable in the vicinity of the sewer trench where Olivia had her students set up their study site. The soil there looked to Solange like accretion, land built up by the sea. She refers to the GPS coordinates of the castle at Pirou just down the road from here as a benchmark that defines where the coastline of your family estate was during the Viking invasions. According to her measurements, where the *fromagerie* sits now would have been on the ocean front, and the carrot field and orchard would be under water. Therefore, during the Viducasse period…" He shrugged, no need to finish the sentence.

"I wonder what Olivia had to say about that." I turned the page and found the first sketches of the skull. "I believe this is where Solange changed her mind about the value of the trench."

"At least they found something interesting." Jean-Paul picked up our snifters and took them over to the sideboard for second shots. "I suppose Olivia was content to create a demonstration dig for her students."

"Two digs," I said. The next few pages illustrated setting up a new dig near the old wall in the pasture. These sketches weren't as polished as the earlier ones, as if Solange were distracted, or maybe just bored by what she seemed to think was futile exercise. In the margins there were random shapes that looked like angular doodles. One of them seemed to be a repeat of something I'd seen earlier, so I flipped back through the pages until I found it again, in the margin of the map sketches.

"Look at this, Jean-Paul."

He set my snifter beside me and peered over my shoulder.

"The archeology students arrived two or three weeks ago," I said. "Early August. Look at the sketches of the climbing rose on the potting shed and at the plants in the garden."

"So?"

"Solange was very meticulous. She made the little thumbnail sketches of various places on the estate in the same orientation you find them on the map. There are no holes or erasures, or drawings crammed in as an afterthought. It looks to me as if she had made a very careful survey of the estate right when she got here. She was looking at that old stone wall in the pasture before they began working along Freddy's trench."

"Is it possible that she made the map first and then drew the sketches later?"

I shook my head. "Look at the climbing rose on the potting shed, and at the asparagus in the garden."

He pointed to the feathery leaves of the asparagus. "Yes?"

"It's finished. Grand-mère pulled it out ten days ago and planted winter leeks. The roses on the potting shed have grown very leggy since this drawing was made."

He thought for a moment. "When did Olivia move her dig to the wall in the pasture?"

"Day before yesterday," I said. "The day before Solange died."

"Hmm." He sipped his brandy as he studied the sketches and the map opposite them. "The wall in the pasture is, I assume, all that's left of an earlier structure, yes?"

"Probably." I looked where he pointed.

"See the way it was constructed? Look at the shape of the stone blocks and then at the pattern the stonemason used when he set them in courses. Now, compare that wall to the compound wall."

"It's different," I said. "The stone blocks in the old wall are uniformly square, and offset in the same way in every row. But the stones in the compound wall are of various sizes, some square, some rectangular."

"Describe for me the pattern you see."

"It looks like the rectangles are twice as long as the squares, but the same height. The pattern is square, rectangle, square, and then it repeats, square, rectangle, square." I studied the sketch of the compound's wall again. "The square stones are darker than the rectangles, so at a distance the wall looks like a bit like a checkerboard."

"That's what I saw," he said. "If I remember my school history, the sequence of known inhabitants of Normandy, after the Cro-Magnon, was first the Celts—the Viducasses and their cousins, or Gauls as the Romans called them. Then came the Romans, followed by the Franks, and after them the Vikings. The Vikings settled here and became the Normans, the north men. Every newcomer brought something to the region, destroyed something of the predecessor, and yet adopted something that was already here."

He leaned over and kissed me. "Have I bored you yet to sleepiness?"

"Not at all." I rested my head on his shoulder. "Tell me more."

"Stones darken with age."

"That's profound," I said, chuckling. "The conqueror destroys, and rebuilds."

"If he stays long enough, yes."

"Which conqueror took down the old structure in the pasture built from square stones," I asked, "then combined them with newer rectangular stones and built the wall around this family's compound?"

He raised his palms and shrugged.

"This is what I know," I said. "It has started to rain and I am very sleepy."

"At last." He took my hand and led me upstairs. To sleep.

—15—

THE AIR ON SUNDAY MORNING after a light overnight rain smelled so sweet, so fresh, that if I could have I would have bottled it to take home to Los Angeles. I was told that until I was two years old and was spirited away to America by my father, I had spent more time living on the estate in the care of my grandmother and my Uncle Gérard and Aunt Louise than I had with Isabelle and her husband in Paris. I do not remember more about the place than the cookies Grand-mère Marie hid in a special place for me to find, and the perfume in the air after a summer shower: ripening apples in the orchard, *eau de* cow grazing in pastures of sweet alfalfa, fresh-turned earth, herbs and flowers in the garden, a stock pot simmering at the back of a stove. Whenever I found that scent on the breeze, I knew that in this place I had once felt safe and happy.

I was still standing in the middle of the compound, still woolgathering, when the family began to assemble for the drive into the village for church. Before mass, the priest would baptize Pierre Dauvin's nephew. I had never met Pierre's sister, the baby's mother, or any of the rest of his family other than his teenage son Gus, but that apparently did not matter to my grandmother. Grand-mère was adamant that all of her family would attend not only the baptism, but mass afterward. Also, because Solange Betz had died while she was a guest of sorts on our family estate we were obligated to stay after mass for recitation of a rosary for her immortal soul. It would be a long morning.

Transportation was an issue. Besides family, several of the students wanted to attend mass, and some of them wanted to participate in the rosary after. The sorting of people into cars became intricate. Antoine would drive the two grandmothers, along with Jacques and Julie Breton, in the Range Rover. Freddy was taking me, Jean-Paul, Olivia, and her student Raffi in the Jag. David was trying to figure out how to fit Casey, Zach, Taylor, and the other three archeology students into Antoine's Mini when a large truck pulled in through the compound gate.

The driver parked in the middle of the space, opened the back of the truck's trailer, pulled down a ramp and backed a shiny silver BMW sedan into the compound. Jean-Paul walked across the gravel, signed some papers on a clipboard, and was given the keys to the car. After a handshake, the ramp went up and the truck drove out. The entire transaction took less than five minutes.

Jean-Paul walked back to the clutch of curious onlookers. He said, "The driver got lost, or maybe he got drunk. He should have delivered the car yesterday."

Passengers were reshuffled. Jean-Paul and I claimed Casey, David, and Olivia in the BMW, leaving Zach and Freddy to distribute the rest of the students between the Jag and the Mini. With Grand-mère's Range Rover in the lead, we were quite a caravan when we pulled out onto the village road. I looked around as we made the turn and saw no sign of the green Toyota, though not seeing it gave me little comfort.

"Should have been delivered yesterday?" I said to Jean-Paul, running a hand over the BMW's leather upholstery.

He nodded. "I ordered the car before I left Los Angeles. I knew I'd need wheels when I came back to France. What do you think?"

I said, "New and shiny."

David, from the back seat, opined, "Monster cool."

The village church was an ancient, dark, and narrow Roman-esque structure. We all converged around the baptistery, a pretty side chapel with tall, Gothic stained glass windows that was obviously a later addition. The baptistery was small, and typically, had no seat-ing, though chairs had been placed on one side of the font for Mme Dauvin, the baby's great-grandmother, as well as my grandmother, Marie, and Ma Mère. As they were escorted to their seats, these four looked to me like the fairy godmothers, sent to watch over the new baby, and all the babies of the women who had survived a particular night more than seventy years ago. There was an interesting dynamic among that quartet, a closeness that went beyond long friendship. They seemed to communicate in a sort of private language that only they understood. And absolutely nothing that happened in that church that morning escaped their notice.

The elderly priest came in from the sacristy, bringing the baby's parents and toddler sister with him. They took their positions at the font. The rest of us clustered around wherever we found space to stand.

A little flurry of activity and a baby's whimper drew all eyes to-ward the back of the church. Grinning broadly, Pierre's father, a tall, handsome, fair-haired man, had the honor of carrying his youngest grandchild to the priest, with the godparents following behind.

I couldn't take my eyes off M. Dauvin. Grand-mère had told me that he had been the first baby to wear the elaborate white silk bap-tismal dress his grandchild now wore. The garment had been sewn by the women of the village using silk from an American parachute recovered at the time of the D-Day invasion. This man, now a grand-father several times over, had apparently been a special baby, born in a difficult time. The four old women held hands as they watched him approach, with tears running down their smiling faces. There was something about M. Dauvin's carriage, his height, and his coloring that made him stand out among the other men in the area. But that wasn't all that set him apart. I just didn't know what that other thing was, yet.

The ritual of baptism was handled with much humor and affection. As if on cue, the baby cried when he was anointed by the priest, and cooed in the arms of the godmother during the blessing. The old priest was only at the beginning of his long morning, so he kept the service blessedly brief and to the point. He did the same during the mass that followed. In his homily, he spoke poignantly about the cycle of life, from the baptism of a tiny baby that preceded mass to the rosary for the dead that would follow, the full cycle of life. The priest looked up sharply when Gaston coughed. As if reminded of something, before the Our Father, the priest asked the congregation to take special heed of the passage that asked us to forgive those who trespassed against us, and to say a special prayer that morning for strangers who died among us. At the end of the request he checked with Gaston, who nodded. Apparently, this was the fulfillment of the request that Jean-Paul had conveyed, a quiet reference in honor of the war dead found in the carrot field. Before the benediction, he announced that all were invited to celebrate the baby's baptism at the Martin family's beach pavilion for lunch that afternoon, as if anyone needed reminding.

When we were finally released out into the sunshine, I spotted Pierre talking with his father under the big oak tree in the church forecourt. I took Jean-Paul by the hand and told him we needed to be introduced to the grandfather. He seemed dubious, but came along. M. Dauvin, Anthony, was very gracious. He had retired some years earlier as the principal of the village *collège*, or middle school. Retirement was wonderful, he told us, but how he wished his dear wife had lived to share it.

There was a line of people waiting to speak with him. We told him we would see him at the party that afternoon, and went to find our passengers. Pierre followed us.

"Don't worry about your friend, Guido," Pierre said when he caught up to us. "There will be a hearing in the morning, a formality, and then I'm sure he will be released. There is no evidence to hold him further."

"Good news," I said, resisting the urge to hug him. "Will he be free to return to the States?"

"The hearing will settle that," he said.

Pierre went off to talk to others, and I looked around for my grandmother. I spotted her across the road in front of the *mairie*, deep in conversation with Ma Mère and Gaston. She looked up, saw me, and gestured for us to join them. Jean-Paul and I were halfway across the road when the old woman from the bakery who had torn up and spat upon the photographs that Erika von Streicher was showing around on market day, pushed past us and made straight for my grandmother and Ma Mère, moving with a purpose as she waved the morning church bulletin over her head.

"Élodie, Anne, look at this," she said, thrusting the bulletin into Grand-mère's hands. She pointed at something printed there and then, in a rapid stream of Norman-accented French that I could barely understand, let it be known that she was beyond outrage. She was so upset that I half expected her to rip up the bulletin and spit on it, too. Instead, still gesticulating and expounding, she turned and walked away toward the bakery.

"What was that about?" I asked Grand-mère, looking over her shoulder at the bulletin. All I saw was the order of worship for the three rites of the morning.

Ma Mère, the abbess, turned to me. "Her name was Betz?"

"Solange?" I said. "Yes, it was."

Grand-mère said, "I thought there was something familiar about the child, but I did not remember the name," she said. "It was so long ago, and they were in another village."

"Solange told me that her family had once lived near here," I said. "Did you know the family?"

The two women exchanged a look that told me they knew something they weren't eager to talk about.

Freddy walked up with a glum-looking Olivia during that very uncomfortable moment. He slipped his hand around Grand-mère's elbow. "Olivia has a headache and would like to go home. I thought you might want a rest before lunch, as well."

"I would, yes." She patted Freddy's cheek. "Thank you, dear."

We exchanged *les bises* and the three of them headed toward the car park, leaving us standing with Ma Mère to wave them on their way. When they were gone, the abbess took my arm and said that she had a few things to take care of before the party: would we walk her home? Jean-Paul took her other arm and we started off toward the convent. We went the long way around, avoiding the crowd still milling about in front of the church.

Glancing back toward the church courtyard, Jean-Paul said, "The name Betz caused quite a stir this morning, Ma Mère."

She leaned into his shoulder. With a sigh, she said, "Will we ever get past that terrible time?"

"The war?" I asked.

She nodded, and changed the subject. "So, have you made a film star of your grandmother? She told me you powdered her nose and lit her up like an angel for the cameras."

I chuckled. "I would never call her an angel, but Grand-mère certainly has star quality. I'm sure viewers will sit up and take notice."

"Be careful, *chérie*, or she'll get a swelled head."

"Are you ready to get your nose powdered and sit down in front of my cameras for a little chat?"

"The bishop gave permission," she said. "But I'm sure I have nothing to add to what Élodie has already told you."

"I think you do." When she held up her palms as a gesture of doubt, I asked, "Who was Betz?"

"Ah, yes, Betz." Her smile was gone. "The child who was killed shared that name, yes?"

"Solange, yes."

She canted her head to look at me. "What do you know about her family?"

"Virtually nothing," I said. "Solange told both me and her professor that her family had roots here, and that they had all moved away. And that's all."

The abbess looked off into the distance as her hands disappeared into the capacious sleeves of her habit, as if she were retreating into a safe place. She sighed, "Oh my."

"Ma Mère?" Jean-Paul laid a hand on her shoulder. "*Ça va?*"

"Yes, yes, I'm fine." She took a deep breath. "You want to know who Betz was, yes?"

"Please," I said.

She thought for a moment, looked from me to Jean-Paul, and

seemed to come to a decision. "My dears," she said, "Élodie told you how it was when a platoon of Nazi soldiers commandeered the Martin home and conscripted some of us village girls as farm laborers. In that situation, the line between victor and vanquished was clear; they were the master, we were their servants. But it also happened, frequently happened in fact, that only one or two soldiers would be billeted in a private home. The Nazis would live side by side with the residents, sharing the same table, passing in the hallways. I believe that most French people in that situation did as they were instructed by the occupiers, but at the same time they did their best to ignore the soldiers living among them, as if the occupiers were ghosts, annoying entities that were not going away."

After a moment, she continued. "Sometimes friendships emerged. And sometimes something more. To gain favors, for love, who can say? Anyway, Betz was a German soldier. And he fell in love with a young woman in the home where he was billeted."

"What happened to them?" I asked.

"D-Day happened," she said. "The Germans lost the war. He was taken prisoner by the Allies."

"What about his lover?" Jean-Paul asked. "Women who collaborated with the Germans were generally treated very harshly by their neighbors."

"Very harshly, indeed. And the woman was. Her head was shaved in public, she was covered in ashes, and shunned. She was also expecting his child."

"Dear God," I said. "What did she do?"

"The old abbess took her in until the baby was born, and gave her charity afterward so that they didn't starve. Her own family turned her out. But it wasn't very long after, maybe only a year, when, to the surprise of everyone, Betz, the soldier, the father, came for her and the child. He took them away, and they never came back."

"I suppose that explains why Solange's family wouldn't come here to collect her belongings," I said.

"I could not say, my dear." We had reached the side entrance to the convent. The abbess took me by the shoulders and kissed my cheeks, and Jean-Paul's, as well. Before I let her go, I had one more question.

"Ma Mère," I said. "My grandmother told me that you women rescued an English pilot. Tell me about him."

"Tony?" She smiled, thinking. "He was a lovely man. Tall and fair, with the deepest blue eyes."

"Tony?"

"Tony." Still smiling, she opened the door.

"What happened to him?"

The smile turned wistful. "He died, shot down over Dieppe in the summer of 1944. A great loss."

"Anthony Dauvin was his son?"

"His beautiful son. The tragedy is, he did not live to meet his boy." With a little bow, she stepped inside, closing the door behind her.

Jean-Paul wrapped an arm around my shoulders as we walked back toward the car park. "You look sad, my dear."

"I was just thinking," I said. "Two mothers from the same area, two soldiers from opposing sides, two babies. One woman was reviled and shunned by the community, the other is cherished to this day. Strange circumstance, yes?"

"Very," he said. "I can imagine how bitter that circumstance could make the one who was shunned."

"Bitter, angry, resentful, vengeful?" I said.

"Murderous?" he said with a soft laugh. "Sounds very Old Testament, doesn't it?"

I suppose it did. We stopped in at the *gendarme* barracks to check on Guido. Once again, he was in the day room instead of locked away in a cell. He was lounging on the cot against the back wall, reading a Mickey Spillane paperback in English that I found at a *brocante*—a flea market—in Cherbourg the week before.

Nodding at the book in his hands, I asked, "Learning anything useful?"

"Tons." He set the book down and got to his feet. "I'm planning to blast out of this pop stand tonight. Meet me around back at midnight, and bring your gat."

"If you can wait until tomorrow morning, we'll just walk out the front door," I said. "In the meantime, it doesn't look like you're being mistreated."

He laughed. "I could walk out the front door right now, go buy some bonbons, and walk right back in and no one would send out the storm troopers. The worst part of this whole thing is the boredom. It wasn't too bad last night because there was another guy in here to talk to. But he was sprung this morning."

"What was he in for?" I asked.

"Drunk in public. When he was hauled in, from the way he was behaving I thought he was wasted. The *flics* gave him a breath test and put him in a cell to sober up. But right away he seemed fine. Talkative bastard, full of questions. It was nice to have someone who could speak in complete English sentences for a change, but I had to roll over and put a pillow over my head to get any sleep."

"American, British?" I asked.

"German," he said.

Jean-Paul's brows shot up. "How old was he?"

Guido shrugged. "Mid-thirties I'd guess."

"Was his name Dieter Schwarz?"

"Something like that," Guido said at the same time I asked, "Who the hell is Dieter Schwarz?"

"Reporter for a right-wing online news agency out of Berlin," Jean-Paul said. "Drives a certain green Toyota."

"When did you find that out?" I wanted to know.

"During mass," Jean-Paul said. "A text came through during the Our Father. I bowed my head and sneaked a look."

"I should have guessed he was a reporter, all the questions he asked," Guido said. "How do you know him?"

"He seems to be tailing us," I said. "What sorts of questions did he ask?"

"Mostly about the German remains we found. He asked what was going to happen to the remains, but he really seemed to be most interested to know about any artifacts that were found, guns and so on. But there wasn't anything much I could tell him other than that there were a lot of charred bones."

"Did you tell him how the bones happened to get charred?" I asked.

"I know better than to volunteer details from a work in progress, Mag. I've been at this game as long as you have." He patted my cheek. "I told him that he'd have to wait for our film to be broadcast."

"Did that satisfy him?"

"I didn't care if it did or not," he said. "But it kind of ticked him off. He told me he was a writer doing research, but he couldn't talk about it. I didn't know if he was being snarky because I wouldn't tell him what he wanted to know about our stuff, or if maybe he wasn't a writer at all. I never really bought the drunk routine so I generally dismissed him as a bullshitter. If anything, I thought that maybe he just needed a place to sleep for the night; rooms are hard to come by around here."

The conversation moved on to the hearing scheduled for the morning. Guido's lawyer had told him not to worry. There were insufficient grounds to file charges against him, and unless charges were filed he couldn't be held beyond the forty-eight hours allowed under *garde à vu*. The last piece the police had been looking into, evidence that Guido had been in a fight, disappeared when Delphine's father affirmed that it was he who punched Guido in the jaw. Guido still did not have an alibi for the night Solange was murdered, but that in itself was not evidence.

"If they give me back my passport," Guido asked me, "are you sending me home?"

"Is that what you want?" I asked.

He shook his head. "I've never abandoned you mid-project. I don't want to start now."

"You won't be abandoning me," I said. "There's plenty you can do from the studio in L.A. More than you could in a French jail."

"Talk it over with your lawyer before you decide," Jean-Paul advised. "But in the meantime, I'll check the airline schedules."

━16━

ANTOINE CALLED WHEN we were on our way to the car park. I thought he'd be asking why we were AWOL from the beach party, and was surprised when he seemed relieved that we hadn't even started out yet. Grand-mère was still at home, he said, and because the rest of the family had been among the first to arrive at the beach pavilion all their cars were now hemmed in by later arrivals. There was no way they could get out until everyone left. The abbess discovered her ride was stuck in traffic, or something, so would we please stop at the convent to pick her up before we left the village to go get Grand-mère? By the way, parking near the beach was abysmal, so he advised that we ditch our car wherever there was space to pull in.

Ma Mère was waiting for us next to the stone fountain in front of the convent, shading herself from the glare of midday sun under a pink flowered parasol. She had changed out of her heavy black habit into a mid-calf-length navy skirt and a white blouse, with a shorter black coif on her head and sandals on her feet.

"Ma Mère," I said as I held the front passenger door for her to get in next to Jean-Paul. "You have legs."

"Have you never seen a nun in beach togs before?" she said with a little giggle and a curtsy. She declined to get in front, though, saying she preferred to sit in back and be chauffeured when a handsome man was driving.

When we pulled into the compound gate, Grand-mère must have heard the car approach across the gravel courtyard. She opened her front door and came out just as we pulled up. Like the abbess, she, too, had changed into clothes that would be more comfortable at the beach than the trim summer-weight suit she had worn to mass. She looked very jaunty in lightweight slacks and a long-sleeved linen shirt. A broad-brimmed straw hat hung from her wrist by its chin strap; there was a stack of folding canvas chairs against the wall.

"I am so sorry for the inconvenience," Grand-mère said as we got out of the car.

"No inconvenience at all," Jean-Paul said. He popped his car trunk and loaded in the chairs. "In truth, you've done us a favor. Your granddaughter was saying that she wanted to swim, but without a suit I'm afraid she'd scandalize the village. So, if you'll excuse us, we'll run upstairs and change."

The two women followed us inside, where it was cooler, to wait. As we hurried up the stairs Jean-Paul and I were laughing about the villagers' reactions if we did go swimming *au naturel*. We weren't on

the Riviera, but it was not uncommon for both sexes among the summer crowd to stroll along the local beaches wearing nothing except
a skimpy bottom, to the amusement or horror of more conservative
year-around residents. I had my hand on our bedroom doorknob
when Jean-Paul pulled me into a very lovely, passionate embrace. He
said, "Alone at last."

"I'm yours," I said, opening the door and pulling him through.
"For all of ten minutes."

"Only ten?" he said before he froze, looking over my shoulder. I
turned to see what he saw behind me.

Erika von Streicher Karl stood in the middle of our bedroom.
Before we had a chance to challenge her for being in a place where
she had absolutely no business being, she began to sputter, trying to
articulate an explanation I supposed. The room seemed to be exactly
as we left it, so if she had rummaged around she had been tidy about
it. Jean-Paul was asking her what the hell she was doing there. It didn't
matter to me what she was after, I only wanted for her to disappear
out of our lives. I pulled out my mobile and called the *gendarme*
barracks; I'd had the number on speed dial since Friday when Guido
was taken in. At about the time someone picked up the call, Erika
managed to utter an actual word: *"Scheiße."*

"This is Maggie MacGowen," I said into the phone. "*Chez* Martin. We discovered an intruder in the house. Please send someone
right away."

I handed the phone to Jean-Paul to deal with the follow-up questions because I thought he would do a better job of answering them.
And anyway, before the *gendarmes* arrived I had some questions for
the woman standing in front of me, sweating like the forward on a
basketball team. My first question was to the point:

"What the hell are you doing here?"

She looked around as if to make sure she knew where she was
before she managed to say, "I thought you would all be at that party."

"Wrong answer," I said. "Try again."

"This was my father's bedroom," was the best she could come up
with. Until that moment, if I had given it any thought at all I would
have assumed that von Streicher had commandeered the larger room

at the end of the hall, my grandparents' room, for himself. But as I thought it through, it made sense that my grandparents would not want to use the same room he'd inhabited. Sometime after the war, I knew, they had done a major modernization of the house, adding central heat and more bathrooms, and had enlarged the master bedroom where my grandmother still slept.

"You say this is your father's room?" I opened the armoire and made a show of looking inside. "He doesn't seem to be here now. What did you hope to find?"

"You have to understand...."

"I'm afraid I do," I said. "Only too well."

Jean-Paul said good-bye to the police, and handed me my phone as he took Erika by the elbow. He said, "We'll wait outside."

When they heard us on the stairs, Grand-mère and the abbess came into the salon from the kitchen. Seeing the Nazi's daughter being impelled down the stairs shocked and confused them.

"Maggie?" Grand-mère said, backing up as we reached the bottom step. "What the hell?"

"She was in our room. We've called the *gendarmes* and they're on their way to pick her up."

Grand-mère nailed Erika with a withering, narrow-eyed glare. "What is it you are hoping to find, madame?"

"My father was so happy here," Erika managed to utter, though the words were no more than a whisper, almost as if she were speaking to herself. "I hoped to find some token of his time in this house, just a little memento."

"A memento?" Addressing her old friend, the abbess, Grand-mère did not take her eyes from Erika. "The major's daughter wants a memento. Too bad, though. I did my best to burn any trinkets the Nazis left behind. And you, Ma Mère? Other than scars and night-mares, have you saved souvenirs from that time that you might share with her?"

The abbess blanched; bad memories stirred. She took out her rosary beads and silently ran them through her fingers.

"My father was not a Nazi," the intruder managed to say in a bolder voice.

Jean-Paul gave Erika's arm a hard jerk. When she looked back at him, he said, "Don't be a fool. Shut up."

"Madame von Streicher Karl," Grand-mère said to get her attention. "Do you think it matters in the least whether your father was a Nazi or not? He wore their insignia, he marched to Nazi orders. He shielded himself behind their power when he abused our people."

"My father was a good and decent man. I knew him."

"He dandled you on his knee," Grand-mère said with a dismissive wave. "You know nothing about the man. But because you are so insistent, I will tell you what you want to know about your father's lovely sojourn in this house."

"Élodie?"

Grand-mère heard the note of caution in her old friend's voice, but shook her head. "I've had enough of this woman's nonsense."

I put my arm around my grandmother and she patted my cheek. Looking up at me, she said, "Yes?" I nodded. She was right. It was time.

"You want to know how your father died," Grand-mère said, taking a step closer to Erika. "That kind and decent man of your fantasies was a thief, a martinet, and a rapist. He forced a child of only fifteen into his bed. And when he impregnated her, he sent her to the village pharmacist and forced the old man, who knew nothing of such things, to terminate the pregnancy. A terrible butchery was done to that precious girl."

Ma Mère groaned. I rushed to her, worried that she might faint. As I hustled to help her into a chair at the far end of the room, I said, "Grand-mère, enough." But the abbess took my hand and said, "No, let her tell it."

After a nod from the abbess, Grand-mère continued. "Only a week after that barbaric procedure, your father tried to force himself onto the girl yet again. She begged him, telling him that she was still bleeding, that she had not yet healed. And he did not care."

"I don't believe you," Erika said.

"No?" Grand-mère walked over toward the arrangement of chairs where the abbess was resting. She grabbed a corner of the Persian rug between the cluster of chairs and flung it back, exposing a big black stain on the gray stone floor. "On this very spot, to stop your father from harming that child further, I slit his throat. You want a souvenir of your father? Here it is. Your father's blood still darkens this place. Shall I rip up the stones for you to take with you?"

Suddenly the only sound in the room were the sobs caught in Erika's throat. Ma Mère looked at the stain at her feet. And then a little smile crossed her face.

We heard a car cross the courtyard. Jean-Paul started toward the door with Erika. "The *gendarmes* are here."

My grandmother sat down on the arm of her friend's chair and reached for her hand as the door closed behind Jean-Paul. She asked Ma Mère, "*Ça va?*"

"Yes, I'm fine. But Élodie, weren't we over there by the stairs when you slit von Streicher's throat?"

My grandmother laughed softly. "Yes, of course. But I thought the stain would be a nice sort of illustration, no?"

"Excellent, yes," Ma Mère said. "But as I recall, you and Henri added this floor years after the war. When you remodeled."

"Ah, yes. So we did."

"Then what caused that big dark spot?"

"It happened just after the floor was laid," Grand-mère said, flipping the rug back into place, hiding the stain. "The stone hadn't been sealed yet. My Gérard—I think he was about ten years old—had that beautiful border collie bitch. Remember her? Henri said she was the best herding dog he had ever trained, so he bred her. Anyway, the dog got in here somehow and dropped her litter right there on the new floor. We never could get the stain out."

"But the rest of what you said happened?" I asked, reminded to keep a close eye on my grandmother.

"Yes," the abbess said. "Except that your grandmother left out the part where she took von Streicher's gun off his belt and shot him in the chest after she slit his throat. Why did you leave that out, Élodie?"

"If I'd told her about it, that wretched woman might have asked for the old Luger as a souvenir." Grand-mère rose. She took out her mobile and checked the time. "We should get to the beach before Antoine calls again looking for us."

"After all this," I said, "you want to go to the party?"

"*Bien sûr,*" she said. "And you, Ma Mère?"

"Yes, of course," the abbess said, rising from her chair. "We have much to celebrate today. If Élodie had not done what she did, I can't be sure this sweet baby would ever have been born. So, let us go and welcome him."

After Erika was driven away by the *gendarmes*, Jean-Paul and I did manage to change into shorts for the beach. As we drove out through the compound gate with the two war survivors nestled into the lush leather of the backseat, the abbess turned to my grand-mother.

"Élodie, that Luger you took from von Streicher? Where is it now?"

"Don't worry, it's in a safe place," Grand-mère said. "Is it not, Maggie?"

─17─

PARTY-GOERS TURNED the usual weekend traffic on the narrow beach road into a gridlocked mess. With no alternate route available, we turned in and claimed our slot in the solid queue of cars, following the rear bumper of a tiny Fiat as we inched forward toward the water. Both sides of the road were lined with dense, thorny gorse that grew as tall as the houses tucked behind it, making the drive feel like being in a train passing through a long green tunnel. Here and there, driveways were cut into the brush and we could catch glimpses of beach cottages that ranged from mere shacks to mansionettes hidden in clearings, sheltered from the wind off the ocean. Most of the cottage driveways had signs warning people against pulling in and parking, though it was tempting to do just that.

Jean-Paul never lost his amiable composure, though I could sense his frustration as we slogged along. Or maybe I assumed he shared my feelings. It was just after one o'clock, but we'd already had a very long day. If we could have turned back, and we could not, I would have suggested that we give up and go home. Grand-mère and the abbess did their best to keep up a conversation, but after a while they both dozed off.

We had progressed no more than a hundred yards when Jean-Paul glanced into the rearview mirror and suddenly tensed. I turned to see what was there but saw only a line of cars stuck in the same slow-motion parade. I caught his eye and shrugged, questioning what he'd seen. A little backward nod let me know to look again. This time, a car slipped out of the queue, maybe to see what was ahead, and I knew what Jean-Paul had reacted to.

"Toyota," I said in a low voice. "Green. German plates."

Grand-mère perked up and turned to see what we were talking about, but by then the Toyota had slipped back into line behind the taller Volvo in front of it.

Jean-Paul put a hand on my knee. "You still have that number on speed dial?"

"I do, but let's wait until we know what the guy's up to. He hasn't actually done anything, yet." We were just edging past a narrow gap in the gorse. The opening wasn't big enough to park in, not if the passengers wanted to open their doors and get out of the car. But I saw a possible use for the space. I watched the progress of the cars behind us until the headlights of the Volvo were near that gap.

"I'd like a little chat with the guy," I said, with my eyes on the side view mirror, I reached for my door handle and told Jean-Paul, "Stop the car, please. Now."

He did. And so did everyone behind us. Fortunately traffic was moving so slowly there was no sound of crashing metal behind us. Over the screech of brakes and blasting horns, Jean-Paul asked, "What are you going to do?"

"Following my grandmother's example, I'm going to end this bullshit."

I was out of the car, keeping my head low as I ran back along the queue. I reached the Volvo's front bumper, went between stopped cars and came up to the green Toyota on the driver's side. I yanked open the door and ordered, "Slide over, Dieter."

"What, what?" His eyes grew wide with alarm and confusion.

I pushed his bony shoulder. "Slide over."

"Who?" He protested, asked questions, seemed stunned, but I just kept pushing him and ordering him to move until he scrambled over the console, negotiating the gearshift, until he more or less fell atop the jumble of old food wrappers and empty bottles, a laptop computer and several ragged-looking notebooks piled on the passenger seat. As he shoved all that crap onto the floor so he could sit in the seat, he asked, "Are you armed?"

"Damn right I am." By then I had waved to Jean-Paul as a signal to drive on and was in the Toyota's driver's seat, pulling the door closed. "I'm at the wheel of maybe a ton of Japanese steel and plastic. Want to see if it can be lethal?"

He started to say "Who?" again, but something occurred to him and he asked, "How do you know my name?"

"Got it through the D.G.S.E." I put the car in gear and started forward as traffic began to move again.

He grew awfully quiet and very pale. The man, thirtyish, hair cropped close, tattoos creeping up both arms and disappearing into his souvenir rock-concert T-shirt, looked scared enough to lose his lunch from either end. He hardly had enough spit in his mouth to speak. "*Direction générale de la sécurité extérieure* gave you my name? I'm not a terrorist. Why did they give you my name? How do they even know me?"

"My turn to ask questions," I said. The gap in the gorse came up on our left front fender. I nosed the little car into the space though there really wasn't room for it. Dieter winced as branches scraped the paint on both sides. When I came to a stop, he tried to open his door, found that he couldn't move it more than a few inches, and gave up the effort.

"How will I get my car out of here?"

"Same way we got in."

With some force, he pulled his door closed. "What do you want from me?" he asked.

"I want you to quit stalking us."

"Stalking you?" he said, looking thoroughly nonplussed. "I'm not stalking you. I don't even know who you are."

"Why is it, then, that when I look into my rearview mirror I keep seeing your bumper?" I pulled out my mobile and showed him the picture I had snapped of his car's registration plates.

After a moment a light seemed to go on behind his eyes, and said, "You were in that car with Jean-Paul Bernard?"

"You know Jean-Paul?"

"No." He shook his head. "I know who he is, I don't know him. I'm a journalist on assignment. I'm following a story lead."

"What's the story?"

"I can't divulge that."

I glanced out the back window at the cars inching along the road past our back bumper. "It'll take a while for this traffic to clear enough for me to back out of here. I can wait. Can you?"

He sighed, crossed his arms over his narrow chest, and slouched down in his seat. "I've been working on a piece about the disrespect that members of the European community continue to show to Germany. All these economically sick nations demand bailout money from us, but what are we offered in return? Nothing. They keep waving the bloody flag of that long-ago war at us as if we're to blame somehow for their bad money management now."

"And so you came here expecting to accomplish what?" I asked.

"Raise awareness, that's all."

"How does Jean-Paul Bernard fit in?"

"I got a tip that the issue came up during an EU trade meeting at the end of last week. When it was mentioned that some German remains were discovered in this area, a German delegate heard one of the French guys at the table say that Germany ought to pay for the cleanup of its war trash, which was a totally disrespectful thing to say. I mean, they're working on open trade agreements among all EU nations, and this asshole thinks it's all right to call dead soldiers from our country trash? I was told that Bernard was sent here with a directive to make certain that the remains were handled with dignity."

"What have you found out?"

He took a deep breath. "No one around here will give me any information about the disinterment or the reburial of the remains.

Bernard seems to be spending a whole lot of time at the estate where the remains were discovered and at the local *gendarme* barracks. I have been trying to discover what action he has taken. Or is trying to take. It looks to me like he can't get cooperation because so far nothing has been done."

"If you had been in church this morning," I said, "instead of in jail pretending to be the town drunk, you would have heard the priest ask the congregation to pray for the strangers who died here, and to forgive the former enemy, as requested by Jean-Paul Bernard and the mayor."

He eyed me. "Seriously?"

"Close enough." Maybe the priest's language was a bit vague about who was to be forgiven and exactly who died, but he had made a gesture.

Dieter asked, "What do you know about what's happening to the remains?"

"That's a question for your own *Volksbund*," I said, and shifted the topic. "What do you know about Erika von Streicher Karl?"

He shook his head. "Never heard of her."

"Or Horst von Streicher?"

He thought for a minute before he asked, "Any relation to Otto von Streicher?"

"I don't know," I said. "Who is he?"

"Maybe you've heard him referred to as the Count of Rutland?"

"You know the count?" I asked.

"That old fraud? No, I've never met him, but I know about him," he said. "A couple of years ago von Streicher took out an ad in our paper offering his title for sale. The editor was curious about it so he sent a reporter friend of mine to check him out. My friend wrote a great story about the old guy. It trended for a while."

"Someone did buy the title," I said.

"Some*one*? How many someones?" He guffawed. "Every time he needs rent money he puts his title up for sale. Except, he has no title. He's some kind of clerk. His father was a schoolteacher, just an ordinary guy."

"What do you know about the father?"

"Nothing. Died in the war I think." He shook his head. "Who is this Erika? A relative?"

"Probably Otto's sister," I said. "Listen to me, Dieter. If you knew what old man von Streicher did here during the war, you would understand why the locals didn't call out a marching band when German military remains were found."

"What did he do?" He shuffled through the junk on the floor, pulled out a ratty-looking notebook and a pen, and looked at me expectantly.

I had gotten everything out of Dieter Schwarz that I needed to know, and had told him all that I intended to. Traffic on the road behind us was thinning out. I kept my eye on the road in the rearview mirror, looking for a gap between cars that would be big enough for me to back the Toyota into. I saw my hole, turned the ignition key and shifted into reverse.

"Whatever he did, Dieter, I strongly advise you against making inquiries around here."

"Why not?" he said, wincing again as the gorse etched our exit path into the car's green paint.

"It could get you seriously hurt."

I left the car hugging the side of the narrow road, facing away from the beach, and got out to walk the rest of the way. It was a bright, warm day and I enjoyed the walk.

The baptism party was in full swing when I finally arrived. The marquee Grand-mère had arranged to have erected on the sand in front of the Martin family pavilion in case of rain made a nice shaded area big enough to accommodate all of the decorated party tables. Food was being served buffet-style inside the pavilion where it was cooler, and where flies could be better controlled. A steady stream of people moved back and forth between the pavilion, the marquee, and the beach.

I had been told that the Martin family had kept a cottage on that piece of beach at Anneville-sur-Mer for many, many years. The original structure was a primitive affair with no indoor plumbing or electricity. At some point, Isabelle, my birth mother, had taken down the old cottage and replaced it with the pavilion, which was a very modern party house rather than a vacation cottage. The only sleeping area was a small loft over one end of the single ground-floor great room that combined a large kitchen, a dining area with a table that could accommodate a crowd at one end, and a seating area arranged around a Swedish fireplace at the other. The pavilion's front wall was made of wood-framed glass panels that could be folded back to open the entire room to the covered veranda in front and the pale sand beyond. Or, in cool weather, opened one panel at a time. Along the side wall there were outdoor showers for rinsing off sand, and inside there were modern bathrooms.

Though the place belonged to the family, over time and after many large parties like this one, people in the area seemed to regard it as a community facility. Indeed, Gaston was lobbying my grandmother to have the potential heirs sign the place over to the regional park system. I wasn't sure I would sign that document, if it was ever drafted, because should the day come when I spent long periods of time in Normandy, I would prefer to stay at the pavilion, alone, rather than surrounded by the family hubbub at the estate.

Antoine walked up to meet me as I came along the path from the pavilion's jammed parking area.

"I was worried," he said, taking my arm. "I asked Jean-Paul if we should send out a search party, but he said he had spoken on the phone with you and that you were on your way. If I'd known you were walking I would have sent a car. Except that's impossible."

He seemed rattled and I doubted it was because I was late arriving. I patted the hand he rested on my arm, and asked, "How's the party?"

"Big. Noisy." He looked around. "As usual."

"Are the students in charge of cleanup later?"

He nodded. "They are."

"The road is clearing up," I said. "If you could get a car out, this would be a good time to escape."

"No, I'll stick around. I might go up to the loft and lie down, though."

As we walked toward the crowd, I told him about Dieter Schwarz. And I told him about finding Erika inside the house

because I thought he should know. And so should Freddy. The way
the family came and went into and out of each other's houses, keeping doors locked was problematic. Until whatever was going on
settled down, though, I thought we needed to be more careful. I
suggested putting up security cameras similar to the ones the students had installed at the camp. Antoine was taken aback: He did
not know that the students felt it necessary to take precautions, and
wished that they had spoken with him about their concerns.

"Antoine," I said, leaning close to him, "you don't have to be
everyone's dad all the time."

He smiled, let out a big sigh. "I miss my kids. I miss my wife. I
need to take care of somebody until they get back."

"Take care of yourself, my dear," I said. "Let the rest of us pre-
tend we're grownups now and then."

All the time we were talking, I was looking around. There were
a couple of soccer games on the beach, some sunbathers and swim-
mers, a mass of people dining or relaxing under the marquee, a
clutch of village women hovering over the buffet tables inside the
pavilion. Casey and David and several other young people were
playing volleyball, using a fisherman's skein for a net. Grand-mère
and the abbess had settled in with Pierre's grandmother and Gaston,
watching over the honored guest who was asleep in a cradle covered
by a bug net. Everyone was accounted for. Except I couldn't find
Jean-Paul.

"Are you looking for him?" Antoine brought his head down closer and pointed to a stand of scrawny trees down the beach. Jean-Paul
stood in the spotty shade, apparently arguing with someone on the
telephone.

"You might as well get something to eat," Antoine said. "That
conversation has been going on for a while."

Jean-Paul looked up just then, spotted me, waved, and turned
back to his call.

"Must be important," Antoine said as we walked inside, where
we separated. He went up the ladder to the sleeping loft. I helped
myself to the feast spread out on the long oak table and took my
plate outside to find a place to sit.

"Hello, Maggie MacGowen!"

I turned and saw Paulette Matson with a curly-haired toddler in her arms, headed my way. I said to her, "Looks like you found a friend."

"This is Monique," Paulette said, smiling into the beatific face of the little girl. "She's the big sister of the little baby that was baptized this morning."

"Hello, Monique," I said, shaking her tiny hand. She reached out and took a chunk of cheese off my plate. While she was busy eating it, I said to Paulette, "You do get around."

She laughed her big laugh. "I told you we found a room with the sweetest family? Well, it's the family of the little guest of honor. They insisted that we come to the party. And here we are."

"Where's Henry?" I asked.

"Probably talking to your builder, Freddy Desmoulins."

"That builder is my brother," I said. "Half brother, anyway."

"Your Freddy is very sharp. Henry loves the concept for his project. They're talking about expanding into other areas," she said. "They're all over the idea of green energy, sustainable agriculture, affordable housing, preserving the charm of village life. Or American small town life. You should hear the two of them go on.

"You have to admit though, that putting up affordable senior housing near existing towns with businesses that are struggling to hang on as young people move away makes a whole lot more sense than building more of those hideous pop-up cities for old people out in the most godforsaken patches of desert in the American Southwest. I wonder if there's a plot to dehydrate the oldsters." She took a breath and smiled prettily at me. "I think that building into existing small towns makes so much more sense, don't you?"

"Are you going to build the village of Rutland, Countess?"

"No way." She laughed as she took a tiny pear tart from my plate and offered it to Monique. "I think it may be time to bury the count and countess. It was fun, though. Henry said he'd buy me a tiara, just as a little memento of this crazy summer."

I wiped Monique's sticky hands with my napkin. "You were a lovely countess, Paulette."

She leaned closer, conspiratorial, and nodded toward Jean-Paul.

"That handsome man of yours has been over there wheeling and dealing for a while now. Something big happening?"

"I have no idea," I said, looking over at him. From his posture and his gestures, I knew that this was not a happy conversation.

"Oh, my!" Paulette waved her hand in front of her face as she smiled down at Monique. "How can such a sweet little girl be making such a big stinky poo? I love you to death, sweet pea, but Auntie Paulette has her limitations. Excuse us, Maggie, it's time to hand this bundle off to a mommy or a grandma with a diaper bag."

"See you around," I said. As I ate, I watched Jean-Paul. His conversation—or was it several conversations?—dragged on. When I was finished, I picked up my plate and dumped the remains into a trash can. Out beyond the expanse of gold sand, the ocean beckoned. I was ready to go for a swim. I glanced again at Jean-Paul, hoping he would join me, but he did not look up.

Raffi, one of the archeology students, who did indeed have curly dark hair and long black eyelashes, as Taylor had described him, bailed out of a soccer game and, panting, chest heaving, dropped onto the sand in a patch of shade and stretched out. Happy for the opportunity to talk to him, I went over and kneeled in the sand beside him.

"You okay, Raffi?" I asked.

He opened an eye, and when he saw who was talking to him, sat right up. "Miss MacGowen."

"Rough game?" I asked.

"Those kids." He gave me a self-deprecating little smile. He had to be all of twenty-three or -four. "I haven't played for a while; I think I'm getting old."

"Not yet, you aren't." I found half a mussel shell in the sand and brushed it off. "Raffi, you know I helped pack up Solange's things."

He nodded.

"We found her notebook, the one she always carried," I said. "Maybe I shouldn't have, but I looked through it."

"She talk about me?" he asked with a wry grin.

"It was all work-related," I said. "I have a couple of questions about some of her notes, and about some of the sketches. Does it bother you to talk about it?"

"No." He gazed off toward the water. "I didn't know Solange all that well. We had a few seminars together at university, but we were focusing on different areas of research."

"Does this mean anything to you?" With the edge of the mussel shell, I smoothed a patch of sand and did my best to replicate the obelisk-like shape Solange had sketched twice. With my fingernail I wrote *FeR* under the shape. He was nodding before I had finished.

"*Fe* stands for iron, of course. And *R* probably means Roman. I found that fragment out by the old wall in the pasture."

"What is it?"

"I can only guess without getting it into a lab, but it looks like part of a shaft, maybe a bolt. I suspect it was cast using a mass-production method commonly found all over the Roman Empire by the third century. I showed it to Solange to get her opinion, but she took it and did not return it. Was it found among her things?"

"We didn't see it," I said. "When did you find it?"

"When?" He shrugged, thinking. "Not long after we arrived here. A couple of weeks ago, I guess. I was just out looking around. I had noticed that the tool marks on some of the sandstone blocks in the wall around your family compound were similar to those found among the ruins of a pre–Roman-era building at a site near Rouen where I worked last summer. The blocks that interested me had been combined in the construction of the compound wall with longer stone blocks cut from a different quarry using more modern tools. I assumed that the smaller stones came from an earlier structure and were repurposed to build the wall. It is still common for people to repurpose building materials, is it not?"

"It is." Used brick and barn wood came to mind as examples.

He continued: "During my walk about, I found a wall, or remains of a wall, out in the cow pasture that was clearly built from the same stone. When I dug down a bit, I found evidence of a foundation for a structure that was at least twelve feet long on a side. I think that if the grass were cut very short you might be able to see the indentation in the soil where there was once a fairly large structure."

"A pre-Roman structure?" I asked.

He shrugged. "We only began to study the site after we had to give up on the carrot patch. If I had to guess, I would say that the older sandstone blocks, the square ones, could easily be pre-Roman. But because stone can be used over and over infinitely, and was frequently transported over long distances, the structure in the meadow could have been built by Celts, Romans, Franks, Vikings, Normans, or by the Martin family. But that site is also where I found the piece of iron, and that is provocative."

"Did you discuss this with Olivia?"

"In passing. She agreed. But at that time, we were still focused on examining the earth turned up during the sewer excavation, so the topic was tabled. I was very happy when we relocated to the pasture wall. It has far more interesting prospects than the carrot field."

I said, "Solange thought that the land around the trench was accreted too recently for you to turn up anything interesting."

"I agreed," he said. "It was a waste of our time. But I think that we set up there as part of Olivia's agreement with Freddy. He is funding us, you know."

I didn't. I asked, "Why did Solange take that piece of iron from you?"

Again, the dismissive Gallic shrug. "I thought she would run with it to Olivia to argue that we should move our study site. When she didn't, I expected her to pull it out at the proper dramatic moment. Or to bury it."

"Bury it?"

"Roman iron might not fit with whatever conclusions Solange had in mind."

"The little stinker. I bet you were pissed."

He shrugged off the suggestion. "All's fair in love, war, and the quest for institutional grant money, yes?"

"I suppose." I got to my feet and brushed sand off my bottom. "Thanks for your time, Raffi."

"My pleasure," he said, shielding his eyes from the sun at my back to look up at me. "If that piece of iron turns up, will you let me know?"

"I will."

He tried to be very cool about what Solange had done to him, but if he weren't angry would he have mentioned it to Casey and David?

I was hot and thirsty as I headed back toward the pavilion. Quite a few people had already left, and others were gathering their families together and saying their good-byes. The women inside were wrapping food and clearing the big table of everything except cheese, sweets, and drinks. I filled a glass with cold lemonade and went out to look for Jean-Paul, hoping he was ready to go home.

He was still on the phone, or on the phone again, but he waved at me and I started walking toward him. As I approached I heard him tell the person on the other end of his phone, "Absolutely not. I'll get there Wednesday." This was followed by, "Tomorrow is impossible." More argument followed. When he was within my reach he abruptly ended the call.

"Trouble?" I said.

He bobbled his head, yes and no, as he slipped the phone into his pocket.

"Did you eat something?" I asked. If he wanted to tell me about the conversation, he would.

He pulled me into his arms, rested his chin on my head, and took a couple of deep breaths. "Will you come with me to Paris tonight?"

"I have waited my entire life for a man to say that to me," I said. "But as you just told someone else, tomorrow is impossible. Why do you ask? What's up?"

"It's complicated." He pulled back enough so that he could look into my face. I thought he was going to explain, but instead he asked, "What happened with Dieter Schwarz?"

"I grilled him mercilessly," I said. "I thought he was just another poor soul looking for the remains of a lost family member or for war souvenirs. But it turns out, he was dogging you."

"Me?"

I told him what I had learned from poor Dieter.

"I hate the press," he said.

"I am the press," I said.

He laughed. "*Merde.* So you are. But not of his sort. Don't think

America is the only nation with some version of Fox News. Fear mongers of the worst sort, and he's one of them. Fair and balanced horseshit."

"Your grasp of American slang is coming along well," I said. "I'm leaning toward using a single multi-purpose obscenity like *merde*, though I have learned some interesting new ones from my grand-mother."

"*Merde* is usually *le mot juste*," he said.

As we walked toward the pavilion with our arms around each other, I asked, "Do you really have to leave tonight?"

"*Oui.*"

"*Merde,*" I said, because it was the perfect word for the moment.

⟶ 18 ⟶

AS ARGUMENTS GO, the little tiff I had with Jean-Paul as he packed his bag didn't amount to much. I could maybe join him in Paris on Tuesday or Wednesday, but I could not go with him Sunday night.

Guido's hearing was set for first thing Monday morning. Because of the language the network used when applying for our French work permit, I was listed as Guido's supervisor. I had to be at the hearing to vouch for him.

Besides that, we were way behind on our filming schedule. Other than hours and hours of background footage the interns had been shooting to stay busy, we had not made any progress since the inter-view with Grand-mère on Friday morning. There was no way I could run off to Paris, or anywhere else, on Sunday night.

"I hate to leave you here alone," Jean-Paul said. "Not until all this strangeness that's going on gets sorted out."

"I'll be fine," I said, cramming his laundry bag into the top of his overnight bag. "I'm surrounded by people day and night, whether I want to be or not. And besides—" I reached over and pulled open the top drawer in my bedside table. "I have Grand-mère's purloined Luger, and it's loaded."

"Jesus, Mary and Joseph." He saw the Luger and pushed the

drawer shut again. "That's the best argument yet for you to come with me. You're more likely to shoot— "

"I know." I held up my hand. "I'll shoot off my own ass before I hit any intruder. But I will make a great, lovely *kaboom* doing it and that will bring everyone running."

"When did your grandmother give you that old cannon?"

"After we found Erika in our room this morning," I said. "She told me that if I found 'that woman' lurking around here again I should put a slug between her eyes. Grand-mère thinks all Americans know how to shoot."

He dropped down onto a corner of the bed and studied me, looking dejected. *"Merde."*

I straddled his lap and pushed him onto his back. "You're welcome to stay, you know."

"There we are, at an impasse." He rolled us over until he was on top, looking down at me. "If all goes well tomorrow, I'll be back on Tuesday."

"And if things don't go well?"

"Just promise you won't shoot yourself in the ass. I'm quite fond of your ass. Exactly where it is."

He pulled us both to our feet and picked up his bag.

"Jean-Paul," I said, holding his arm as we walked downstairs. "Exactly what is it that you do when you aren't the consul general? Every time I ask you, you say you're a boring businessman. But what sort of boring business are you in? And don't say that if you told me you'd have to shoot me because we have already delegated that little job to me."

He laughed. "It's complicated."

"Should I take notes?"

He let out a long breath as he worked on his answer to the question. "Could we just say that I am in the business of statecraft?"

"What does that mean?"

Grand-mère was waiting for us at the bottom of the stairs. Jean-Paul kissed my cheek and said, "It will take more time than we have to explain."

"Jean-Paul," Grand-mère said, "your driver is here."

I tugged his arm to hold him back. "You have a new car. Why do you need a driver?"

He reached into his pocket, pulled out the keys to his new BMW, and folded my hand around them. "You need wheels. Just remember to watch six. And leave that damn Luger in the drawer."

There was neither time nor privacy for a passionate good-bye. The driver put Jean-Paul's bag in the trunk and opened the back door for him. A round of kisses and then a wave as they drove out the compound gate. Grand-mère stood beside me and watched them leave. When they were out of sight, she heaved a great sigh.

"I have come to hate good-byes," she said.

"He'll be back in a few days," I said.

"A few days?" She seemed unusually wistful. "This morning when I woke up I said to myself, as I have said every morning for the last several years now, Well Élodie, old dear, you've been given another day. Will I see another? Or one after that? Every good-bye sounds final, and every hello is a little surprise."

"*Chère* Grand-mère." When I wrapped my arm around her shoulders, for the first time she seemed fragile. "Don't be sad. And don't you dare talk about leaving us for a very long time yet. Hell, we haven't finished the film."

She laughed, a big, strong laugh. "Then I promise I won't call the undertaker just yet. Would you like a cold cider?"

As I followed her into the kitchen, she told me that we were having dinner at Freddy's house, at seven. Olivia wanted to reciprocate for all of the meals she'd eaten with the family by cooking for us. She hadn't the confidence to prepare a meal for the usual mob, but that Sunday night there would only be a few of us for dinner, so she had volunteered.

"I have a question about something Jean-Paul's mother said to me." I sat down at the table and watched her pour cider into two tall, narrow glasses.

"Yes?" She sat down beside me.

"Madame Bernard told me you advised her to keep her daughter, Karine, away from Pierre Dauvin. What were your issues with Pierre?"

She let out a surprised little laugh. "Issues with Pierre? No, dear, the issue was with Karine. She was a silly, romantic girl, and Pierre was, and is, a serious boy. But he was also a normal teenager full of hormones and she was both very beautiful and very available. We did not want the girl's pursuit of Pierre to end in a situation they would both regret for the rest of their lives."

"We? You, the other grandmothers, and Ma Mère?"

"Of course. But I could hardly say that to the girl's mother, could I?"

Of course not. What would the village do when the grand-mother mafia was gone?

The topic shifted to the winter, which she usually spent in Paris at the house in the Marais district that she inherited from her parents. She wanted me to come and stay with her. Sometime in early September I would have to go home to California to take care of business, but I planned to be back in Normandy that fall in time to film the apple harvest. After that, I had work to do, but I promised to spend at least part of the holidays with her in December, in Paris. Exactly when that would be would depend on my daughter and my mom. And possibly Jean-Paul.

Grand-mère and I had our mobile phones on the table, comparing calendars. I was thinking how nice it was, and how rare it was, to be alone with my grandmother. For the second time, though no one else was in the house, I heard water running through the plumbing.

"Where does that noise come from?" I asked her.

She shrugged. "Probably someone using the outside tap."

I got up to see, following the sound of rattling pipes from the kitchen to the mudroom, and out the back door, with Grand-mère following. Antoine was washing mud off a pair of bright blue muck boots using the faucet that extended out the back wall.

"Did I see Jean-Paul leave?" Antoine asked, shaking water off the boots. When I said he had, Antoine said, "Better let Freddy know there's one fewer for dinner."

"I called," Grand-mère said. "Though when did one more or less for dinner ever matter?"

Antoine set the boots in a sunny patch next to the house. "Maybe this archeologist is a nervous cook."

"Poor child, volunteering to feed this bunch," Grand-mère said with a little laugh. "Whether she can cook or not, Olivia is an interesting woman, is she not?"

"She seems to be," I said. "But what makes you say so?"

"Driving back from mass this morning when the rest of you went on to the beach, she had questions about the house. How old is it, who built it, when was it remodeled? I gave her a little tour, because she seemed interested."

"That was generous of you," I said

She patted my hand. "Perhaps it was generous of her, my dear. I have come to hate being alone as much as I hate good-byes."

"You didn't run into Erika von Streicher during your tour, did you?" Antoine asked with a smirk. "She was probably already inside."

"We didn't go into bedrooms, dear. Olivia was interested in the structure of the house; its bones and its stones."

It was early evening and the sun was low in the sky. I was watching the play of shadows cast by the roses on the arbor against the side of the house when I stopped to take a good look at the stone blocks used to build the foundation. I wouldn't have noticed if I hadn't spoken with Raffi earlier. A couple of them looked as if they had recently been scrubbed.

"Grand-mère, how old is the house?" I asked.

"I doubt anyone can answer that with confidence. Parts of the house have been here for several centuries, at least."

"Which parts?"

She chuckled. "Would you like the tour as well?"

"I would."

She stepped away a few paces, looking up at the structure. "You can see where additions were made over time by differences in the colors of the stone. This kitchen end of the house is, I think, the most original. The kitchen, at least, has always been where it is now on the ground floor, though it has undergone many modifications over the generations. However, until my father-in-law, Giles, became master of the estate, the area where the salon is now traditionally was the cowshed."

"Where was the house?" I asked, looking around.

She pointed up; Antoine laughed at my question. He said, "You know that, traditionally, tradesmen lived above their shops. Well, farmers lived above their livestock. The animals and cooking fires on the ground floor heated the rooms above. Having the livestock underfoot, as it were, also kept them safer from thieves and poachers."

"Warm, maybe, but very stinky," I said.

Grand-mère shrugged. "There was no plumbing, so bathing was a great inconvenience. I suspect the animals smelled no worse than the people who lived among them."

"French perfume," Antoine added, "is a case of necessity driving invention."

I said, "One of the archeology students told me that some of the stones in the compound wall are very old, maybe Roman or pre-Roman. The blocks he was talking about look to me like the foundation stones at this end of the house. He thought that they might have come from whatever structure that old wall in the pasture used to be."

"I would not be surprised," Grand-mère said. "Perhaps that is why Olivia was so interested in the foundation. She wanted very much to see under the house at this end, but I told her that was impossible."

Antoine's brow furrowed. "But why, Grand-mère? She would be able to see the foundation more clearly below than she can up here. There's nothing down below except a lot of old furniture. Unless you're hiding more bodies you haven't told us about."

"You and Freddy knew better than to play down there," she said shaking a finger at him. "You were severely chastised when you were caught by your grandfather, were you not?"

I caught Grand-mère's eye. "It wasn't the foundation you didn't want to show her, was it? It was the unclaimed ends of von Streicher's loot that's stored in the basement, yes?"

"Merde," Antoine muttered, thinking that through. "Is that what all that stuff is?"

"Bien sûr," she said, of course, what else could it be?

"But why not let her have a look?" he asked.

Grand-mère laid her palm against his cheek. "My angel, Antoine. There has been altogether too much interest of late in that reprobate von Streicher and his hoard of stolen objects. This young archeologist seems to be genuine in her interest, but I don't know her. Our basement is not a curiosity shop. Everything down there represents the genuine suffering of people. Why, my dearest dear, would I simply throw the doors open to a stranger?"

"Maggie is not a stranger," he said, taking her hand, grinning impishly. "I can see from the look on her face that she is dying to get a peek down there. You can't deny her."

I said nothing, but he was right. Grand-mère took a glance at me, and then told Antoine, "Go get the keys from the cupboard by the back door, and a couple of flashlights."

The basement door was very sturdy, made from what looked like old solid oak. Grand-mère said the door hadn't been opened for years, but the key turned readily in the lock and the bolt retracted. The hinges squealed like crypt doors in a B-grade horror movie, but Antoine managed to pull the door open. A wave of cold, clammy air rose up from below.

The lintel was so low we had to duck our heads to get past the doorway. Once we were inside, a vast, black space opened below us at the bottom of a steep stone stairway. The light from my flash barely disturbed the dark beyond the stairs.

"Grand-mère," I said. "This space is huge. What is it?"

"This was the original *fromagerie, chérie.* There was a milking shed out in the yard, and here there were two levels, the *fromagerie* above and the cheese aging room below, where the temperature is always constant."

"Constant like a dungeon," I said.

"Exactly. When my father-in-law, Giles, moved the cows out of the house, he also moved the *fromagerie.* The construction when he added the new wing destabilized the old wooden floor between the levels, and eventually the floor collapsed. Now there is nothing but a cavern."

"I could use it for brandy storage," Antoine said.

She shook a finger at him. "Brandy is a fire hazard. Better that it stay out in the cider house."

"Let's go see what's below." Antoine picked up a tool of some sort that was leaning against the wall just inside the door. He went down first, holding the tool by the head and using the handle to break through the veil of cobwebs that draped the stairs.

When I reached the bottom step, I swept my flashlight from one side of the basement to the other to see what was there. Even though Grand-mère told us to expect only old furniture, I still held out hope for chests full of jewels. Or maybe shelves lined with antique clocks; she said that von Streicher was fond of clocks. What I saw was, indeed, old furniture. Ornately carved tables and chairs, massive bed frames, silk-upholstered settees and chaises, inlaid chests, a few huge paintings, some sculpted garden nymphs, and beautiful but very tall armoires. All of it was heavy, old-fashioned, over-sized and swathed with dust and spiderwebs.

"We could open an antiques store," Antoine quipped.

"No, *mon chèr*," Grand-mère said. "All of this was stolen from French homes by the Nazis. This is not ours to sell."

"It's Miss Havisham's dining room," I said. "All we need is the wedding cake."

"Someone you know, dear?"

"From Dickens. *Great Expectations.*"

"Whoever she was," Antoine said, swiping at a low-hanging web. I wondered, did French schools assign Dickens? Maybe *A Tale of Two Cities*? "If her dining room reminds you of this place, she needed a housekeeper. How did it get so dusty?"

"How many years has it been since you last played down here?" Grand-mère asked him. "Thirty, perhaps?"

"At least."

I lifted the top of a chest inlaid with mother-of-pearl and caught a faint scent of lavender. Inside there was a stack of linens trimmed with handmade lace. I said, "How beautiful."

Grand-mère looked around me to see. She reached in and pulled up a beribboned sachet. "These linens were probably part of a young woman's trousseau. We can only wonder if she lived to spread them on her marriage bed. Or if her young man survived to join her. I hope that doesn't explain why the chest wasn't claimed."

"How very sad," I said, putting an arm around her.

She trained her light on random pieces. "Everything here has a story. The tragedy is, we don't know whose stories they are."

"It's another sort of graveyard," I said.

"Seriously, Grand-mère, what are you going to do with all this?" Antoine asked.

Grand-mère patted his arm. "Leave it for my heirs to figure out."

I was playing my light along the intricately carved whorls of a headboard that was at least ten feet tall. It was beautiful, but ornate to the point of decadence. Many of the pieces in the basement were. And all of them were hand-selected by von Streicher, a humble schoolmaster. I wondered if he thought he could take any of his acquisitions home with him. Could he have had a bedroom large enough to accommodate such a piece? Not many people would. Not then, not now.

"Seen enough?" Grand-mère asked.

I turned to her. "Will you let me film down here?"

"Why would you want to?"

"Because what's here belongs to your story."

She looked to Antoine, who I assumed would one day be in charge of clearing everything out.

"Why not?" he said. "Maybe someone will recognize some of this stuff and come and claim it."

She raised her hands in a what-are-you-going-to-do gesture. "When will you come with your cameras? I'll have it all dusted for you."

"No, no. I want the dust. And the spiderwebs." Something scurried across a far corner. "But if you have some mousetraps, I'll use them."

"I am going to sneeze," she said and headed toward the stairs. "Antoine, please give the keys to your cousin."

He had his flashlight in one hand and the tool he'd picked up in the other. He handed me the tool so he could reach into his pocket for the keys. That's when I got my first look at its business end.

"What is this thing?" I asked, shining my light on it.

He shrugged, as if everyone would know what it was. "It's a mattock."

──19──

"PIERRE," I SAID when he picked up my call. "This is Madame Sherlock Holmes."

"Ah. Maggie MacGowen," he said with a tired little laugh. "How does the detecting progress *chez* Martin?"

"A little too well, I'm afraid. There's something I think you should take a look at."

"Something?"

"A mattock."

"A very common tool," he said.

"So it seems. But this one is marked as property of *l'école du Louvre*, just like the tools we found in Solange Betz's tent. It turned up locked in my grandmother's basement."

There was a long silence broken only when he muttered *putain de merde*. Finally, he asked, "Did you handle it?"

I told him about Antoine using the mattock handle to break through cobwebs. He had given it to me, and that was when I saw the markings. This information did not make Pierre any happier. He said he would come and take a look, but in the meantime, would I please not use it to chop weeds or to crush ice for cocktails. I tried not to laugh at his sarcasm, but I did. And then I asked for a favor.

"When you come to look at the mattock, Pierre, can we please be discreet about why you're here? I don't want to alarm my grandmother or to alert certain people about what's in the basement." Then I told him about Harry and Vincent and my concern about overly eager souvenir hunters. Yes, I was going to film the furniture, but I was not going to disclose its location.

He understood my concern. If this mattock turned out to be the murder weapon, knowing that it was hidden in Grand-mère's basement where possessions that had been stolen by the Nazis were kept would upset his grandmother, as well. After all, she was a party to the original operation also. I told him that we would probably be at Freddy's when he arrived, and that I would have the keys to the basement with me. When he came, he would at least need to come by and say hello, such were the customs of the region. As a cousin of a cousin's cousin by marriage, he was, after all, nearly family. And when he came to the door, I would slip him the keys.

"I'll think of an excuse to be there," he said, adding that he would arrive within the hour.

Freddy greeted Grand-mère, Antoine, and me at the door with *les bises* and glasses of Spanish *rioja*, a very dry wine full of pepper. Leading us toward chairs, he said, "Maggie, I heard you got the historic house tour. Antoine and I never found anything down there that we thought needed to be kept under lock and key, but we were always hopeful."

"Still the same old stuff," Antoine said, dropping into a leather wingback chair. "Just dustier."

Grand-mère glanced nervously toward the open kitchen door, checking to see where Olivia was. After all, she had denied Olivia access to the basement immediately before taking me down. Olivia came out to greet us, stopping first to place little bowls of olives on side tables beside the chairs. I thought she was too nervous about the meal she was preparing to have anything else on her mind. She said her hellos, declined my offer of help, and retreated back into the kitchen.

Freddy wanted to show us some of the marketing ideas for his building project that our Uncle Gérard was working on, so we followed him into the small study off the main salon that he was using as his office. While he was working on the project, Freddy was staying in the house that Isabelle built for the two of them, long after I had been taken to America.

Isabelle's was the smallest of the three houses built inside the compound walls. Grand-mère's rectangular pile of stone, the largest house, was at the far end of the enclosed quadrangle, and the other two faced each other between hers and the gate that led out to the village road. Where the original cider house had been until my great-grandfather burned it to the ground, my Uncle Gérard built a pretentious faux château, planning for the structure to be used one day as the sales office for a grandiose housing project that never got off the ground, fortunately. Antoine, though chagrined by the façade's lavish presentation, currently lived there with his family and Grand-mère Marie.

Isabelle built the third house. After her divorce from Freddy's father, she took down an old carriage house to build her modern, ecologically green pastiche on the design of the original old family home: time and weather had rounded the edges and roughened the surface of the stones in Grand-mère's house; Isabelle's stones were cut to have sharp edges and smooth faces. She used steel where the old house had wood. Her house was the most functional and comfortable of the three, cooled in summer by temperature-activated attic fans and vents, and warmed in winter by radiant heat installed under the floor.

As a child, Freddy had lived in that house with his mother, our mother, so he felt perfectly at home. But I was always a bit uneasy there. Though she was my mother, I had no memories of Isabelle from the brief time I was with her. And from what I had learned about her since her death, I knew that I was better off not remembering. The irony was, because of the arcane French inheritance laws, legally the house was as much mine as it was Freddy's.

I wasn't concentrating on the conversation about Freddy's sales campaign. I'm sure that because a hefty portion of my share of Isabelle's estate was at stake, I should have been paying close attention, but I was too distracted knowing that we were in the room where Isabelle had spent much of her time. If it were up to me, the furnishings, obviously expensive, certainly carefully chosen and well used, would be consigned to the basement with the rest of the ghostly relics.

When I heard the distinctive crunch of a car driving across the graveled compound, I volunteered to go see who it was. I was fairly certain it was Pierre Dauvin, but whoever it was I was grateful for an excuse to leave the room. As soon as the others heard Pierre's voice at the door, they followed, so there was no opportunity to pass him the basement keys without being seen and then needing to explain.

Pierre had come in his own car, and he still wore the same shorts he had on during the baptism party instead of his two-tone blue uniform. To all appearances, this was a friendly visit, not an official one. And he had come up with a good excuse for dropping by: he was returning the platters Grand-mère had lent to his sister for the party that afternoon. He apologized for interrupting so close to dinner time. He would, he said, go put the platters away in Grand-mère's kitchen and be on his way.

Quick visits were unheard of. Freddy insisted that Pierre come in for a drink. It would hardly be polite for him to say no. But first, the platters, Pierre insisted; wouldn't want to have one too many drinks and drop them. Like the eager student in the front row, once again I volunteered, this time to help Pierre because I knew in which cupboard the platters were kept.

The platters were quickly stowed in their places so that we could get to the real business that brought him. On the way through the mudroom, I picked up a couple of flashlights and handed Pierre the ring of household keys.

He walked straight to the cupboard by the back door where the keys usually hung from a nail and opened it. The nail was empty. "This is the main set, then?"

I held up my hands. He seemed to know more about them than I did.

"Anyone had access," he said. "If they knew where to look."

"Apparently, it was no secret."

Holding the back door for me, he said, *"Allons-y."*

He led the way to the basement access. Without fanfare, he pulled on latex gloves, turned the bolt, and pulled the door open, cringing at the squeaky complaint made by the hinges. We did not go through the doorway. With my light, I showed him the mattock resting against the wall next to the door frame where I left it. First he took pictures from several angles. He asked where the tool was when Antoine picked it up, so I pointed out the disturbance in the dust on the floor just a foot further along the wall. Using his flashlight, he studied the floor and the wall, and took more pictures before he pulled a folded plastic bag out of a back pocket, opened it, and collected the mattock. Last, he sealed the bag with red evidence tape and signed his name diagonally across it.

"You'll need to come down to the barracks to give us samples of your fingerprints," he said, closing and locking the door again. He dropped the keys into his pocket. "Tomorrow when you come for your friend's hearing will be soon enough. Tell Antoine to do the same."

We were headed toward Pierre's car when my phone rang. I checked caller I.D. It was Vincent from the war salvage shop I visited on Friday.

"You might want to hear this," I said to Pierre, putting the call on speaker when I connected.

"Vincent?" I said into the phone.

"Righto." There was a moment of silence. "I was, uh, just seeing if maybe you're ready to sort out a deal."

"As I told you," I said. "I don't have anything to deal with."

"You would say, luv, with that wanker Harry looking on. But I think you and me can sort a deal to our mutual benefit, if you know what I mean."

"Not really," I said. "But that doesn't change my answer."

He started to say something but then asked me to hold on, he had another call. Pierre held up his palms, asking what Vincent was talking about.

"He's looking to buy German war artifacts," I said. "Especially firearms."

Pierre scowled.

"Oi, miss." Vincent was back. "What's that your friend is carrying? All wrapped up careful like."

I looked around, and so did Pierre. "Where are you, Vincent?"

"We'll talk later, then?" He hung up.

From somewhere not very far away, I heard a motorcycle rev and speed off, but I saw no one.

Pierre took my phone from my hand as he hit speed dial on his own set. When the call was answered, he opened my call log and read Vincent's number to whoever was on the receiving end. Then he called his barracks and ordered an alert to be sent to all units for a Kawasaki motorcycle headed north away from the estate. He wanted every Kawasaki in the vicinity to be stopped, and for the rider to be identified. If there was anything out of order in the driver's license, bike tags, or proof of ownership, he wanted the rider to be held and the bike to be impounded. Then he ended the call and handed me my phone.

He asked, "Have you found any German artifacts this man might be interested in buying?"

"Not unless he wants a tarnished brass button."

"Does it have a swastika?"

"It does."

"Then you can't sell it," he said with a surprisingly jaunty shrug as he locked the mattock inside his trunk. "I'm sure you found dozens of those buttons in the dirt when you and your grandmother went nighttime digging among the remains. We did. We tossed them into the bags with the bones. Where is yours?"

"My daughter did something with it."

He smiled. "An interesting souvenir of her summer with Grand-mère, yes?"

We hadn't been gone more than fifteen minutes, but Grand-mère opened the front door and came outside to meet us as we walked toward Isabelle's. "I was going to send your brother to search for you."

"We were just talking," I said.

She looked from me to Pierre, and said, "Hmm."

"Madame Martin," Pierre said with a courtly little bow. "I was just informing your granddaughter that she will be asked to testify tomorrow during the arraignment of Madame von Streicher Karl. Nothing to worry about. She only needs to say that she found the woman in her room and had not invited her to be there."

This was news to me. I was glad that Grand-mère was watching Pierre's face and not mine because she would have seen surprise and dismay written all over mine. He offered her his arm and we walked back inside where Freddy plied us with more of that very good Spanish wine.

"Where's Gus tonight?" Freddy offered olives to Pierre to accompany his drink.

"Out with friends," Pierre said. "There's a new video game."

"Well then." Freddy patted Pierre's shoulder. "You'll stay to dinner."

Without waiting for an answer, Freddy went off to tell Olivia that there would be one more at the table. Antoine and Grand-mère got into a crop-related discussion, leaving Pierre and me to entertain each other.

"Pierre," I said, deciding on an opener for a conversation that I hoped would have nothing to do with buried Germans. "Is it common for national police to be assigned to their home towns the way you and Jacqueline Cartier are?"

He shook his head. "No. In fact, effort is made to prevent such an assignment, for reasons I understand only too well. My job would be much easier without the advice of so many grandmothers."

"So, how did you land this assignment?"

He stalled, sipped some wine, looked for a place to deposit an olive pit. But in the end, he decided to answer. "Jacqueline and I were both allowed transfers for reasons of compassion. My wife was ill, she needed constant care for what could be an extended period. And we had a child to think about. Jaqueline is my wife's sister. We both offered our resignations so that Gus and my wife could be with family when we needed them close by. Instead, we were offered posts at the barracks here. It meant a demotion for me, but it has worked out well."

I had met his son, Gus, but never the wife. I was curious, but I hesitated to ask what became of her. He provided the answer, himself.

He lightly touched his fingertips to his temple. "I understand that your husband also died from…"

"Your wife?"

He nodded. Brain tumor, like my Mike.

"I'm sorry," I said. "I didn't know."

He smiled. "Then I overestimate the grandmother information system. A very old system, you know. No network is speedier than their word of mouth."

I had to chuckle. Indeed, there seemed to be very few secrets among this elderly mafia. I asked, "How are you and Gus doing?"

"We feel that a great hole opened up and something wonderful disappeared into it. But we are getting by. I can't say we got over losing her, but we are getting used to the reality that she is not with us any longer." He tipped his head toward me. "And you?"

"That describes the way I feel very well."

"But you have found a new love." The statement sounded more like a question. "It has been five months for me. I figure that I have about seven more months before the grandmothers begin trying to find someone for me. Long before then, however, I will have been posted somewhere far, far away."

"You're leaving?"

"*Bien sûr*. There is nothing keeping me here any longer. Gus will leave to begin his university prep course the first of September," he said. "As for me? I am choosing between wrestling with smugglers in Marseille and becoming an instructor at the national training academy. Either will be fine with me, as long as I never have to investigate another murder."

"After this one?"

He took a deep breath. "Please, God, never again a case like this one."

Olivia came in from the kitchen carrying a large salad bowl and announced dinner. She was a nervous cook, so she wisely kept her meal simple. We were to have a salade Niçoise and pizza made on the backyard grill using a cooking technique she had perfected while camping at remote archeological dig sites. Grand-mère was skeptical, but the pizza was delicious. Olivia had topped a thin crust with soft goat cheese, fresh tomatoes and basil, and finished it with a drizzle of truffle oil. She began to relax when it was clear that the meal was a success.

"So, tell me," I said to her, forking the last sliver of sardine from my salad, "how did you become attached to Freddy's project?"

She glanced at him, shrugged, and said, "This is a designated heritage area, so it was required. There is concern that important historical sites will be paved over, as so many already have. So, every building project of a certain size must have an archeologist on staff during the excavation phase. Freddy applied to the government registry, and my name came up."

"That explains why you're focusing on the sewer trench area," Antoine said. "Otherwise it makes no sense because that land hasn't existed long enough to be covering up anything except old seashells."

"Even so," she said, gesturing with her fork, "there is important information to be discovered. My students have taken core samples of soil every five meters along the progress of the trench. There is an interesting and very old history in this region of farmers harvesting and composting seaweed to create arable soil where there had been nothing but tidal marshland. Study of those samples may show us migration patterns, development of agricultural technology, changes in the regional diet, and so on."

"But no Viducasse remains?" I said.

She laughed. "Not unless they fell overboard. That area was still underwater when the Romans arrived."

"Sounds like tedious work for young people to be very happy about," Grand-mère said.

"You should hear the kids complain," Freddy said. "Grumble, grumble, all day long."

"Of course," Olivia said with a dismissive little shrug. "They all hope to uncover a Viking burial ship or some other holy grail of the profession to pave their way to publication and from there to appointment on a university faculty. But for young graduates in this discipline, in this economy, such an appointment may be as unlikely as finding a Viking ship. By the work we are doing here, I hope to ground my students in the realities of employment in their chosen field. And right now, the best positions available to the majority of them will involve temporary gigs either following behind excavation equipment at building sites or playing the saxophone in the Paris Metro."

Antoine laughed. "I'll counsel my son to aim toward an employable major."

Olivia leaned forward to catch his eye. "I don't intend to discourage my students. I only hope that being forewarned will save them from despair when their fantasy discovery, and therefore life path, never materializes. And for the vast majority, it simply won't."

"Do they get bitter?" I asked.

"They may."

Pierre had been listening intently. "If there are so few positions, even the brightest students must be very competitive with one another. How cutthroat does it get?"

"You mean would they kill each other, *monsieur l'agent?*" After a pause, she said. "Sabotage, *bien sûr*. Murder, no."

At that point, Freddy shifted the conversation to the imminent availability of the swimming pool in his new community center. "Maggie, if the water chemistry is balanced, you'll be able to swim tomorrow afternoon."

I was very happy to hear that. On Monday, after I had sprung Guido from Pierre's lockup and testified at Erika's arraignment, a long, hard swim would be most welcome.

Freddy cleared the table and Olivia brought out a tray of cheese and fruit. The *digestif* was iced Limoncello served in narrow stemmed glasses, the perfect end to a Mediterranean-themed meal. Soon, Grand-mère was nodding off.

"I'll take her home," I said, rising from my chair. Antoine needed to be there when David brought Grand-mère Marie home; she was having dinner with David's parents and my daughter. Pierre said that it was time for him to go as well. He'd had a long day and faced another long day on Monday. All of us had had a long day. We thanked Olivia for the meal and Freddy for the hooch, kissed every cheek, said good night, and were shown out.

At about midpoint in the compound, after another noisy round of good nights, Antoine turned to walk home while Pierre continued with Grand-mère and me all the way to our door. As soon as I had the door open, Grand-mère went straight on inside, announcing that she was going right up to bed. I held back, and so did Pierre. I thought he had something to say, but I spoke first.

"Pierre, Solange Betz kept a notebook about her work this summer."

"Yes, I saw it."

"It's locked up in my studio with her personal things. I wonder if we could take a look at it together."

"If you wish."

We locked the front door and walked through the house and out the back door, headed for the little studio building. There was only a sliver of a moon in a star-filled sky. I flipped on outdoor lights as we passed them; the floodlight over the back door, the low-watt bulbs on strings under the rose arbor, the strong work light beside the grill. The path lights were solar-powered and came on automatically at dusk. When we came around the side of the studio to the front, the shadows were deeper. But there was certainly enough light to know that the studio door gaped open. My first thought was that the interns were inside, but it was too quiet. And then I saw a little palm recorder lying in the dirt next to the door mat.

"Bloody hell," I said, almost afraid to look inside. Pierre put out an arm and held me back. He reached for his belt where ordinarily his sidearm would be. But he had come straight over from cleaning up after the baptism party and was not armed. Cautiously, he peered around the door jamb to look inside before he motioned me forward.

"Take a look, but don't go in," he said, flipping on the light switch with a latex-gloved finger. "Tell me if you can see that anything is missing."

I came around beside him, steeled myself, and looked in. The single room was full of very expensive equipment, from cameras to computers. Drawers and cupboards that didn't have locks stood open and their contents were heaped on the floor, mostly cords and converters and various sorts of jacks and connectors, none of it worth locking up. The middle door of one of the tall steel lockers bolted to the back wall had been crudely broken through and a pair of laptops was missing. Expensive ones, property of the TV network. The thief had made an attempt to open the next locker over, but we'd had heavy-duty combination locks installed on the lockers when we ordered them. To get in, the thief needed to go through the door itself, like opening a can.

Except for the laptops, the camera that was dropped on the way out and two very similar to it that we'd left on a shelf above the work counter, everything seemed to be intact. In a mess, but intact.

"They ran out of time," Pierre said.

"How did they get in?"

"Picked the lock," he said. "Considering what's in here, you should have had a better lock on the door."

"Except for the computers on the counter and the little palm recorders, everything that's valuable is inside those lockers," I told him. "I wanted the interns to be able to get at the equipment they need without having to hunt down the guy with the keys. Or worse, to have multiple key sets floating around to get lost or stolen. The irony is, the key to the front door is under the flower pot beside the mat."

"Any ideas about who did this?" he asked.

"You might give that artifact buyer, Vincent, a call."

"Anyone else?

"Not specifically, but I would like you to take the things we packed up from Solange's tent with you tonight. I planned to ask you what to do with them tomorrow, but since you're here you should take them now."

"Why, Maggie?"

"Because having them around is beginning to worry me," I said. "This idiot, Vincent, and apparently some others including your guest Erika von Streicher Karl, seem to have decided that I have, or know where to find, something that they want very much. But of course, I don't have anything except that button, and even that I can't put my hands on at the moment."

"How does any of that relate to the personal effects of Solange Betz?"

"I can think of half a dozen scenarios, but I know only one thing: she's dead. Is there a connection? That's for you to figure out."

He peeled off his latex gloves and gave them to me to put on. "Touch nothing else, but get them."

I tiptoed in and opened the locker where we had stowed Solange's bags. Everything was as we had left it. I tossed the duffel to Pierre, who remained standing in the doorway, and lifted out the suitcase and the notebook. After closing the locker and twirling the combination lock, I took another look around from that vantage point, saw nothing else missing or amiss, and tiptoed back out carrying the bag so that it wouldn't leave tracks on the floor. When I was outside again, I asked, "What now?"

He shouldered the duffel and pulled up the handle of the case. "Now, while we wait for my people to arrive to take over the crime scene, I would like for you to show me what we came out here to retrieve."

I made tea and we sat at the big kitchen table with Solange's notebook between us. I showed him the two sketches Solange drew of the obelisk-shaped piece of iron Raffi found near the old wall.

"When you searched her tent, did you find anything like this?" I asked him. "I understand that it's about as long as my thumb."

"A small scrap of iron? If I had seen it, I wouldn't have thought it important."

"It was important enough that Solange stole it from another student, a man named Raffi."

"*Oh là*, these academics. The smaller the stakes, the bigger the fight, eh?"

"I don't know how big the stakes are," I said, opening to the pages where Solange had complained about Olivia. "Or how big the fight was. But what I found interesting was that Solange had decided right after she arrived that the area around an old stone wall out in the cow pasture was a far better site to study than the path of Freddy's sewer was. She and Olivia argued about it. I doubt that any rationalization Olivia delivered to her students about getting a dose of reality by doing archeological grunt work at a construction site would have held much sway."

"You don't buy that Olivia was giving them the advantage of a real-world experience?"

"Not for a minute." I refilled his teacup. "Pierre, these are elite graduate students, from a premier university program. Raffi, the kid who found the iron shard, spent last summer working on a Gallo-Roman dig at Rouen. He must have expected something of that caliber here, or he would not have applied. The same for Solange and probably the others. Like Solange, my question is, why are they digging in marsh fill when they expected to be excavating a possible pre-Roman Celtic village?"

"Are they paid for their work?"

"I understand that their living expenses are covered and there is a small stipend. But what they were doing won't advance their research in any way. It's a waste of their time."

"I'll talk to Freddy about the arrangements."

I heard the front door and Casey came into the kitchen.

"Mom, the compound is swarming with cops," she said, taking a mug out of the cupboard. "Oh, hi, Pierre. What's up?"

I told her, "Someone broke into the studio while we were having dinner at Freddy's."

"Oh my God." Though she escalated straight into a flight of teen dramatics, she still managed to fill her mug and sit down. "How awful. Did they trash it?"

"They only managed to get a couple of laptops and two palm recorders." I pushed the tin box of Grand-mère Marie's shortbreads toward her. "I think we may have scared them away before they could do real damage."

She had her phone in her hand and her thumbs ready for action. "Did you see them? Mom, they didn't hurt you, did they?"

"None of the above." Pierre took the phone from her hand and laid it face down on the table. "We aren't releasing any information. No instant messages. Facebook ignored. No comment, *comprenez-vous?*"

"Oh." I thought she seemed disappointed that she couldn't post this bit of news, but she rallied enough to open the tin and eat a cookie.

There was a knock at the back door. Casey started to rise, but Pierre waved her back down into her seat and went to answer. To my great surprise, Zach and Taylor were ushered in by a uniformed *gendarme.* They didn't seem upset, but they did seem perplexed as they walked through the mudroom and into the kitchen.

I gestured for them to come in and sit down. They did, but their police escort hesitated at the kitchen door. *"Capitaine,"* he said, "I located this pair at the brewpub in Périer, recognized them as the kids up on the ladder with cameras on Friday. Will they do?"

"Nicely, Sol," Pierre said. "Good work. Are Jacqueline and Denis set to go in their place?"

"All set."

"Did Jacqueline give you a bag for me?"

"I have it in the car, sir." He came in far enough to put the *gendarme's* version of an American policeman's Sam Browne belt, with holstered sidearm, on the table. "Where do you want me to put your bag?"

"Leave it on Antoine's doorstep," Pierre said. "I'll be staying there tonight."

In the meantime, Casey was serving tea and shortbreads to Taylor and Zach. After Pierre locked the back door behind Sol, it was time for him to answer their questions.

He apologized to my interns for any inconvenience. And he apologized for any embarrassment caused when the police took them away from their friends at the pub before anyone explained why. He told them, "We're imbedding two of our officers in the student camp. They will be staying in your tents until we get things resolved. And you will be staying here as the guests of Madame Martin."

"Does Grand-mère know this?" I asked.

"You'll explain it to her in the morning," he said.

Taylor plucked at her shirt, the one she'd worn all day. "We don't have, like, clothes or anything."

"We'll get your things to you tomorrow sometime," he said. "In the meantime, I am certain that Madame and Mademoiselle Mac-Gowen will do what they can to make you comfortable."

"What happens to us tomorrow?" Zach asked.

"Just go about your work as usual. At the end of the day, you'll come here instead of going to the camp. Understand?"

"And you'll be at Antoine's?" I asked him.

"Tonight, I will."

He gathered Solange's things and left by the front door. After he was gone, there was a quiet moment. Mentally, I was working out sleeping arrangements. I knew from the surveillance tapes at the student camp that Zach and Taylor were sharing a sleeping tent. But they didn't know I knew this, and we were in my grandmother's house and I didn't know what she might have to say about young guests cohabiting in her house. I was still dithering when Casey stepped forward.

"Taylor," she said, "do you want to bunk with me? I can lend you some PJs."

"Thanks, that would be great." Taylor yawned.

My turn: "Zach we'll put you in the room my cousin Bébé uses when he stays here. I think we can find something for you to sleep in. Before you two go to bed, we'll toss your clothes into the washer for you to wear tomorrow. There are new toothbrushes in the top drawer of the hall bathroom upstairs. Help yourselves."

"Okay," Zach said. "But what's this all about?"

"The studio was broken into tonight."

"Oh, my God, no." Taylor looked as if she might topple over, she was so upset. Zach wrapped a supportive arm around her. "All our work? Who? What did they do?"

"Everything is okay, kids," I said, giving her arm a little squeeze. "All they took were a couple of laptops that were in a locker and two palm recorders. They dropped a third recorder on their way out."

"Hold on a sec." Zach reached into the messenger bag he usually carried and took out two palm recorders. "We only have four of these."

This was happy news. "I should have known you two wouldn't go out unequipped. Good. Damn great, actually."

I texted Pierre and told him to take the two missing palm recorders off his list.

Taylor was not ready to be reassured. "They didn't take our photo cards, or flash drives, or—"

"No," I told her. "I think they were looking for something very specific, something other than video equipment. They wasted a lot of time breaking into one of the lockers. When they left, they left in a hurry, and I think they took the laptops they found in the locker just because they were there. They probably scooped the palm recorder off the shelf on the way out and dropped it making a getaway."

"You keep saying 'they,'" Casey said. "But if there were more than one of them, wouldn't they have taken more stuff?"

"Good point," I said.

Zach put the cameras back into his bag. "Unless the other guy was the lookout."

"Let's leave that to Pierre's people." I got up from the table feeling stiff and thoroughly exhausted. "Zach, Taylor, I don't know if this is good news or not, but we won't be able to get into the studio for equipment or editing until the police are finished with it."

Good news, apparently, from the looks they exchanged with each other.

"What's up?" I asked.

"They're burying the German remains tomorrow morning at La Cambe, the German military cemetery near Bayeux," Zach said. "We want to film it."

"Fantastic idea," I said. "Think you can make do with the palm recorders?"

"No problem," Taylor said. "But we don't have wheels."

"We'll figure that out in the morning," I said. "Right now, I'm going to bed."

My phone vibrated. I picked it up, saw the number on the screen and groaned. But I answered.

"Oi," Vincent said. "You called the coppers."

"Damn right I did. You broke into my house."

"Not me, luv," he said. "What'd they get?"

"Not much."

"Good. So before anyone else has a go at it, why don't you and me sort out terms, if you know what I mean."

"Actually, Vincent, I don't know what you mean. What the hell are you guys looking for?"

"You know," he said. "So quit fucking around saying you don't."

—20—

THE FIRST QUESTION the hearing judge asked me Monday morning was to state my full name, for the record.

"My entire name?" I asked.

He said yes without looking up from the papers on the table in front of him. He was about my age, forty-something. Renée told me that he presided over hearings of this sort in a different village every day of the week, and that he was not a local. It was only Monday morning, but already he looked as if he'd had a long day. There was no courthouse in the village, so the proceedings were being held in a large conference room in the *mairie*. And because the setting was casual, there were no robes or white scarves. The judge, Renée Ferraro the prosecutor, and the defense attorneys representing the suspects waiting in the next room to hear the charges against them, all wore ordinary business suits.

Guido's case was the first up. He sat with his *avocat*, his French lawyer, at the next table over from me.

The judge finally looked up and seemed to join the proceedings. "Madame?"

I took a breath and began. "My full legal name is Marguerite Eugènie Louise-Marie Duchamps MacGowen Flint."

He smiled, leaned over to the court reporter sitting next to him and asked him, "Did you get that?"

"Oui," the reporter answered with a sardonic little smile of his own.

"And how shall we address you, madame?" the judge asked.

"I usually answer to Maggie MacGowen."

Again he referred to the paper atop the stack on the table in front of him. "Maggie MacGowen, are you acquainted with Monsieur Guido Patrini, seated at the table to your right?"

"I am."

"For what duration?"

"About twenty years."

"In what capacity?"

"We work together."

"Madame MacGowen, do you attest before this court that Guido Patrini is a man of good character?"

"I do," I said.

"Monsieur Patrini," he looked at Guido over the top of his glasses. "As there is no charge filed against you, you are herewith released from the custody of this court."

The judge tapped the table with the end of his pen in lieu of a gavel, and announced the next case.

Guido and his lawyer, Étienne Moss, rose from their seats and I rose to follow them. At the rear of the room, Guido kissed my cheek and thanked me for supporting him.

"I know you have to stay for the next case," he said. "But I'm getting the hell out of here before the judge changes his mind."

Guido walked out, but Moss, the local *avocat* referred by a friend of Jean-Paul, stayed. He ushered me to a seat in the spectator section among weeping mothers and wives who were waiting for their loved ones to be arraigned before the judge. Moss took a seat next to me, sticking close. I knew Jean-Paul had a hand in that, and I was grateful.

Erika was led in from the next room looking like someone dragged in from a homeless camp. Her long gray hair hung in greasy hanks and she still wore the same dress she had on when I found her in my bedroom Sunday morning. There was no facility for holding women overnight at the local *gendarme* barracks, so she had been taken to St-Lô overnight and driven back early that morning to appear at her arraignment. I doubted she'd gotten much sleep.

A young policewoman walked her to the chair Guido had recently vacated and sat her down. I assumed that the gray-haired woman who took the chair next to her was her lawyer. They bent their heads together and I wondered if this whispered conference was their first meeting.

Someone seated in the row behind me leaned forward and rested his elbows on the back of the chair next to mine.

"Oi, Miss Hollywood Star. Fancy running into you here."

I turned my best scowl on Harry, the collector of war salvage this-and-that. I said, "Why am I not surprised to see you here?"

He flicked his chin toward Erika. "Can't wait to hear what the old girl has to say, huh?"

"Do you know her?"

"We've talked," he said. "It's time for us to talk again."

The judge tapped his pen on the table, calling the court back into session, and all conversation stopped. Harry leaned back into his own seat. Next to me, Moss was sending a text on his mobile to Jean-Paul. He had snapped a photo of Harry.

The judge asked the prosecutor to state the charges being filed against the defendant. Renée Ferraro rose and read them aloud:

Criminal trespass of a private residence, burglary of an inhabited structure, brandishing Nazi paraphernalia or images at a public meeting or gathering. The charges were repeated for Erika in German. When she was asked if she understood the charges, her lawyer answered that she did, though Erika sat as still as stone as Renée listed her offenses.

Erika was asked to identify herself, and to give both her legal place of residence and her local place of residence. That last caused a little ripple through the room when she said that she supposed her local address was the jail in St-Lô.

Renée was called to the judge's table for a conference. Étienne Moss took that opportunity to explain to me that the last charge was tacked on because of the photographs of her father in Nazi uniform that Erika had shown around at the Saturday market. It was a bogus charge, he said, but it was there to allow the prosecutor to get information about Erika's purpose for being in the area into the record.

I saw Ma Mère slip in through a side door and take a seat at the far end. She caught my eye and gave me a little smile. When I thought about it, I was surprised that she had come.

"Call the first witness," the judge intoned. Renée motioned me back to the same chair at the front table where I'd sat before. Moss came with me and took the chair beside mine.

"You again," the judge said, pulling his glasses further down his nose to look at me. "It pains me to do so, but I must ask you state your full name for the court."

Before I could speak, though, he held up a finger for me to wait. Then he asked the court reporter if he had sufficient paper. When he got the little twitter of laughter from the crowd that he apparently was after, he nodded at me. "Madame?"

Before I began, I looked for Ma Mère because she was among those responsible for the long string of names I had to carry through life. She put her fingertips to her lips and blew me a kiss.

I said, again, "My full name is Marguerite Eugènie Louise-Marie Duchamps MacGowen Flint."

"Phew," the judge said for the crowd's benefit. "*Madame le procureur*, please proceed with this witness."

Renée stood to one side of the open area between the judge's table and mine, the area that would be the well of the court in a formal courtroom, and read her questions off an electronic pad.

"Madame MacGowen," she began, "are you familiar with the prisoner seated to your right?"

"I am."

"Old friends?"

"Not friends at all."

"What is the circumstance of your acquaintance?"

The judge leaned forward and addressed me. "This is an arraignment hearing, madame. Our goal is to determine whether the charges filed have sufficient merit to bring Madame Erika Karl to trial. In your answers, I would like for you to feel free to answer fully. What our prosecutor is asking you, one little drop at a time, is, how is it that you came to know Madame Karl? Please, start at the beginning."

He sat back and Renée, chastised by the judge's comment, nodded at me to go ahead.

Moss patted my hand, I took a deep breath, and began.

"I first became aware of Madame Karl on Friday morning of last week," I said. "She left a note on my grandmother's door relating that she had learned of the German war remains that were discovered near my family's carrot field Thursday. She said that her father had lived in our home during the war and had spoken fondly of the place. He went missing during the war. She asked for permission to come calling."

"Was she then invited into your home?" Renée asked.

"Absolutely not," I said, trying to keep the heat out of my voice. "Madame Karl's father was Major Horst von Streicher, the commanding officer of a platoon of German SS Occupation troops that commandeered my family's home during the war and put them into forced labor. My grandmother wanted no contact with her Nazi occupier's daughter. But Madame Karl began to hang around the estate, uninvited. Saturday morning when my grandmother was working in her garden we saw Madame Karl sitting outside the garden gate."

"What was she doing there?"

"Weeping."

"Weeping?"

"Sitting and weeping."

"Did you speak with her then?"

"No," I said. "The first time I spoke with her was later at the market in the village. Madame Karl was showing photos of her father in his full Nazi uniform to various elderly people at the market, asking them if they knew her father. As it happens, some people did. One of the vendors slapped Madame Karl's face. Another tore up the photos and spat on them. I thought that someone needed to get Madame Karl away from the immediate area before the situation escalated, so I took her by the arm and walked her to a place where the crowd would not see her. She told me then that she was only trying to find out what happened to her father. She pleaded with me to ask my grandmother for permission to see the house where he was last known to be alive."

"Your grandmother is Élodie Martin?"

"Yes."

"Did you ask Madame Martin if she would speak with Madame Karl?"

"I told Grand-mère what happened at the market. She told me that she would not speak with Madame Karl because what she would have to tell her, no child should know about her father."

"Your grandmother said that?" the judge asked.

"She did."

He scribbled a note while Renée asked her next question.

"Did you see Madame Karl again after the Saturday market?"

"Yes. On Sunday morning after church I came home and found her standing in the middle of my bedroom."

"Had you invited her into your home?"

"No one invited her in. What really alarmed me was that my ninety-two-year-old grandmother arrived home an hour before I did, and was alone in the house while Madame Karl was upstairs searching around."

The judge was eyeing Erika over the top of his glasses, trying to reconcile my story with the bedraggled woman sitting in front of him. I wondered if she had made herself look as unkempt as she did that morning as a ploy to present herself as more dotty and harmless than she was.

Renée asked, "At some point Sunday morning, did your grandmother encounter Madame Karl?"

"She did. I called the police and walked Madame Karl downstairs to wait for them outside, hoping my grandmother would be spared. But Grand-mère saw her. Madame Karl begged my grandmother to tell her what she knew about Major von Streicher, whom she described in idyllic terms. Grand-mère decided to set her straight about her father's character."

Renée held out a hand as an invitation for me to elaborate. First I checked on Ma Mère. When she gave me an encouraging nod, I began.

"My grandmother told Madame Karl the many ways that Major von Streicher had abused the power bestowed upon him by the Nazis. Grand-mère called him a thief, a martinet, and a rapist. And then my grandmother told Madame Karl how she slit the major's throat with a pruning knife."

"And killed him?" the judge asked, eyes wide.

"If that didn't kill him, the bullet Grand-mère put in his chest immediately after did."

"Was there a precipitating event for that act?" he asked, brow deeply furrowed.

"It happened during the war," I said. "Von Streicher was an enemy combatant. As if that weren't reason enough, Grand-mère walked in on von Streicher as he initiated the rape of a fifteen-year-old girl. Grand-mère stopped him."

The judge, transfixed, muttered, *"Mon dieu."*

Erika dropped her head into her arms and wept. Ma Mère crossed herself.

"What happened next, madame?" the judge asked.

"The police came and took Madame Karl into custody."

"Yes, yes," he said impatiently. "But what happened next with your grandmother and Major von Streicher?"

"She dug a hole in the turnip field and buried him."

The courtroom crowd erupted and the judge pounded the table with his fist to quiet them. When order was restored, he asked me, "Is von Streicher still in the turnip field?"

"The field is planted in carrots at the moment. But, no. His remains were discovered on Thursday." I looked at the clock on the wall behind the judge. "Just about now, volunteers from the German *Volksbund* should be putting what's left of Major von Streicher into an unmarked grave at La Cambe military cemetery."

"Ah, yes. The carrot field." The lightbulbs seemed to come on. "He was not the only Nazi buried under those turnips, then, was he?"

"No, sir. There were sixteen others."

He turned to Renée. "You are finished with this witness, yes? I want to hear what Madame Karl has to say for herself."

A brief recess was called so that Erika could pull herself together. She blew her nose and tossed back a small brandy her lawyer provided to her. I went back into the spectator section, choosing a seat as far away from Harry as I could. He skewed around and waved to get my attention. In a stage whisper that the entire court must have heard, he said, "Now it comes, aye? You just get ready."

After a conference with the judge, Renée resumed her place. "Madame Karl, will you explain to the court how you came to be inside the Martin home on Sunday morning?"

"I needed to get something," she said.

"And what was that?"

"Some personal property that belonged to my father," she said. "I thought that while everyone was away at a party no one would mind if I just popped in and got it."

"Are you a friend of the Martin family?"

Erika turned in her seat and searched the room until she found me. Facing forward again, she said, "No."

"Did any member of the Martin family invite you into their home or give you permission to retrieve this property?"

"No."

"You are from Germany, are you not?"

"I am."

"Is it customary in Germany for people to pop into stranger's homes uninvited to retrieve items?"

"No, it isn't."

"What do you call that sort of activity in Germany?"

"*Einbruch.*"

"That means burglary, correct?"

"Yes."

"What happens when burglars are caught in Germany?"

"They go to prison."

Renée turned to the judge. "I am finished with this witness."

He nodded, but he was watching Erika closely. "Tell me, Madame Karl, exactly what were you looking for?"

"A box." She held her hands as if she were holding something about the size of a shoebox. "My father put it under the floor in his room to keep it safe so he could bring it home to us."

"And what was in the box, pray tell?"

She hesitated. Then in a tiny voice that was barely audible at the back of the room, she said, "Gold rings and watches."

"Your father brought this box of gold rings and watches with him to France from Germany?"

"No," she said, squaring her shoulders and looking him in the eye. "He acquired them during the war."

"He told you where to find this box?"

"He wrote to my mother about it," she said. "After the war, whenever life seemed too harsh for my brother and me to bear, my mother would tell us about the treasure that our father had hidden away for us. She would promise that as soon as we could, we would go get it. And then everything would be as it had been before the war was lost."

That did it for the judge. The room had erupted again but he paid no attention to the chatter. He said, "Prisoner is to be held on remand, no bail. A trial date will be set by the master of the court. Officers, please take Madame Karl in charge. Next case, please."

Étienne Moss took my elbow and we rose to leave. On the way out, I spotted Paulette and Henry Matson among the crowd with their heads bent close together, deep in conversation. I didn't stop to speak with them, or with anyone, but continued on until we were outside in the sunshine.

"What will happen to her?" I asked Moss as we walked briskly away from the *mairie*.

One of his shoulders went up, a twitch more than a shrug, the French version of an American saying "Um" while he thought. "Most likely, she'll be put into the charge of her consulate and invited out of the country. But first, she'll probably need to sign a pledge never to return. In exchange, the case will not come to trial. After all, she took nothing and did no damage."

"That's probably the best solution," I said, offering him my hand. "Thank you for staying for the hearing."

"My pleasure," he said with a little bow, just a slight bend from the waist, but a courtly gesture nonetheless.

Still holding on to his hand, I asked, "How do you know Jean-Paul Bernard?"

That shoulder twitch again. "He was a university classmate of my older brother. Do say hello for me. And tell him that Suzanne and I will expect the two of you to come for dinner very soon."

Knowing Jean-Paul as I did, I had expected the answer to be something in that vein. We said our good-byes and I started off toward the *café tabac* where Guido texted that he was waiting for me. I was about halfway there when the Matsons caught up with me.

"Maggie," Paulette said, a bit breathless as she slipped her hand around my arm and walked along close beside me. "What a story! And what a crazy woman."

"Double that." Henry had her other arm. "I think that both she and her brother, the count, must live in fantasy land. Quite the pair. After hearing what that woman had to say, I wonder if our count actually believes that his title is legitimate."

"I've been humming 'Somewhere over the Rainbow,' ever since her big finish." Paulette leaned her head closer to mine. "So, do you think there really is a box of gold stashed under the floor in your grandmother's house?"

"No. It would have been found during the big remodel fifty years ago," I said. "Though no one would have been surprised if something like that had turned up. Major von Streicher stole all sorts of things, including a houseful of furniture. After the war, my grandparents and the priest cleared his loot out of their house and did their best to return all of it to the original owners."

"So tragic for so many people," she said with an angry shake of her head. "I suppose the man got what was coming to him, but holy Jesus, Mary, and Joseph it took some balls for your grandmother to do what she did to him. I only hope that in the right circumstance I would have the fortitude to do what she did."

"Honey," Henry said, "I have no doubt that in a battle of the *cojones*, you would come out on top."

She paused to think about that for a moment, and then she let loose her big, American laugh. I thought that poor Henry would melt with pure joy just hearing it.

Still smiling, Paulette leaned forward to catch Henry's eye. "Well, my prince, I think it's just about time for you to summon the coachman and carry me away."

"Where are you two off to next?" I asked.

"Saigon," Henry said. "Not for fun this time, just business."

"I enjoyed meeting you," I said. "Have a safe trip."

Paulette gave my arm a squeeze. "Don't think you've seen the last of us."

"I hope not."

We managed to pull off a round of *les bises* as if it were perfectly natural for us to do so. With a last wave, they headed off toward the car park behind the *mairie* and I continued on my way toward the *café* to meet Guido. Before I went inside, I found a shady spot and called Jean-Paul.

"I like your friend Étienne Moss," I said.

"He's good at what he does. Tell me about the hearings."

"Guido was sprung, as expected." We went over the testimony during Erika's arraignment, but I had the feeling that he already knew the essentials. "Moss thinks she'll be sent home with a warning. I expected her consul to be there. Maybe I missed him."

"No, he wasn't there," Jean-Paul said. "Ordinarily in a case where there was no actual damage, a woman of a certain age and with a clean record, like her, would be reprimanded and turned over to her consul, who would put her on an airplane home. But Germany is very sensitive about its image, especially when there is any reference to its Nazi past. And while France loves tourist dollars, it does not encourage tourists from Germany who are openly interested in nostalgic pilgrimages into Papa's World War Two stomping grounds."

"Stomping grounds is a descriptive word choice," I said. "So, the German consulate left Erika to twist in the wind?"

"If that means what it sounds like, yes," he said. "It was decided that the best way to make her cease and desist would be to allow an open airing of not only her reprehensible behavior, but also that of her sainted father. Let the public stone her in a metaphoric sense."

"And then put her on a plane headed home," I said.

"Exactly," he said. "Do you think she got the message today?"

"I don't know. I'll be happy when her plane leaves French air space. So, tell me about your day," I said. "Are you at lunch?"

"I'm lying on a beach with a mai tai resting on my bare belly."

"Interesting image," I said.

"I lied. But if I lean way out I can see a bit of water. Or is that just a puddle on the pavement below my hotel?"

"Where are you?"

"Paris still," he said. "Maggie, I've been offered an interesting position. But before I accept, you and I need to talk."

"Do we?"

"Don't tease, *chérie*. My poor heart won't take it; I haven't had lunch yet."

"I'm all ears." Actually, I was all nerves. When someone says, "We need to talk," something damn serious usually follows.

"Not on the telephone," he said. "I will need all the weapons in my arsenal for this particular discussion: dimples, boyish charm, maybe a little pout if things don't go my way."

"Your only dimples are on your backside."

"Be warned, I will launch them if necessary."

"When will this launch take place?"

"Maybe tonight. I'll call when I know."

My hands actually shook when I put the phone away. Was I

ready for this conversation? Feeling the need for a bracer, my first stop when I went inside the *café* was at the zinc-topped bar for a *petit blanc*, a short glass of wine. I slugged it back the way the locals did, letting it hit the back of my throat without landing on a single taste bud until I exhaled the fumes afterward. I suppose that it's the shock of the alcohol hitting bottom all at once that steadies the nerves.

After a few deep breaths, I went in search of my old friend, Guido. I found him drinking coffee and reading his Mickey Spillane novel at a table in a far corner, next to a window that looked out onto the street. The duffel bag we had taken to him at the barracks was on the floor next to his chair.

"Fine literature?" I asked, pulling out a chair. I waved at Clothilde, the proprietress. She set a demi-tasse in front of me filled with coffee so dark I swear the spoon could stand on its own.

"That'll put hair on your chest," Guido said, laying the book aside.

We spent the next hour filling each other in. It had only been three days since he was picked up by the police, but so much had happened that it felt like a month had gone by.

His first question was, "Do you want me to pack up and fly home?"

"I hope you don't want to go, Guido. We're so far behind and now with everything shut down because of the break-in, we're pushed back even further. I can't finish this film without you."

"Seriously?" he said. "You want me to stay?"

"Seriously." I nudged his hand with my fist. "Though I must say that the interns have really stepped into the breach. They've taken enough background footage that we could junk all this serious shit we've filmed so far and make a really hot film about the summer scene in Normandy. Zach's bikini shots alone would sell it."

He laughed. "Okay, we're back. What's first?"

"Know where we can get some decent video cameras?"

"There's an electronics store over in Pérrier."

I held up Jean-Paul's keys and gave them a shake. "We have wheels. Let's go do it."

He looked at his watch. "Lunch first, okay?"

I called Grand-mère and told her that I had Guido with me and that we would be eating in the village. She thought it was just as well that we were. The police had made the entire backyard off limits so lunch would be served to the workers and students in the dining room of Freddy's community center. She and Grand-mère Marie would have lunch at Julie and Jacques Breton's house.

The local word-of-mouth information service had already given her all the gory details from Erika's arraignment. I apologized for testifying in public that she had slit von Streicher's throat, but she promised that it didn't matter. After all, she said, I had already filmed her talking about the same incident, but in far greater detail than I had revealed to the judge, and that film would be broadcast to the public soon enough.

There were only two restaurants in the village center. My favorite was on the ground floor of the only hotel in town, a workingman's hotel that offered long-term guests a package deal that included lunch and dinner. The restaurant off the lobby was open to the public. All meals were served family-style at long tables, and just like home, everyone who sat down was served the same meal. It was always surprisingly good and surprisingly cheap, and the dining experience there had a certain earthy charm about it. You never knew who would sit down next to you.

The lunch fare posted on the board outside was rosemary-roasted chicken and fried potatoes, so we went inside and found seats among the mix of working men, village locals, and tourists. If the food was simple, the mix of languages and conversational topics was rich.

A man with a florid face and a too-tight collar reached past me for the carafe of red wine on the table in front of Guido. He pulled a well-read newspaper out from under the edge of his plate and slapped it with the back of his hand to show us an article about Chinese imports.

"You see how it is?" he said, washing down a mouthful of food with wine. He told us he was a salesman for a company that made knives and scissors. At one time the factory and corporate headquarters were in Germany and he reported to a French supervisor in Lille. But now the factory was in China, his boss was English working from an office in Brussels, and the company's headquarters were in Singapore. He complained that he was no longer treated like a valuable asset, but had become an easily replaceable cog in a huge machine. Worst of all, the product he now had to sell was crap. And so on.

Of course, this conversation was entirely in French so Guido understood virtually none of it. But he responded to the tone of the man's voice, nodded during pauses, and *tsk*'d when the man *tsk*'d. When the man finished his lunch, he complimented Guido on his grasp of the problem, shook his hand, saluted me and went on his way.

"What was that about?" Guido asked me.

"Do you really want to know?"

"Probably not." He scooted a little closer to ask, "Anything new on Solange?"

"If there is, I wouldn't know. Antoine told me that all of the students were questioned individually, but Pierre isn't sharing his thoughts. Not with me anyway."

I retrieved the wine carafe and refilled our glasses. "I have a hunch, though, that Pierre is using the break-in at our studio as an excuse to move his officers onto the estate because he's closing in on a suspect or he's worried something else will happen. Last night, he imbedded two officers in the student camp. He wanted them staying in the tents, so he moved Taylor and Zach into Grand-mère's with us. Get up early, my friend, because you can expect a line for the hall bathroom."

"So that's what Jacqueline was up to," he said. "She came in last night dressed in jeans, with her hair in a long braid. I thought she was headed for a barbecue or something with this other officer who was dressed in shorts and old sneakers. But she picked up a uniform for Pierre and headed out again. I wondered if she was going under-cover. Is she at the camp?"

"She is."

He leaned in close. "She and Pierre are really tight, you know. I think there's something going on with them."

"There is," I said. "But it's not what you're thinking. She's his sister-in-law."

That cheered him up. "So, she's single?"

"Guido." I took a deep breath. "Give it a rest, huh? Could you wait until you've been out of the slam for maybe a full day before you get yourself into something?"

"No harm in asking."

Lunch taken care of, we got up to leave. Through the door into the adjoining bar, I saw a familiar Hawaiian shirt. I took Guido by the arm and led him in.

"Oi, Harry," I said, perching on the stool next to his; Guido stood beside me, leaning an elbow on the bar. "Things turn out the way you expected today?"

"What a bunch of bollocks, huh?" He looked Guido up and down. "The old bird promised me she had something really big, gold worth half a mill easy, she tells me. Antique jewelry. But what does it turn out to be? Some crappy little box full of wedding rings this bloody Nazi ripped off the fingers of war widows. I like a good deal when I can get it, sure. But I have my limits. And something like that? Makes my blood curdle, I tell you. Makes my blood curdle."

"Did she ever offer you any proof that the gold existed?"

He reached into his pocket and pulled out a folded envelope, which he dropped onto the bar in front of me. "Treasure map, she said. She neglected to tell me she had no access to the house on the map. Another cock-up for Harry."

I picked up the envelope and took out a photocopy of a letter written in German, addressed to Frau Streicher. Neither Guido nor I speaks much more German than we need to order a couple of beers and a sausage, so the hand-written text meant nothing to us. But the diagram of the upper floor of my grandmother's house was clear enough. The date on the top of the letter was January, 1944, so the diagram did not include the alterations my grandparents had made to the house after the war. But by following the map a person could still find his way to the spot marked by a star in a corner of my bedroom.

I slipped the letter into my pocket without bothering to ask if I could keep it. "What now for you, Harry?"

He shrugged as he signaled for another shot of scotch. "I stay at it. There's always another deal down the road. You just have to keep your options open. I learned my lesson though. I'll never give anyone a finder's fee up front again."

"You gave Erika Karl money?"

"For travel expenses," he said. "But never again."

I slid off the stool and started to leave, but turned back.

"Harry, does your friend Vincent know you were expecting to get gold, and not maybe German weapons?"

"In the first place, that cockhead is not my friend, so get that straight. He's just another bloke out there looking for this and that to buy and sell. Except he has that shop up there near where tourists coming to see the invasion beaches can't miss it. The farmers up around there know they can take the war junk they dig up out of their fields over to Vincent and he might buy it from them. Now and then he takes a special order from a collector and puts out the word. Right now he's got a buyer looking for old firearms in top condition, offering top price for them."

"He seems to think I have something he wants," I said.

"Well, you can lay blame for that on the crazy lady. That's where I met her, in Vincent's shop, where I met you just a day later." He tossed back his scotch and tapped the counter asking for another. "Not much of a coincidence if you think about it. Vincent has the biggest signs on the road and he's the first shop you come to when you get out of Caen headed toward the beaches."

"Okay, but why can I blame the crazy lady for having Vincent on my back?"

"So, she comes into the shop end of last week when I happen to be there looking for old aircraft parts, and she asks if Vincent would be interested in some stuff her father put away during the war. She says she hasn't inventoried it yet—that was her word, inventoried—but it was quite substantial, she said, and it hadn't seen light of day since the war. She said there would be antique gold jewelry and there would be military stores, meaning firearms to me. So me and Vincent say, sure we're interested. Later, the two of us divide things up. I'll check out the gold and leave him the firearms."

"There are no firearms," I said. "If you talk to Vincent, I'd appreciate if you passed that along to him."

"Well here's some news: there's no gold either. Not anything that I'd have truck with, anyway." He wrapped his fist around his new drink. "Now bugger off. I'm going to get seriously pissed."

Jean-Paul's car was still in the lot behind the *mairie*. As we came out of the hotel, I heard a motorcycle speed off down the side street.

"Nice," Guido said, straining to get a look at the motorcycle. "A Kawasaki."

—21—

"THE FLOOR IN your bedroom was never touched during the renovation," Grand-mère said, looking from von Streicher's handdrawn map to the corner of my bedroom that corresponded to the star on the drawing. "Nothing was done to this room, except that your grandfather cut a door in the wall for access into the old nursery next door when he converted it into a bathroom."

"Then maybe there actually is something under the floor," I said.

"Merde," she sighed, handing von Streicher's letter back to me. "What does the letter say?"

"Jean-Paul found someone who could read it for me. The letter is the usual miss you, love, kisses to the children wartime stuff. But von Streicher also says that he will try to send more to his wife. He doesn't say more what, but he admonishes her to bargain more aggressively than she has in the past because it's difficult to get packages through, especially now that the Allies are dropping bombs on Germany."

"I wonder what he sent her."

"Grand-mère, may I take up the floor in my room?"

"Of course. I'll call Antoine to bring some tools."

"And I'll call Pierre," I said. She started to protest, but in the end she didn't.

I crossed the hall and roused Guido from his nap. When he came to the door, I said, "Grab your new camera, matey, it's show time."

Guido and I pushed all of the furniture in my room against one wall to give Antoine and Pierre more room when they came with tools. When we moved the bed, we found a tire iron on the floor.

"You have a Luger in your drawer," Guido said, looking at the tire iron. "Why do you need a tire iron under your bed?"

"I didn't put it there, but I have an idea who might have. Don't touch it. There might be prints."

"Whose?"

"Erika von Streicher Karl's. She was in here, I told you, on Sunday. I have a feeling that we interrupted her before she could get at the floor."

"She could have swung that thing at your head, Maggie," he said with sincere concern.

"We never got within her striking range."

The tire-iron discovery slowed the start on the floor demolition for a few minutes. Pierre dutifully dropped it into an evidence bag, but he said there wasn't much point in sending it for prints. Erika was on her way to Orly Airport and, if her flight was on time, she would be out of the country before any results came back. He set the tire iron inside the armoire to get it out of the way and set to work with Antoine lifting planks of the old, and very solid, oak floor.

Guido brought a stepladder up from the kitchen. Standing on the top rung with one of the new video cameras on his shoulder, and a happy grin on his face, he recorded the proceedings.

I stood to the side with Grand-mère to watch. Like serving the first slice from a pie, it took a lot of finesse for Antoine to remove the first plank without damaging it. After the first plank was up, its neighbors came more easily.

Pierre, on his knees beside Antoine, turned to look up at me. "Maggie, that man who was calling you, Vincent something. I asked a colleague from the Caen barracks to send some officers out to search his shop. I wanted them to shake him up a bit, let him know that they were keeping an eye on him for illegal firearms sales as well as contraband Nazi paraphernalia."

"Thank you," I said. "I hope that scares him off."

"Don't thank me. Before they arrived, Vincent had already been taken in for interrogation by the D.G.S.E. When the anti-terrorist unit comes for you and asks questions about ordnance and weapons, you know you're in trouble."

"Fancy that." I saw the hand of Jean-Paul Bernard at work. Just who did he know in the anti-terror organization that he could call and get such a service provided? In more than a few ways, his network of connections was just a little bit scary. Useful, but scary.

All of the planks in the area the map seemed to mark were up and neatly stacked against the wall. Antoine sat back on his haunches and looked over at Grand-mère. Shaking his head, he said, "Sorry, nothing here."

She went over for a closer look into the opened space under the floor, as did I. There was a tiny scrap of paper caught on a nail. I bent down and pried it loose. Hand printed, I could make out the number fourteen, and part of a word: *taschenu.* I typed the word fragment into the search engine on my phone.

"I think it said pocket watch," I said. "Fourteen pocket watches."

"Antoine," Grand-mère said. "Pull up some more floor, please."

Two planks further, a floor board, though tightly fitted, wasn't tacked down. Antoine pulled it up and the edge of a box appeared. Grand-mère had to sit down on the edge of the bed when she saw it. I sat beside her and put my arm around her as we watched Antoine and Pierre pull up another plank, a second loose one, so that they could get the box out of the space between the joists.

Guido came down from his stepladder and leaned over Pierre's shoulder for a close-in shot as Pierre, wearing latex gloves, pulled the box out from its nest under the floor and turned it over to look at it from all sides, rattling the contents. The box was made of heavy metal painted light brown, longer than it was deep, with a hinged lid and a wire fastener. On the sides, a series of numbers and letters and a German eagle were stenciled in black.

"It's an ammo can," Pierre said. "It was meant to transport Luger shells."

"Bring it up here to me." Grand-mère patted the bed beside her. She reached toward the wire latch to open the box, but her hands shook. In the end, she asked me to open it. I folded the lid back on its hinges and we all leant in for a look.

A jumble of gold rings and gold pocket watches glimmered in the light from Guido's camera. I reached in and took out a plain gold band that was so worn that the back was no thicker than a fine wire. With a gasp that was nearly a sob, Grand-mère took the ring from my hand and slipped it onto her finger.

"That despicable beast," she murmured. "Whose precious ring did he steal?"

"During the war, everyone was required to turn in their gold," Antoine said.

"True," she said, plucking another ring, one with a small stone, out of the jumble. "But the gold was intended to be used for Germany's foreign trade, not to buy potatoes for Madame von Streicher or music lessons for her children."

Carefully, she upended the can onto the bed and spread out the contents. Some of the rings had inscriptions inside the bands, but most did not. Antoine opened watch cases, looking for inscriptions that might identify the owners.

"What will we do with this, Grand-mère?" Antoine asked.

"If we can identify any of the owners, we'll return what we can. For the rest, I'll call Gaston and Ma Mère. They'll know what to do."

"What do you think all that's worth?" Guido asked.

Pierre shrugged. "A few thousands at the most. Hardly worth that woman's efforts."

Guido was on his knees behind Grand-mère, shooting down over her shoulder at the array of gold. Antoine's brow furrowed as he watched my partner work. He said, "Grand-mère, does that camera bother you?"

She leaned to the side to get a better look at what Guido was doing. Then she shrugged and told Antoine, "The camera is just fine, dear. People should see this. Fear enabled that man's corruption. If we don't take him out of the dark and expose him for the cheap, venal tyrant he was, then men like him will always have the power to make us afraid."

She looked back at Guido again. "How do you say it when you have to ring a bell to cover bad language on television?"

"Bleep," he said.

She laughed. "Maggie, my dear, you may have to bleep my words, but I say piss on that pissant von Streicher."

"What is all this, then?" Jean-Paul appeared at the door wearing a beautifully tailored suit and a perfect red tie. His overnight bag was at his feet. "What have I missed?"

"A treasure hunt." I went over to him for a better kiss than the glancing pecks of *la bise*. I took him by the hand to show him what we had discovered.

"So, it exists." He picked up a watch and opened the cover, read the inscription, and sighed. "A larger fortune in imagination, perhaps, than in reality. But the marvel is that it does, in fact, exist."

"That reminds me. Pierre," I said to get his attention. "Erika Karl apparently told the two dealers who have been such a nuisance, Harry and Vincent, that there was half a million in gold here. We know of course that there isn't. But she also said that there were military stores in pristine condition that have been hidden away since the war. The two collectors interpreted her to mean firearms. So, as Jean-Paul said, we've found that a cache of gold does exist. But what about the other? Can there be weapons stashed somewhere?"

Pierre looked at Antoine. They both shrugged. Antoine spoke first.

"Grand-mère, shall we pull up the entire floor?"

"Merde," was her response.

Jean-Paul spoke up. "Pierre, do you have access to a metal detector?"

He did. He made a call and within half an hour an officer was lugging the necessary equipment up the stairs. First, they put the empty ammo can back between the floor joists where it had been found, and then laid loose planks over it to see how the metal detector would register. When the base line was established, the detector was run over the rest of the floor. I think that we all stood at once when the metal detector signaled that it had found something. Again, there was a floor board that was tightly fitted but not tacked in place. Antoine pulled it up and underneath, wrapped in an oiled cloth, was a pristine Luger and three boxes of bullets.

Pierre laid claim to the Luger immediately and sent us all out of the room because the gunpowder in the ammunition was old and probably unstable and could explode in unpredictable ways if moved. He called in an explosives removal team from the barracks at Carentan to come and get it. Ignoring the tire iron in the armoire for the moment, Pierre scooped the rings and watches, shimmering on the bed in the sunlight from the windows, back into their box, and sealed the box in an evidence bag. When he turned to leave the room, he seemed surprised that we all still stood there, watching him.

"Allez, allez," he ordered, shooing us all down the stairs.

In the kitchen, I took a bottle of cold cider out of the refrigerator. "One Luger hardly amounts to a stash of pristine military stores any more than a couple of handfuls of rings is half a million in gold. But once again, something was there."

Jean-Paul pulled off his tie. "If you tried to persuade the Karl woman that this was all that was found, she would never believe you."

"I'm happy that I'll never need to persuade her of anything."

"Maggie, Jean-Paul." Antoine pulled cider glasses out of a cupboard. "You're welcome to stay with me tonight. We'll get the floor fixed in your room tomorrow. I have to warn you, though, that Grand-mère Marie snores like a jackhammer. But I can put you at the far end of the hall."

"Antoine, *mon chèr,* I prefer that you take the film students home with you," Grand-mère said. "Zach and Taylor are perfectly lovely, but their padding back and forth across the hall in the middle of the night was annoying. Maggie, why didn't you just put them in the same room to begin with?"

I would have raised my hands to connote "coulda shoulda" but I was pouring cider so all I could do was shrug.

"Maggie and Jean-Paul can go into Bébé's room," Grand-mère said, settling any issue about where we were to sleep that night.

Jean-Paul was being very quiet. I knew he wanted to talk with me, but we had been surrounded ever since he arrived. On the pretext that I could use some help setting up for a film shoot, I invited him to come with me down into the basement. It was hardly a romantic place, but we could be alone there.

Pierre's crime scene people had come and gone from the backyard by early afternoon so there was no legitimate reason for Pierre to keep us away from our studio. He had Grand-mère's permission to post a few officers on the property, but they were doing their best to stay out of sight.

Earlier that day, while I was still in the village for the arraignment, a locksmith was called in to put a new lock on the studio door, a hefty bolt that took a little muscle to turn. I asked Jean-Paul to come with me to the studio to help me collect extension cords and spotlights we would need to film in the basement first thing in the morning. When we went into the studio, it was a relief to see that everything in the studio had been returned to its place, a task that had been handed to Devon and Miller, the quieter of our interns. I showed Jean-Paul the spotlights that we would use for filming. Manfully, he picked up two of them at a time and carried them down the basement steps while somehow managing to hold onto a flashlight.

With a roll of gaffer's tape—duct tape—on one arm and a reel of heavy-duty extension cord on the other, I went in search of an electrical socket. The first one I found was at the near end of the rose arbor. I plugged in the cord, taped it in place, and began unreeling the cord, taping it down as I went so that no one would trip over it in the yard or on the basement steps. When I reached the bottom step, Jean-Paul already had four lights set up on adjustable stands. I plugged in the lights and an entirely new scene opened up before me. It was eerily beautiful: long shadows disappearing into the darkness beyond the lights' reach; lacy cobwebs draping down from the ceiling fourteen feet above us; heavily carved old pieces softened under a layer of fine, gray dust.

"Wow," I said. "I am dying to see how this looks on film."

He laughed. "There are no bodies down here, are there?"

"Just us, as far as I know."

"I had something a little more romantic in mind," he said, running a finger through the dust on a table top. "Candlelight, flowers, a nice wine maybe."

"A beach, a naked belly, a mai tai?"

"Either would do." He reached out and took my hands. "But if this is what we have, this is fine."

"Why are my knees knocking?"

"Because you know I'm going to ask you something important."

"Do I know how I'm going to answer?"

"You do or you wouldn't have brought me down here, alone. I saw you fast-talking Guido out of joining us."

"So, then, Jean-Paul, you've driven a long way to ask me this question. But maybe first you should tell me about the job offer. A woman wants to know if a man has good prospects before committing to him."

He laughed and pulled me into an embrace. "I've been asked to head an international trade commission. On its face that sounds a bit dull, but international trade is a deliciously dirty affair, so I think we'll find it quite interesting."

"We, huh?"

"Depends on your answer, does it not?"

"Where would we live?"

"I told the committee that I need to be in Los Angeles through the first of the year, time enough for you to finish the film. After that, Paris for six months. We'll have plenty of time to figure out where to go from there."

"Could be interesting," I said. "Now, I understand you have a question to ask."

"Yes, but my knees are knocking."

"Oh, Jean-Paul." I gave him the best kiss I had. "We both know the answer. But before we make any announcements, I'd like to speak with Casey and with my mom in California."

"Of course, but Casey says she couldn't be happier, and your mom says it's about time."

"You spoke with them?"

"What can I say? I'm traditional enough to want the blessing of the people you love."

"If you called Mom, I suppose you called your mother, too?"

"Oh yes. She insisted on meeting you first, but she's delighted."

"What's left to do, other than the deed itself?"

"We need to go upstairs. Your grandmother has prepared a surprise for us."

"She knows?"

"Of course. My mother called her."

There was a small party waiting for us in the salon. All the usual suspects had gathered, the family and the nearly family, along with Gaston, and Ma Mère. Zach and Taylor were there, and Guido, of course, and Pierre and Jacqueline, though they were both on duty and could not drink more than the three glasses of wine they were allowed to consume while on duty. The event was memorable, not only because the food and drink were delicious, and everyone was so happy, but because the bomb squad from the *gendarme* barracks in Carentan stomped through in all their Kevlar garb when they came to remove the old ammo. They stayed for cakes and Champagne without needing any persuasion, and offered us their best wishes.

Once the ammo was removed, I was able to go into my room to collect some clothes, though I am happy to say that certain garments spent most of the night on the floor beside the bed.

Eventually, Jean-Paul and I fell asleep wrapped around each other like puppies in a basket. I don't know what wakened me. I lay quiet in Jean-Paul's arms, and listened. The old house creaked and sighed in the night as it cooled off from the day, as it always does. But there was something else beyond our heavy bedroom door that was not a part of the usual house noises. I nudged Jean-Paul. He rolled on his back to look over at the face of the clock on his nightstand. It was three-thirty.

"What is it?" he whispered.

"Listen."

We both sat up and listened. A low-pitched creak—almost a groan—then a thump. He slipped out of bed first and groped around on the floor for his pants while I grabbed my robe off the back of a chair and pulled it on. In bare feet, he padded around to my side of the bed, the door side, stopping to take Grand-mère's Luger out of the drawer where I stowed it when I brought my clothes across the hall from my room. Slowly, being as quiet as he could, he turned the knob and opened the door enough to see into the hall. I was close behind him.

The door to my room across the hall was closed, but something or someone moving around inside interrupted the sliver of light visible under the door. The strange groan became more defined, the sound of a nail being pried out of wood. Someone was pulling up the plywood that had been hastily tacked over the bare floor joists so that no one got hurt until the floor could be repaired. The original wooden planks were stacked against a wall.

Holding the Luger down beside his leg, Jean-Paul slipped out into the hall with me close on his heels. He gestured for me to go left when he went right so that we flanked my bedroom door, me on the hinge side, he next to the opening. On a signal, I reached over, turned the knob, and pushed the door open. Whoever was in the room began to scramble. Jean-Paul rushed in, hit the light switch and then all hell seemed to break loose. Wooden floor planks flew past the open door and Jean-Paul cried out when something must have hit him. I ducked low and slipped inside. Jean-Paul was on the floor with blood on his head as I opened the armoire and grabbed the tire iron, still sealed in a clear plastic evidence bag. Out of the corner of my eye I saw movement and swung at it.

Something hard gave inside whoever I hit. He went down with a thud that shook the flimsy plywood underfoot. Jean-Paul was on his feet, Luger still in his hand, so I knew he was all right. I went over to the moaning pile of clothes lying crookedly over re-exposed floor joists. I nudged the man with the tire iron and he rolled onto his back and looked up at me. Tears rolled down his lined face.

Jean-Paul was beside me. There was a gash on the point of his temple that was already swelling and turning blue. I asked if he was okay, but it was the man on the floor who answered.

"You broke my arm."

He had to be at least eighty, too old to be doing second-story work. And he must have been awfully desperate to be out prowling in the middle of the night. One of his arms, encased in a beautifully tailored, if threadbare, jacket, bent sharply about midway between his wrist and elbow. I should have felt bad about that—he was a very old man—but I didn't.

I wrapped an arm around Jean-Paul's naked middle and centered the end of the plastic-shrouded tire iron on the man's chest as if he were a big-game trophy.

I said, "Jean-Paul, meet 'Count' Otto von Streicher."

—22—

THE ARREST ON Tuesday morning was a very quiet affair. When Pierre drove into the compound with a warrant from the court, Antoine had just returned from the village bakery with the croissants he picked up at dawn every morning for all three of the family houses as well as for the workers at the *fromagerie*. I had not been able to go back to sleep after Pierre came in and hauled Erika's brother, Otto von Streicher, off to the village lockup. I suspected that this member of the von Streicher family would not get off with a slap on the wrist and a plane ticket home.

Zach and Taylor found me in the kitchen during that hour after dawn when they came in from a morning run with Casey and David. I was making coffee, proud to have mastered Grand-mère's *cafetière*. When I went out to collect our croissants from Antoine, my interns ran upstairs to get their laptops so they could show me some of the footage they had taken the day before. They were very excited about it.

Pierre looked like hell when he got out of his car that Tuesday morning. He couldn't have had much sleep the night before. Jacqueline was with him, back in uniform after two nights at the student camp. She seemed nervous, and I found that curious.

Antoine stopped to talk with them in front of Freddy's house, holding the three muslin bags of warm croissants over his arm. I walked over to save Antoine the few steps to Grand-mère's door, and to see how Pierre was. Though the morning was cool, he already had sweat rings under the arms of his freshly pressed uniform shirt. I asked if he wanted to come in for coffee. I told him that Zach and Taylor were going to show me the footage they shot of the burial of the German remains at La Cambe Cemetery on Monday. He said no at first, but Jacqueline put her hand on his arm and told him that he should go ahead, that she would keep an eye on things. When Pierre hesitated, she took one of the croissant bags from Antoine and gave it to him.

"Eat something, Pierre," she ordered. ""Have some coffee. I'll be right here. Go."

The interns had set up two laptops on the kitchen table. One had footage of the burial at La Cambe, the other a burial ceremony at the American military cemetery at Coleville-sur-Mer for a recently deceased American veteran of the D-Day landings. The juxtaposition showed the stark contrast between the two events. The former was brief and colorless, and witnessed only by the men who delivered the remains and the men who laid them all in a single grave in the section for unidentified German soldiers, and covered them over. At the latter, hundreds of tourists visiting the perfectly manicured American cemetery overlooking Omaha Beach joined the family for the burial. There was an honor guard escort, a twenty-one-gun salute, a bugler to play "Taps," and a small military band that played the national anthem at the close.

Pierre seemed distracted, drinking his coffee, picking at his croissant. He commented that even the sky looked dark during the burial at La Cambe.

I told Zach and Taylor how impressed I was by their work. There was a place in the film for the La Cambe footage, and they would certainly have a line in the credits. "You need to get your union cards, kids," I told them. "It's time for someone to pay you for your work."

They bounced off upstairs for showers, excited about shooting in the basement later in the morning.

When we were alone, Pierre thanked me for putting him onto an important line of inquiry for the Solange Betz murder case. Before I could ask him what it was, his phone chirped.

"It's time," he said, putting the phone away. On his way out of the kitchen, he said, "I need this to be my last murder investigation."

I admit I was a little slow that Tuesday morning, not enough sleep, not enough coffee. But even I understood that when Pierre said "It's time" that something having to do with the murder of

Solange was about to go down. I followed him out and stood beside him on Grand-mère's front steps.

Jacqueline knocked on Freddy's door. Freddy answered, spoke briefly with Jacqueline and then stepped back inside, leaving the door ajar. Olivia appeared in the doorway, dressed for work in khaki shorts and a long-sleeved blue chambray shirt. Jacqueline motioned for her to come outside. Standing on the gravel in front of Freddy's house, reading from a signed court order, Jacqueline informed Olivia that she would be charged with the willful murder of Solange Betz. Olivia nodded when she was asked if she understood the charge, followed instructions to turn around with her hands behind her back, and did not speak or struggle when Jacqueline slapped handcuffs on her slender wrists.

Olivia was placed in the backseat of Pierre's official blue-and-white Renault Mégane. She was looking down toward her lap when Jacqueline drove her away.

Pierre stood watching them go, not moving even after they were gone. Freddy had watched the arrest from his open front door. He came outside and walked across the gravel to join us.

Freddy wrapped an arm around Pierre's shoulders. "I know that was difficult, old friend."

Pierre looked over at me. "You're not surprised?"

"I'm not. I'm sorry, but I'm not surprised."

"It was what you said about the work she was having her graduate students do that planted the germ," he said. "I got in touch with her university. Olivia had applied for a summer research grant and put in for seven students to work with her. But the grant was denied late in the process. Instead of cancelling, she went out and got hired by this company that places archeologists with builders. She lucked into Freddy because of all the students that are on the estate all summer. Hers could just get folded in."

"But why did she kill Solange?" I asked.

"Desperation?" Pierre said. "Solange was unhappy about the work Olivia was having her students perform. She called her tutor or mentor or whatever, and complained. That got Olivia into difficulty. But the thing is, Olivia was already in trouble at the university, and that's why she had lost her grant. She hadn't published enough or published recently enough, or whatever she's supposed to be doing. Her position was in jeopardy. I believe she was afraid of what Solange was telling people about her. Olivia waited for an opportunity to speak with Solange alone. They must have argued, and Solange lost."

"Then Olivia washed the mattock she used, and hid it in the basement," I said. "The mattock that was checked out to Solange."

He nodded. "The key for the potting shed she used to store her tools was on the same ring as the keys for the basement."

"How ironic," I said. "If Olivia hadn't mentioned that Solange's mattock was missing, I wouldn't know what a mattock is, and I would never have suspected its significance when Antoine picked it up."

"Fortunately for us, she was an amateur in the business of murder." He canted his head and gave me a little upside down French smile. "When she comes out of prison she will be looking for a new career. Please, Madame Sherlock Holmes, do not offer to tutor her in the art of criminal investigation."

Jean-Paul came outside just then, carrying a coffee mug. He looked a little sleepy still, and I adored him.

"You missed the morning's drama," I said.

"That's perfectly fine with me." He kissed the back of my neck. Then he yawned. "I've had all the drama I need for a while."

A motorcycle sped past on the village road.

"A blue Kawasaki," Freddy said. "German registration. That's the third time this morning I've heard it pass. He was around yesterday, too."

"Merde." Pierre pulled out his phone and called for an alert to go out. Blue Kawasaki headed north away from the village. Stop and question, please.

"Tell me we've seen the last of the treasure hunters," I said.

He shrugged, just a twitch of one shoulder. "I wish I could."

fin

— —

ABOUT THE AUTHOR

Edgar Award–winner Wendy Hornsby is the author of eleven previous mysteries, nine of them featuring documentary filmmaker Maggie MacGowen. She is a retired professor of history and lives in California. She welcomes visitors and e-mail at www.wendy hornsby.com.

More Traditional Mysteries from Perseverance Press
For the New Golden Age

K.K. Beck
Tipping the Valet
ISBN 978-1-56474-563-7

Albert A. Bell, Jr.
PLINY THE YOUNGER SERIES
Death in the Ashes
ISBN 978-1-56474-532-3
The Eyes of Aurora
ISBN 978-1-56474-549-1

Taffy Cannon
ROXANNE PRESCOTT SERIES
Guns and Roses
Agatha and Macavity awards nominee, Best Novel
ISBN 978-1-880284-34-6
Blood Matters
ISBN 978-1-880284-86-5
Open Season on Lawyers
ISBN 978-1-880284-51-3
Paradise Lost
ISBN 978-1-880284-80-3

Laura Crum
GAIL MCCARTHY SERIES
Moonblind
ISBN 978-1-880284-90-2
Chasing Cans
ISBN 978-1-880284-94-0
Going, Gone
ISBN 978-1-880284-98-8
Barnstorming
ISBN 978-1-56474-508-8

Jeanne M. Dams
HILDA JOHANSSON SERIES
Crimson Snow
ISBN 978-1-880284-79-7
Indigo Christmas
ISBN 978-1-880284-95-7
Murder in Burnt Orange
ISBN 978-1-56474-503-3

Janet Dawson
JERI HOWARD SERIES
Bit Player
Golden Nugget Award nominee
ISBN 978-1-56474-494-4
Cold Trail
ISBN 978-1-56474-555-2
What You Wish For
ISBN 978-1-56474-518-7

TRAIN SERIES
Death Rides the Zephyr
ISBN 978-1-56474-530-9
Death Deals a Hand
ISBN 978-1-56474-569-9

Kathy Lynn Emerson
LADY APPLETON SERIES
Face Down Below the Banqueting House
ISBN 978-1-880284-71-1
Face Down Beside St. Anne's Well
ISBN 978-1-880284-82-7
Face Down O'er the Border
ISBN 978-1-880284-91-9

Sara Hoskinson Frommer
JOAN SPENCER SERIES
Her Brother's Keeper
ISBN 978-1-56474-525-5

Hal Glatzer
KATY GREEN SERIES
Too Dead To Swing
ISBN 978-1-880284-53-7
A Fugue in Hell's Kitchen
ISBN 978-1-880284-70-4
The Last Full Measure
ISBN 978-1-880284-84-1

Margaret Grace
MINIATURE SERIES
Mix-up in Miniature
ISBN 978-1-56474-510-1
Madness in Miniature
ISBN 978-1-56474-543-9
Manhattan in Miniature
ISBN 978-1-56474-562-0
Matrimony in Miniature (forthcoming)
ISBN 978-1-56474-575-0

Tony Hays
Shakespeare No More
ISBN 978-1-56474-566-8

Wendy Hornsby
MAGGIE MACGOWEN SERIES
In the Guise of Mercy
ISBN 978-1-56474-482-1
The Paramour's Daughter
ISBN 978-1-56474-496-8
The Hanging
ISBN 978-1-56474-526-2

The Color of Light
ISBN 978-1-56474-542-2

Disturbing the Dark
ISBN 978-1-56474-576-7

Janet LaPierre
PORT SILVA SERIES
Baby Mine
ISBN 978-1-880284-32-2

Keepers
Shamus Award nominee, Best Paperback Original
ISBN 978-1-880284-44-5

Death Duties
ISBN 978-1-880284-74-2

Family Business
ISBN 978-1-880284-85-8

Run a Crooked Mile
ISBN 978-1-880284-88-9

Hailey Lind
ART LOVER'S SERIES
Arsenic and Old Paint
ISBN 978-1-56474-490-6

Lev Raphael
NICK HOFFMAN SERIES
Tropic of Murder
ISBN 978-1-880284-68-1

Hot Rocks
ISBN 978-1-880284-83-4

Lora Roberts
BRIDGET MONTROSE SERIES
Another Fine Mess
ISBN 978-1-880284-54-4

SHERLOCK HOLMES SERIES
The Affair of the Incognito Tenant
ISBN 978-1-880284-67-4

Rebecca Rothenberg
BOTANICAL SERIES
The Tumbleweed Murders
(completed by Taffy Cannon)
ISBN 978-1-880284-43-8

Sheila Simonson
LATOUCHE COUNTY SERIES
Buffalo Bill's Defunct
WILLA Award, Best Softcover Fiction
ISBN 978-1-880284-96-4

An Old Chaos
ISBN 978-1-880284-99-5

Beyond Confusion
ISBN 978-1-56474-519-4

Lea Wait
SHADOWS ANTIQUES SERIES
Shadows of a Down East Summer
ISBN 978-1-56474-497-5

Shadows on a Cape Cod Wedding
ISBN 1-978-56474-531-6

Shadows on a Maine Christmas
ISBN 978-1-56474-531-6

Shadows on a Morning in Maine
(forthcoming)
ISBN 978-1-56474-577-4

Eric Wright
JOE BARLEY SERIES
The Kidnapping of Rosie Dawn
Barry Award, Best Paperback Original. Edgar,
Ellis, and Anthony awards nominee
ISBN 978-1-880284-40-7

Nancy Means Wright
MARY WOLLSTONECRAFT SERIES
Midnight Fires
ISBN 978-1-56474-488-3

The Nightmare
ISBN 978-1-56474-509-5

REFERENCE/MYSTERY WRITING

Kathy Lynn Emerson
How To Write Killer Historical Mysteries:
The Art and Adventure of Sleuthing
Through the Past
Agatha Award, Best Nonfiction. Anthony and
Macavity awards nominee
ISBN 978-1-880284-92-6

Carolyn Wheat
How To Write Killer Fiction:
The Funhouse of Mystery & the Roller
Coaster of Suspense
ISBN 978-1-880284-62-9

Available from your local bookstore
or from Perseverance Press/John Daniel & Company
(800) 662–8351 or www.danielpublishing.com/perseverance